F
WOO   Woods, Paula L.

           Strange bedfel-
           lows

DUE DATE		B697	23.95

Strange Bedfellows

Strange Bedfellows

A Charlotte Justice Novel

Paula L. Woods

One World
Ballantine Books
New York

Published in the United States by Ballantine Books, an imprint of
The Random House Publishing Group, a division of
Random House, Inc., New York.

BALLANTINE and colophon are registered trademarks of
Random House, Inc.

LIBRARY OF CONGRESS CATALOGING-IN-PUBLICATION DATA
Woods, Paula L.
Strange bedfellows : a Charlotte Justice novel / Paula L. Woods.— 1st ed.
p.   cm.
ISBN 0-345-45702-1—ISBN 0-345-45703-X (pbk.)
1. Justice, Charlotte (Fictitious character)—Fiction. 2. Police—
California—Los Angeles—Fiction. 3. Fascists—Crimes against—
Fiction. 4. African American police—Fiction. 5. African American
women—Fiction. 6. Los Angeles (Calif.)—Fiction. 7. Toy industry—
Fiction. 8. Policewomen—Fiction. I. Title.

PS3573.O6414S77 2006
813'.54—dc22   2005045232

Printed in the United States of America

www.ballantinebooks.com

2 4 6 8 9 7 5 3 1

FIRST EDITION

Book design by Nicola Ferguson

For Felix, as always

Smiling faces, smiling faces
Tell lies and I got proof.

—*The Undisputed Truth*
"Smiling Faces Sometimes"

One lie calls for another and another.

—*Cecilia "Grandmama Cile" Justice (1908–   )*

Strange
Bedfellows

1

Ain't Nobody's Business If I Do

When Aubrey Scott invaded the bathroom where I had retreated that Monday morning, I knew I was in for a surprise. It just wasn't the kind I was expecting. For starters,
he was fully dressed. And what was worse, instead of taking off his
clothes and joining me in the steam room like he had some sense, he
dragged me out of my warm cocoon by the hand.

"Check this out," he ordered as he turned on the television in the
bedroom.

An early morning talking head was blabbering about the aftermath
of a multicar accident on Route 219 near Modesto, some three hundred miles north of Los Angeles. Saturday morning, he informed us,
"tule fog, that monster weather condition peculiar to California's Central Valley, had spread like a cancer, causing a sixty-five-car pileup that
claimed the lives of nine people, including a CHP officer, and injured
twenty others," including the subject of the news bulletin Aubrey was
so intent on me seeing.

"As reported on Channel Four this weekend," the newscaster went
on, "the driver of one car, a late-model Toyota, had disappeared. Police
speculated that he may have wandered away from the scene and died
from his injuries. Well, the mystery driver has been found alive and

identified as nineteen-year-old Nilo Engalla, wanted for questioning in a shooting that occurred eight months ago right here in Los Angeles."

Aubrey stroked my arm. "Isn't that the Filipino kid you were looking for last summer?"

I mumbled a reply, surprised Aubrey would remember a case I had investigated during the early months of our relationship. I pulled on my robe and sat on the edge of the bed to try and figure out how to handle this unexpected curveball.

An exterior shot of a one-story concrete-and-glass building was on the screen. "Engalla showed up last night at this urgent care center in Ceres, some five miles south of the scene. He was transferred to a Modesto area hospital, where he's listed in critical condition. Police are hoping Engalla regains consciousness so they can determine how he found his way to the urgent care center and how he came to have over twenty-seven thousand dollars in cash concealed in the wrecked car."

I was still staring at the television when the bulletin ended, concerned that they'd revealed too much about Engalla, and concerned about something else, too. "This is great news!" Aubrey exclaimed, putting an arm around me. "Nothing like getting back into the swing of things after a tough case."

"Nothing like." Thankfully, Aubrey was sitting on my right because my left eye had started twitching again, as it had regularly since I'd left the Parker Administrative Building last Wednesday. Twitching in response to a sight I never wanted to see again, but which kept playing in my dreams in a continuous loop of blood and brains and tears.

Which was why I was sitting here instead of "getting back into the swing of things," as Aubrey so quaintly put it. But how could I tell him the truth? My dilemma reminded me of an old saying of my grandmother's: *One lie calls for another and another.*

Aubrey kissed my neck and kneaded my shoulders. "The steam seems to be helping these knots."

If it would only stop the racing of my heart. "What're you up to today?"

"Typical Monday. Meeting with the CEO over at White Memorial to review the short list of candidates for their new ER director. But I'll be home early to start cooking for tonight. Unless you want to cancel."

Cancel what? Then I remembered, said, "No, that's fine," hoping he hadn't realized that I had forgotten March was our month to host Film Night. It was a tradition that started in the Justice family years ago and now included Aubrey in my family's cut-'em-low critique of new and classic movies. "Did we decide on a movie?"

"I've got that handled. You need to call your lieutenant."

My heartbeat accelerating way past the legal limit, I rubbed my left eye to stop its spasmodic dance. "I will, later."

"If you do it now, I can drop you off downtown."

As encouraged as I was about this new development in the search for Engalla, my boyfriend driving me to work was just about the last thing I needed. "I can drive myself."

"In what?"

It was Aubrey's way of chastising me about not picking up my car from the Parker Administrative Building since wrapping up that case on Wednesday. I had put it off, saying I had been given a few days off to get some rest and was planning to take ultimate advantage of it by not doing battle with L.A.'s hellacious traffic.

But now it was Monday, and I had run out of excuses for not picking up my car, for not going back to my office in the PAB, for not telling Aubrey the truth. "I can catch a cab."

"Don't be silly, Charlotte! I'll walk the dog while you get dressed and check in with your lieutenant, then I'll drop you off myself, okay?"

I half-turned and gave Aubrey the smile he was expecting. "Sure."

A half hour later, we were headed for the PAB, rounding a hill on the interchange that would take us past Chinatown and into the belly of the Civic Center beast. "Your lieutenant say if he was sending you up north to interview that Engalla kid?"

On our left sat one of the taller buildings in Chinatown, as silent and ominous as a grave. "He wasn't sure." I started fiddling with the radio. "They might get somebody else to do it."

"But you worked that case with Steve Firestone and Gena Cortez. I would think that with both of them out . . ."

Perspiration pricking at my armpits, I found a station playing jazz and turned it up, trying to get lost in a Billie Holiday song.

Lieutenant Kenneth Stobaugh had caught me at my house in the Fairfax District that Friday eight months ago. It was a sweltering July evening, and the city's nerves were still humming from the Rodney King riots, every minor dustup fraught with the potential to spark and scorch the wings off the City of Angels once again. I was on call for the third time that summer after solving the homicide of Cinque Lewis, leader of the militant Black Freedom Militia, who'd disappeared after gunning down my husband and baby daughter years before. I hadn't caught a case since returning to duty, which was fine with me, given I was still nursing physical injuries from the riots and a psyche that craved doses of single-malt Scotch, despite the ministrations of the department's Behavioral Sciences Services—or what the guys on the street called Bullshit Shrinks. But I was pressing my luck to think I could escape what those same guys called the busy season in a city that was home to over four hundred homicides a year. Those kinds of statistics affected everyone, even a specialized division like Robbery-Homicide, which was assigned only the highest-profile or most complex homicides that floated up from the city's ever-growing cesspool of crime.

"It's a madhouse down here," Stobaugh said by way of preparing me. "Chuck Zuccari and a couple of his dinner companions were shot in front of the Oviatt Building on—"

"Olive near Sixth." I put down my glass of Cragganmore and shook my head to focus. "I'm familiar with the location." Four years before, my parents had thrown me a thirty-fifth birthday party at Ristorante Rex, the pricey restaurant on the ground floor of the Oviatt, but I didn't tell my lieutenant that. "Who's Zuccari?"

"CEO and chairman of CZ Toys, headquartered down in Irvine."

"And he's ours because . . . ?"

"He's chairman of an ultraconservative wing of the Republican Party down in Orange County. The governor's office has already been notified by the chief."

"Great." While Zuccari's political connections were a bit of a surprise, I knew the company well. CZ Toys had created a line of chubby-cheeked talking dolls in the sixties and had expanded over the years to include toy trucks and video gaming devices as well as the highly collectible dolls and accessories my mother and uncle prized. I wondered how they'd feel if they knew Zuccari's politics.

As it turned out, that was only the half of it. "How'd it happen?" I asked.

I heard pages rustling. "Zuccari, a black male by the name of Malik Shareef, and their wives were coming out of Ristorante Rex when someone wearing a smiley face mask drove by and shot up the place."

The clash between the yellow pop art image and the Art Deco landmark was jarring. "How many DBs we talking?"

"None so far, but the paramedics think they could have as many as four dead before the night is over."

I rummaged in a drawer for a fresh notebook. "Status?"

"Zuccari sustained a GSW in the head and chest. They took him over to County/USC for emergency surgery. His wife is there, too, with a gunshot wound to the abdomen. Shareef was hit in the chest and is undergoing surgery at California Hospital right now."

A riot-related injury had sent me to California's emergency room the previous spring, and into Aubrey's life. But that memory was replaced by a more immediate concern. "That's only three."

There was dead air on the line, making me wonder if we'd lost the connection. When Stobaugh finally spoke, his voice was oddly muffled: "Zuccari's wife is six months pregnant. She's undergoing an emergency C-section now, but they don't hold out much hope for her or the baby."

My heartbeat started to thrum in my ears as I fought back the rising nausea I always feel when a child is involved. "Any wits?"

"The uniforms are interviewing one of the parking valets now. He was the closest to the car as it approached. And Firestone and Cortez are en route to the scene to interview Shareef's wife and some other wits who were on the street. But a banquet was just breaking up next door at the Biltmore when the shooting went down, so there's a hell of a lot of them. How soon can you get here?"

I checked my watch and my breath, blowing into my cupped hand. Eight-ten, and nothing a little toothpaste and Listerine couldn't handle. "I'll be there in twenty."

I tried to intercept Aubrey, who was on his way over for dinner. Takeout was more accurate—that night, I'd bought Mexican-style soul food from Sky's the Limit. But Aubrey wasn't at his office or at home, and he wasn't answering his cell phone. I left a note on the door, telling him to ask Mrs. Franklin across the street for the key, and called to let her know what was going on.

"The cards tole me you'd be back in action soon," she drawled.

"I don't recall requesting a reading, Mrs. Franklin." My neighbor had a storefront on Pico where she read tarot cards, tea leaves, and coffee grounds under the dba *Sister Odetta, Your Neighborhood Psychic.*

"You didn't, but I was tired of seein' you mope around the house so much after the Uprisin,' I consulted the cards on my own."

"Just keep an eye out for Aubrey, will you?"

"Only if he brings that Sky's over here. Miz Burrell and that boy a'hers make some of the best damn tacos on God's green earth!"

It was a fair enough trade, given that my Houston-born neighbor had always had my back, from the day my husband Keith and I moved into our Fairfax District home sixteen years before. Mrs. Franklin had seen me through everything from changing gardeners to fixing a leaky roof, not to mention funeral services and a shoot-out in front of my own house during the riots. She sometimes felt more like a mother to me than my own. But the maternal association became a little too real when she'd started needling me about when I was going to cook Aubrey a real meal.

"You know what they say," she'd warned that night. "The quickest way to a man's heart is through his stomach."

If that's what it took, I'd thought, I was up the creek without a paddle.

But Mrs. Franklin and the little voice in my head had been wrong. Aubrey turned out to be a man who could cook better than I ever would, who knew what I did for a living but invited me to move in with him anyway, less than a year after we met, who deserved to be told the truth of what was going on with me now.

I'll tell him after this song is over, I promised myself. But after Billie Holiday's song ended, Aubrey switched to an all-news station and started talking about his upcoming meeting. I buried myself deeper in my seat and thought about mine.

I had Aubrey drop me off at the corner of first and Los Angeles Streets, about thirty yards away from the PAB. "I don't need the boys seeing me roll up in a Benz. Some of them already know I've moved up to Los Feliz."

"Ain't nobody's business if you do," he snapped, paraphrasing the Billie Holiday song we'd just heard. "Besides, I work damn hard to afford this car!"

"You don't have to justify it to me. I just don't need any more grief on the job than I've already got."

"What do they think I am, a pimp or something?"

"You know better than that! It's just that most cops are so . . ."

"Racist?"

"No, *paranoid* that something as flashy as a Mercedes would attract the wrong kind of attention."

"You talking about their paranoia or yours?" Aubrey turned left and pulled the car to a quick stop near the northeast corner. "If I were you, I'd stop worrying about what other people think, Char, and live my life for myself."

"Well, thank you, Dear Aubrey!" I clambered out of the car, slammed the door, and made a show of walking north toward the PAB, checking every few feet to see if my advice-giving lover had driven away. But Aubrey hadn't moved, had even pulled out his cell phone and appeared to be making a call. Shit, what would I do now?

Ahead I could see my lieutenant walking toward the parking lot, where he shook hands with a curly-headed, mustachioed guy who used to work RHD. Stobaugh couldn't be trying to get Harry Bosch transferred back to Robbery-Homicide, not after that case he'd screwed up.

Or maybe, my voice proposed, *Bosch can fill the spot on Stobaugh's team you'll be vacating if you don't get your act together.*

Avoiding the two men, I edged into the lobby and hovered just inside the door, keeping watch on the traffic outside while ignoring the inquisitive gaze of the uniforms on the desk. My mouth sour, I reached in my pocket for my Altoids tin while I rocked on my toes and waited. After Aubrey's car finally slid by the building, I counted to twenty as a precaution, then escaped the building to a DASH bus idling at the curb.

2

Chinatown

'd been to the site of the present-day Chinatown from the time I was a kid—impromptu Sunday dinners when my mother didn't want to cook, shopping for Chinese herbs with Grandmama Cile, field trips in high school. I knew from a paper I'd written in the tenth grade that what people called the area north of the 101 Freeway between Broadway and Hill Streets was in fact the third Chinatown. The first had been established east of the old town plaza. Was it a coincidence, I asked in my paper, that those first Chinese immigrants, brought to California to build wagon routes and railroads for next to nothing, were called coolie slaves and forced to live in a run-down part of town anchored by Calle de los Negros, or what I speculated that less-tolerant Angelenos of the time probably called Nigger Alley? The second "China City," where parts of *The Good Earth* were filmed, was more of a tourist attraction than a community and had mysteriously burned to the ground. The third, "New" Chinatown, where I was headed now, was Chinese-owned and had prospered from Day One. As the bus pulled up to one of those tall buildings I had glimpsed from the freeway I wondered if it was a bad Freudian joke or some bizarre form of karma that I would end up at the Depression-era landmark, the intersection of my past and present, trying to figure out whether I had a future.

Maybe I should have had Mrs. Franklin do a reading for me and saved myself the trouble.

The third-floor reception area was empty, the dozen or more chairs lining the walls in quiet judgment. *Knew she'd be back*, they whispered to each other. I rapped on the receptionist's window, wondering why anyone would be fool enough to sit in this waiting room exposing themselves, where even the chairs knew your secrets.

A manicured hand slid back the glass to reveal a young woman with dark hair and double-lidded eyes. "Are you Detective Justice?"

"You got more than one black female coming in today?"

I regretted the crack when I saw the receptionist's eyes flicker and the corners of her mouth tighten. "Just a moment." She turned to say something to a colleague as she slid the window closed.

"I'm not waiting out here all day!" I warned the frosted glass. When I got no response, I walked the perimeter of the room, studying the art on the walls, pictures drawn by schoolchildren of uniformed men riding in cars, saving kitties, helping kids cross the street. But, after circling the room a few times, I noticed there were no women in the drawings and no one with skin deeper than Crayola's infamous flesh color. Were females and minorities really that invisible?

I was about to leave when the window slid open again. "He can see you now."

"*He?*" I walked through a door on my left and into a colorless hallway that looked worse than my OB/GYN's office. *Better pregnant than this.* I was greeted by a tawny-complected male, five-nine, maybe mid-forties, with a softness through his midsection that told me he spent more time on his butt than he did in a gym.

He stuck out his hand and told me his name. "Where's Dr. Betty?" I demanded.

He hesitated for only a moment before withdrawing his hand. "Let's go to my office. It's just down the hall."

On the left was Dr. Betty's corner office. Her collection of Georgia O'Keeffe posters was still hanging in the darkened room; her African violets were still massed on the coffee table. The only thing missing was the gold-framed quote that usually sat next to the violets, something O'Keeffe had said that I couldn't recall at the moment. "Where is she?" I repeated.

His office was three doors down from Dr. Betty's and smaller by a third. But that was because Dr. Betty ran the place, while this guy, from the looks of him, was a mid-level automaton. Was this soft-gutted fool all I merited this time around?

He gestured to a love seat against the wall while turning around a guest chair that fronted the desk to face me. I chose to stand. "I'd rather see Dr. Betty."

"That's not an option." He turned in his chair and reached past a gold picture frame and wooden clock to grab a folder in the middle of his desk. When he found me still on my feet, he said, "You can stand there all day, Detective, but it's not going to get you out of here any sooner." The blandness in his voice concealed a steeliness beneath that made me want to put my fist in his solar plexus.

I parked myself at one end of the love seat, opened the tin of Altoids, and popped a couple. While slipping the tin back in my pocket I checked out the collection of masks that covered the wall behind his desk. There were some wooden ones from Africa and Central America, one of painted batik whose origin I couldn't place, even a few that looked as if they had been made by children. But for all their political correctness, they told me nothing other than that their owner didn't mind being scrutinized by these frozen imitations of life. "What's your name again?"

He reached into a woven basket on his desk and handed me a card. PABLO WYCHOWSKI, PH.D. I looked at him and then reread the card, twisting my mouth to conceal the smile.

"Something wrong, Detective?"

"I'm sure you've heard this before, but you've got quite a name, sir."

"Please, call me Dr. Wychowski, or Pablo. And what do you mean, quite a name?"

"Wychowski is Polish or Jewish, right?"

He stared at me, his eyes emotionless pools of brown.

"And with a name like Pablo . . ." I paused, squinting to interpret the tint of his skin. "I'd guess someone in your family is Latino."

"Or likes Pablo Picasso's art."

"Possible, but I don't think so, sir."

The mustache above the Polish Picasso's lip twitched a bit. "Is it that important?"

I crumpled his card into a pocket. "I'm just trying to level the playing field here." I gestured to the file in his lap. "You're the one with the information advantage."

"This?" His tapered fingers touched, but didn't open, the file in his lap. "This is just paperwork."

"On me, correct? Paperwork that could get me bounced out of the department."

He folded his hands over the file. "I'd much rather hear what's in here from you than read a bunch of reports."

I had the distinct sensation of ants crawling along the back of my neck. "I've covered a lot of this territory before with Dr. Betty. Don't you people believe in continuity of care?"

"When it's in the best interests of the client, yes. But in your case, I don't think it would hurt to revisit some of this territory, as you call it, with someone new. Besides, Dr. Frasier is out of town."

One point for our side. I'd gotten him to tell me something he hadn't intended. But my victory was short-lived when I realized he was just staring, waiting for me to say something. I couldn't figure out which was worse—him or those damned masks. I preferred Dr. Betty's sensual O'Keeffes to these lifeless faces, taunting me with their fixed gazes and gaping mouths. Like looking at a corpse. "We could save a lot of time, sir, if I could talk to Dr. Betty."

"And why is that?"

"She knows my—what do you people call it?—my history."

"Is that the only reason you want to talk to her?"

I resisted the urge to brush those ants off my neck. "What else could there be?"

He considered me with eyes as vacant as the sockets in his mask collection. "I don't know. Perhaps you object to my being male, or maybe what you believe to be my ethnic background makes you uncomfortable. Weren't your former partners Jewish and Latino?"

I shot to my feet. "Don't you dare try to peg me as some kind of bigot, because you don't know the half! With the crap I've had to put up with from folks in the department, I should be the one questioning *your* motives, not the other way around."

His eyes sparked a bit. "I see the thought of being considered prejudiced upsets you. Why is that, Detect—or may I call you Charlotte?"

"I'd prefer *Detective* Justice."

He raised a hand in a gesture of truce. "Okay, Detective Justice, sit down and take it easy. My objectives here are the same as yours, or at least I think they are."

I crossed my arms over my chest and tried to ignore those masks staring at me. "Go ahead. You seem to have all the answers."

Undeterred, he ticked off on his fingers: "One, to ensure that you're fit to return to active duty. Two, to ensure that as a consequence of what you've been through on your last case and"—he gestured to the file in his lap—"some of these others, you don't lose your concentration and endanger yourself or your co-workers. And three—"

"That's a crock of shit!"

"May I finish?"

"No! You talk like I'm crazy or something."

"Going to a therapist doesn't make you crazy . . ."

Aubrey called you paranoid.

". . . despite what people say," he added, as if in response to my inner voice.

"I don't need people talking about my business all over the department!"

"They won't, but I'm interested in why you would care."

Now he was really beginning to sound like Aubrey. "Get real! A cop with a history like mine is bad enough. Add a few visits to Chinatown, and my career could get permanently sidetracked."

"Don't worry, Detective, our sessions are completely confidential."

"Except what you tell my superiors."

"You should know from before, Detective Justice, that I only discuss with them your readiness to return to work, not the content of our sessions. As for your career concerns, it may comfort you to know that eighty percent of BSS clients come to us voluntarily."

"So what does that say about me? I've been ordered in by my superiors to see you people three times in the past year!"

He rolled forward in his chair, almost close enough to touch my knee. "It says that you've been through an incredible amount of stress, Detective Justice. It says you've seen way too much death."

I shrugged and edged away. "Occupational hazard. It's no big deal."

"Only if you're a television or movie cop. In the real world, the violence like what you've encountered, year in and year out, can get next to the best of us."

My stomach flipped. "Shit happens. Far as I'm concerned, only the strong survive."

"Which is why a lot of cops get their fill of working homicide after a few years and move on to something else."

"Like what?"

"Burglary. The special theft squads. Even command positions."

My sour stomach gurgled in protest. Who did this guy think he was—my tenth-grade guidance counselor? "I'm a homicide detective first, last, and always will be."

"You say that as if there are no other options."

"There aren't for me!"

He studied me for a long moment. "Well, if that's your desire, then let me do my job."

"Don't let me stop you."

His brown eyes locked on mine. "I gave you my first two objectives. You wouldn't let me give you the third."

I squirmed deeper into the sofa. Something lower than those ants on my neck was beginning to itch, and listening to this idiot was only making it worse. "Your superiors care enough about you as a person and as a resource to this department," he was saying, "to want to ensure that you're not going to end up like some of your colleagues. What's the term cops have for it?"

Unbidden, a red-hued image of blood and brain matter exploding from the back of someone's head. My nightmares come to life—was it the memory of a previous case, or a premonition of things to come? Whatever it was, the thought of eating a gun sandwich made me stop, the snappy phrase frozen on my lips.

"If you don't want to talk . . ." Misinterpreting my silence, he flipped open the file. I became aware of the clock on his desk, measuring out the hour in maddening ticks. My God, how much more time would I have to spend here?

While I reminded myself to breathe, my captor was reading. "It says here you investigated a case against the orders of your superiors during the riots and ended up discharging your weapon against a fellow officer."

His comment made me see red all over again. "What would you have done if someone had threatened an innocent child?"

"I'm not judging you, Detective, I'm just reading what's in the file. And you investigated another homicide last fall where you were involved in a shooting and witnessed a suspect's suicide."

"The shooting and the suicide were not related. And, besides, the Board of Rights cleared me on both incidents."

"And last week, I understand you witnessed your second suicide in four months."

He says that like you had something to do with it. That sour taste began to rise at the back of my throat, but I resisted the urge to reach for my Altoids tin. "And your point?"

He closed the folder. "In the eyes of many in the department, that kind of history would put you squarely on the path to joining the List of Forty-Four."

His voice was calm, but I knew he was laying out the bait, seeing if mention of the infamous list of "problem officers"—developed by the Christopher Commission in their post-riot investigations—would make me go off on him again. Instead, I recited to myself a snippet of a psalm my grandmother once gave me—*The Lord is my strength and my shield*—and took a deep breath. "That's what it might look like to an outsider, or someone reading a bunch of CYA reports in a file. But, covering their asses or not, I'm betting my superiors briefed you on the background behind those reports. If they did, you know the *real* reasons behind each of those incidents. Maybe they're not in your files, or in my personnel jacket—"

They're damn sure in those diaries I keep.

"—or in the proceedings of the Board of Rights hearings I was subjected to which, I *repeat*, ruled my actions were within procedure. But, if after what I've been through, anybody tries to brand me a rogue cop like the guys on the List, a cop to be bounced because of my 'potential for future abuse of LAPD regulations,' then rest assured I'll be taking somebody down with me!"

He regarded me somberly. "I hear a lot of anger in your voice. Do you hate the department that much?"

No he didn't! "After dedicating almost fourteen years of my life to the job, is that what you people think?"

Even as I deflected his challenge, that damned voice in my head was saying: *Good question!* I took in another breath to regroup. "Actually, I love what I do. Every day I have a chance to be one of the good guys. I get to solve murders, bring the scum who commit them to account. I get to give some measure of closure and, excuse the pun, justice to the families whose lives will never be made whole because of losing their loved ones."

He looked me dead in the eye. "That's a very noble-sounding rationale. When I hear cops say something like that, there's usually more to it than meets the eye."

His words drew me back some fifteen years, to an image I'd tried hard to forget, to blood pooling among the jacaranda blossoms in my driveway, to me cradling my husband Keith and baby Erica and screaming for help that came too late. I took in a breath to steady myself, and tasted chalk at the back of my throat. "That's your interpretation, sir, not mine."

The shrink allowed himself a small smile. "I've just been observing you today, Detective. And from where I sit, despite your superficial politeness, I can see you're sitting on a lot of anger. I suspect you probably do a good job of hiding it from the untrained eye, but it's there nonetheless. Which brings me to my treatment plan."

He paused. *What the hell was he waiting for, a drum roll?* "I think if we spend some time exploring where that anger comes from, what it might be hiding, we can make your job a little easier. I can also help you develop some tools that you can use to cope so the anger doesn't eat you, or your stomach lining, up alive."

"My stomach lining is fine!"

He glanced in the direction of my pocket. "Hiding antacids in candy tins is an old trick, Detective."

I could feel the Altoids tin resting in my pocket, could remember the number of times I'd resorted to eating the Rolaids I'd secreted inside it in the past few months. The past few hours. I gave the shrink's words some thought, weighing the pros and cons of the situation and calculating how much bargaining power I had. "I guess that's a fair trade," I replied. "But I'm a pretty quick study. Why can't you give me these tools now, so I can get out of here and back to work?"

"What's your hurry, Detective Justice? You're on medical leave until I sign off on your clearance to go back to full duty. Why don't we take some time, make sure we really see what's going on with you?"

His words sparked a memory, directing my gaze to the gold picture frame on his desk. I realized that it wasn't a photo at all, that I'd seen it before, but not in this office. "May I?"

"Be my guest."

It was that Georgia O'Keeffe quote that had been on Dr. Betty's coffee table the first time I was ordered in for therapy. *Nobody sees a flower, really*, it read. *It's so small. We haven't time, and to see takes time.*

To see takes time. It was something Dr. Betty would say in our sessions. Although I didn't know where my former therapist was at that moment, I did know one thing—she and what's-his-name were in cahoots, probably talking behind my back about "objectives" and "treatment plans" and God knows what else. So, like it or not, it was this funny-named pudgeball, not earth mother Dr. Betty, who held the keys to the kingdom I longed to reenter. And if I wanted to get back to the work I saw as my calling, I was going to have to do what the ex-wife of a victim once said: *go along to get along.*

I had one more card of my own to play, but I'd have to do it carefully. "How much time is this going to take?"

"Why do you ask?"

Don't be too eager. Just lay it out and let him do the rest. "There's been a development on a cold case that I think is going to need my involvement."

He shifted in his chair. "Why is that?"

As the excitement rippled through my stomach I realized how much I wanted to win another round of this match, beat what's-his-name at his own mind games. So I told him about the Smiley Face shootings and Nilo Engalla, about how important it was for me to interview him. "Finding Engalla is the first break we've gotten in seven months. And I'm the only one left in the department who worked the case originally. They need me on this one."

"What about the case files?"

"There's a lot of information that's not in the files. It's up here." I tapped my forehead. "You know, like continuity of care in your field, there's stuff I know about this case that could make a difference."

Watching him stroke his beard, I wasn't sure if he was still listening. But after a while he murmured: "It *would* be a way for us to examine your reactions in a controlled environment."

Toss him a bone, now! "And it would be nice to have someone outside of the job to talk to while I'm working a case."

I realized it was the wrong thing to say when he said: "You don't talk to your family about your work?"

"Not that much." I was reminded of my mother's opposition to my being a cop, her alarm at the "murder and mayhem" I'd insisted on bringing into her spotless View Park home for the past thirteen years. Or my "quit now" brother Perris, who had left the LAPD after being shot on duty the same day my husband and daughter were killed. With a chip on his shoulder the size of a sequoia tree, Perris had become a successful attorney specializing in criminal law and cases against the department. And he was not above getting ammunition for his plaintiffs by any means necessary, whether it meant picking my brain about harassment in the department or, in his latest stunt, stealing some of my late husband's files on gangs and black militant groups when he and my family were at my house, supposedly helping me pack up some odds and ends for storage.

"What about a significant other?"

I noted his use of the politically correct term and wondered whether he was trying to be polite or infer something about my sexuality or his own. "I moved in with my boyfriend a few months ago, but he's not a cop," I replied, knowing that Aubrey was a listening ear but that his sympathy came too often with a dose of unsolicited advice.

He made a note. "Sounds like something we can talk about in a future session."

"Whatever you think," I said, trying to keep my voice agreeable.

He didn't say anything for a while; then, more to himself than me: "Perhaps something could be arranged with your superiors. Maybe get you an inside assignment."

I almost told him I'd rather be back in the field, but I knew that was a lie. Much as I hated riding the paper or fielding phone calls, if it was all I could do to get back on the Smiley Face investigation, I'd do it gladly. Anything to crack one of those unsolveds that keep you up at night with the feeling that some murderer is out there laughing while you twist in the wind of your failure.

"Detective, are you sure you're up for this?" Wychowski said, regarding me intently.

"Call me Charlotte." I took note of the slight crinkle of satisfaction around his eyes. *Two points for our side.* "And I *am* up for it, sir. I've had almost a week off after that last case, and I did nothing but sleep."

"Which could be a sign of something other than tiredness."

I knew where he was headed, but I was willing to let him have his little victory. "Like what?"

"Depression, for one thing."

"Isn't that where *you* come in? I come and talk to you once a week, work out this anger or depression or whatever it is you think you see."

He shot me a look that said he'd caught the disparaging edge in my voice. "And you can show me how to use some of those tools you mentioned," I hurried on, afraid I might have tipped my hand. "I could try them out, you know, in real-time situations, see if they can keep me from ripping the heads off of some of these idiots I have to deal with." I rattled the antacids in my pocket. "Maybe I can even get rid of these."

He didn't respond. Instead, he sat leafing through my file for what seemed like hours. He eventually pulled an LAPD form from a drawer and started writing.

"So?" I could feel the weight of those antacids in my pocket.

"I'm going to go along with this on a short-term basis."

"With what? Desk duty only or can I go back into the field?"

"Into the field, but only for this one case. And only under the close supervision of a senior detective."

"But I was supervising on my last case! I don't see why I can't—"

"Take it or leave it, Detective. I'm not going to let you put yourself, or anyone else, in danger until I'm satisfied you're ready to resume a full schedule." While I grumbled acquiescence, he went on: "You will report to this office and me twice a week. See Yuki on your way out—she'll help you arrange for days that fit your work schedule."

I started to protest that the appointments would interrupt what I expected would be intense work weeks, but decided to bite my tongue. Go along to get along.

Bullshit the bullshitters.

"*Are* we clear, Detective?"

"As a mountain stream, Dr. P."

His mustache twitched upward, letting me know there might be a human being in there somewhere. "Soon as we're done, I'm going to phone your CO and tell him of my recommendation, and that the paperwork is on the way." He put down his pen and looked at me the way my father would when he'd let me stay out past my normal curfew. "But don't mess this up for yourself, Charlotte. Or this department. We don't always allow an officer back in the field during therapy, especially not one who's been through as much as you. So you've really got to do the work this time. No breezing through here for three or four sessions, half-stepping and telling me what you think I want to hear, and then getting back out there and going into meltdown. You got it?"

So Pablo Wychowski *had* been talking to Dr. Betty. And had read my file more closely than he'd let on.

"Despite what you cops say," he added, "BSS does *not* stand for Bullshit Shrinks."

And he wasn't as clueless as he looked. "Got it," I said.

"We're going to look at every aspect of your life on the job and your family life in a way I suspect you never have before. Think of it as a chance to take stock."

"Take stock."

He rose and extended his hand. "You'll work as hard in here as you do on your cases, so get ready."

If shooting the shit with this shrink helped me get back to the work I loved sooner, I was willing to give this therapy idea another shot. I took his hand this time and squeezed it. "I'm ready, Dr. P."

3

Family Business

should have used the ride back to the PAB to focus on Engalla and the Smiley Face shootings, but my thoughts kept returning to something Dr. P had said. And as much as I wished miracles were possible, I held out little hope that therapy or anything else could improve my relationship with my family or keep them out of my business.

The first-born daughter of a high-yellow Angeleno and her darker-skinned, Arkansas-born husband, I had felt like the ball in a Ping-Pong match, ricocheting between the competing interests of the blue-veined Currys versus the down-home Justices.

It had started over my choice of a career. I'd grown up with a natural love of history, a love my father, Matt, encouraged me to turn into teaching—a profession revered by his side of the family.

Whack.

But that wasn't good enough for my multi-degreed, Talented Tenth mother, who felt that nothing less than doctors or lawyers should number among the fabulous Curry clan.

Whack.

Buffeted by their arguments, I veered toward a life of crime almost by default, spurred as much by the need to break out of my family's prison of expectations as by the desire to murder a conniving heifer who'd trapped Aubrey Scott, my brother's best friend and my high school crush, at the altar.

An undergraduate criminology class was just the ticket, allowing me to understand crime and the mind of the criminal without actually becoming one. The benefits of that class were many—I finally found something I was actually interested in, as opposed to having something drummed into my head by my parents, and I was able to transfer my affections from Aubrey to Professor Keith Roberts, a more mature brother who sported a big Afro and who lived in an apartment in the then-fashionable Jungle, down the hill from my parents' home in View Park.

But even after I graduated and we began to work together professionally, it looked as if my interest in Keith would go unreciprocated until I invited him to a barbecue at my parents' house one Fourth of July. To my surprise, he not only accepted but suggested we go out to a fireworks display afterward.

While I was shocked, my mother Joymarie was all atwitter, impressed that a full professor from the most prestigious university in town would deign to attend a Justice family gathering. "She's drivin' me crazy," my father reported on the preparations. "I've had to rearrange the furniture in the livin' room three times and have the pool cleaned twice! I hope this professor friend a'yours is worth my sanity!"

Another reason we kids called our parents' home the Nut House.

My brother was excited about Keith's visit, too, but for different reasons. Perris had joined the LAPD a few years before and worked out of Southwest, one of the busier divisions in the city. I couldn't say police work suited my politically left-of-center brother, but my mother had determined he was even less suited to Vietnam, which he had an excellent chance of seeing, given his low draft number. So Joymarie had pulled some strings to get her favorite child on the department and safely ensconced under the watchful eye of my father's best friend, Henry Youngblood, who also happened to be at the time commanding officer of the LAPD's Southwest division and my godfather.

Perris had heard me talk about Keith's research, and thought his

knowledge of street gangs could benefit him and his partner, Burt
Rivers, in their patrol work. So Perris descended on poor Keith the
minute he hit the door, dragging him out by the pool to talk about
Crips and Bloods, Deathstalkers and Royals. As the afternoon progressed I saw Keith warm to Perris, as people inevitably did, as se-
duced by my brother's probing questions as I was repelled by them
when they were directed my way.

But, a week later, when Perris dubbed Keith "a brilliant brother"
while looking at the photos taken of Keith and me during the barbecue, my venture into the world of crime was somehow sanctioned, my
chosen career as a criminologist suitable for admission into Joymarie
Justice's List of Approved Professions, even if Professor Roberts was a
few shades darker than desirable in a potential mate for her fair-
skinned daughter.

At least he has a Ph.D., she consoled herself.

And I was on that path, too, was what my father called ABD—all-
but-the-dissertation—when Keith and our baby, Erica, were murdered
in our driveway, victims of what law enforcement would come to call a
drive-by shooting. Their deaths drove me over the edge and out of the
ivory tower of academia to face crime where it lived—in the streets and
houses of the City of Angels, in the hearts and minds of criminals who
perpetrated more evil than I could ever imagine. Hunting them down,
seeing them taken off the streets became the driving force of my life,
as necessary to my survival as air. And I was willing to do whatever it
took to keep doing it, even if it meant dredging up the past with Dr. P,
reliving the sights of blood in my driveway, blood on the walls, blood
on my hands.

But as the bus pulled up to the PAB, bile rose in my throat again,
and I realized that "whatever it took" could be more distasteful than I
had anticipated.

I t was a blessing in disguise that I spotted Billie Truesdale as I entered the lobby. In a department where watching your back was as
necessary to the job as carrying a weapon, Billie was one of the people

I never had to worry about. In addition to being a sure-nough sister from the 'hood, what made me like Billie was the fact that she was a warrior, cunning enough to have survived both the violence-prone streets of her neighborhood and the testosterone-laden halls of South Bureau Homicide, where she'd worked for several years before getting called up to RHD. I'd been privileged to work a couple of cases with Billie while she was in South Bureau. I also knew her from the Georgia Robinson Society, an L.A. sisterhood of black females in law enforcement that meets every few months to console and cajole its members into staying the course. But it wasn't until Billie transferred to RHD that I realized how deep the sisterhood went, how she had my back even when I thought it was covered.

So seeing her emerge from the elevator and cross the lobby that day allowed me to breathe a little easier and focus on the case ahead instead of the one just completed—the one that had taken me up those same elevators and into hell, then sent me back to BSS for another stretch in their padded offices. But no one knew about BSS but me, my commanding officer, and Dr. P., and I intended to keep it that way. Even if it meant keeping a secret from the closest thing I had to a friend on the job.

I slipped up behind her as she was buying some donuts from the snack shop. "Step away from those pastries and put your hands where I can see them!"

"Charlotte! Girl, how are you?"

"Fine, but you won't be if you keep eating those fat pills."

She smiled crookedly, hiding the package in a pocket. "Did you get my phone calls?"

I accepted her warm hug, giving her a sisterly pat on the back in return. "We've been letting the machine pick up the calls." Calls from Billie, from my girlfriend Katrina, from exclusive-seeking reporters—and especially from my thieving drunk of a brother, whose bullshit and excuses I just wasn't up to facing.

Billie snorted her approval as we headed for the elevators. "Fine as that man of yours is, I can understand that! So, what are you doing back so soon?"

I was amused at how Billie could appreciate men yet be so attracted to women. "It's Aubrey's fault. He saw Engalla on the news and made me watch the story."

Billie cocked her head to the side. "And now you're here because . . . ?"

"I figured I could help out."

"Won-der Wo-man!" Billie sang and twirled an imaginary lasso over her head.

But after I explained how the Smiley Face shootings had haunted me, she changed her tune. "I'd rather eat broken glass than have a cold case on my conscience," she admitted. "And I hope you do get assigned to it, 'cause we're sure 'nough going to need someone around who worked it before."

I paused at the elevator, lightheaded at the memory of the last time I'd ridden it upstairs. "We? Stobaugh's already put you on it?"

"Given the department's workload and Middleton wrapping up the Vicki Park homicide, I'm the only available detective from our team— and a successor of sorts to the original folks who worked it." The elevator doors opened, and Billie walked past me. "Speaking of Park, we each got a letter of commendation from Chief Youngblood for how we handled that case. I think it's a bit of a power play on his part to keep the old guard from taking all the credit, but I'm not complaining."

"Me either." My feet rooted to the ground, I could not follow Billie into that elevator. "But that's great for you and Middleton. Your first case out of the gate at RHD and a commendation to show for it. Solving the Smiley Face shootings will be another feather in your cap."

Billie turned to see the look on my face. "Don't look so upset! No one's saying you can't work the case. It's just that . . ."

Realizing she'd misread my body language, I waved away her apology, and slipped inside. "Don't even trip it."

She pushed the third floor button. "You sure you feel up to it?"

"You're the second person to ask me that today!"

"Sorry," Billie mumbled and faced the front of the elevator. "I just remember the wiped-out look on your face when we found you in that interview room with that cop last week. Kind of the way you look right now." When I didn't respond, she repeated her concerns about my readiness to return to the job.

"Don't be silly!" I managed to laugh this time. "Who's the new lead on the case?"

But instead of Harry Bosch, Billie gave me someone else to worry about. "Thor."

Knocking on seventy, Larry Thorfinsen had solved so many cases in his thirty-odd years in RHD that he'd attained mythic proportions in the LAPD pantheon of crimefighters. And while I'd learned a lot from him on our last case, Thor had some very human foibles, including a bad habit of turning a deaf ear when it came to confronting the wrong-headed slurs made by some of our colleagues. The most recent, which had tagged Billie and me as the Dykenamic Duo, had motivated me to bet the senior detective a hundred dollars that we'd solve the Park case, which we did in record time. And although he'd paid up, I had the lingering feeling that Thor was not on my side.

Billie unearthed the package of donuts from her pocket as we got out of the elevator. "I just came downstairs to get some sustenance before going to the briefing he's called on the case."

As if he knows anything about it. "Well, let me check in with the higher-ups, see if they'll let me join you."

"That'd be great." Billie's smile told me she meant it.

4

Then Engalla Popped Up

The CHP have any leads on where Nilo Engalla's been for the past eight months?" I asked.

After a brief conversation with my captain and Lieutenant Stobaugh, I had joined Billie and the legendary Thor at his desk in a section of the Homicide I bullpen where he held court. And although the three of us spoke in hushed tones, I could feel the attention of every detective at our end of the big room, straining to glean some little tidbit of information, not the least of which was how the hell did I get returned to duty so soon.

Thor answered my question with a shrug. "The Chippies are trying to reconstruct his movements, but it's difficult to get information from someone in a coma."

"They think he'll come around?"

"He's not showing any signs yet, but the hospital and the CHP know to call us as soon as there's any change."

"Maybe we ought to head up there, see what we can find out on our own."

Thor raised his hand. "Hold your water, Justice. How seriously were you looking at him?"

"Not at all in the beginning. We first thought the shooting was part of a busy gangbanging weekend. But there were no wits who could definitively ID the car or its occupants, and we could never trace the M.O. to any of the usual suspects in our gang databases. So then we started looking at each of the vics, see if anyone wanted them dead."

"Zuccari's an Italian name. Any chance he's mobbed up?"

"The name *is* Italian, but the family is German, came to the States in the thirties. Interestingly enough, there was some background noise about the family being tied to the Nazis prior to immigrating."

"What 'background noise'?" Thor asked.

"A letter was sent to Zuccari about six months prior to the shooting, containing a German magazine article about his father making uniforms for the Hitler Youth Brigade—"

Thor raised a craggy eyebrow. "The Hitlerjugend?"

"Yeah. Zuccari's assistant said the letter shook up her boss pretty badly, convinced him someone was out to get him. So much so he hired an outside PR firm and additional security, too. The company's attorneys thought it was either extortion or maybe had something to do with the venture with the Shareefs, but there were never any follow-up letters or leaks to the press, so they blew it off."

"You got the letter?" Thor asked.

"The assistant saw Zuccari put it in his desk, but she couldn't find it among his papers after the shooting."

"I know why," Billie said. "Imagine the fallout in the stock market if the public got wind that the founder of CZ Toys was a Nazi! It'd be as bad as Procter & Gamble and the Satanism rumors in the eighties!"

"Was there any truth to the Nazi accusation?" Thor asked.

"About as much as Procter & Gamble and the devil." I spoke easily from memory. "Of course, we spent some time on it, but we couldn't confirm the Nazi connection. What we did learn was that Claus Zuckerman, the father's real name, was a down-on-his-luck dollmaker who became very successful supplying uniforms for the Hitlerjugend. But Zuckerman lost the contract and ended up changing the family name and fleeing to the U.S. when Hitler made membership in his youth brigade mandatory, and his son was coming up on that age. As Carlo Zuccari, Zuckerman reestablished his doll-making business in New Jersey. His son Chuck moved it to California in 'sixty-eight, took the company public ten years later, and has never looked back."

Billie grunted. "With a family history like that, I wouldn't either."

"How's the company doing today?" Thor asked.

"Still publicly traded, although eighty percent of the stock's still held by the family. And they're fairly successful, in that second tier of toy companies behind Mattel and Hasbro, growing from increased sales and aquisitions like the Shareefs."

"Anything else?" Thor asked.

"The company's a huge corporate supporter of the arts in Orange County, several hospitals, too. And from all accounts, Zuccari himself is a pillar of society down there, a big deal in some ultraconservative wing of the Republican Party."

Next to me, I heard Billie mutter something under her breath about the berry not falling too far from the bush, which I chose to ignore, adding: "His net worth's about one hundred fifty million, depending on the value of the company's stock."

Thor whistled while Billie said: "Not too shabby. What about the wife? She piss off anybody at the country club who carried a grudge?"

"Which wife are we talking?"

Billie's eyebrow shot up. "How many are there?"

"The one who got shot, Alma Zuccari, is number three."

"What's her story?"

"Born Alma Gordone, from some little berg in New Jersey, only child of a physician dad and a socialite mom, both deceased."

"So we can assume no mob connections with her, either," Billie stated more than asked, sneaking a glance in Thor's direction. "What about the other wives?"

"The first wife died when their son Mario was two. Zuccari remarried in the late fifties but divorced Number Two three years before the shooting. She landed on her feet, though, and remarried a venture capitalist even richer than Zuccari."

"So Number Two's got no motive to have him shot," Billie said, ignoring the exasperated glare Thor cast her way.

"She's got a personal net worth of about sixteen million herself, mostly in the company's stock, as do his son Mario and a daughter, Gabriella."

Thor asked for a rundown on the Zuccari siblings. "Both of them work in the business. The son, Mario, should be forty now. He's the CFO, unmarried as I recall, upstanding citizen, a lay leader in one of those born-again megachurches in Orange County that his father supports. The daughter, Gabriella, is about ten years younger and does something for the company over in Europe, I can't recall. We never met her."

"This third wife," Billie asked, referring to the notes she was taking, "Alma—she a trophy wife, gold digger, or both?"

"She was working as a trade show model when they met. Thirty-seven to Zuccari's sixty-six at the time of the shooting, so you do the math."

"Pretty?" Thor asked.

"Reasonably so, if you're into blondes."

Billie raised her hand. "Then I vote trophy wife. Anything else on her?"

"They'd been married a little over a year at the time of the shooting, and she was pregnant with their first child."

Thor made a noise between a snort and a laugh. "She didn't waste any time."

"The scuttlebutt we picked up around the company was that Zuccari wasn't too thrilled about having a baby so late in life, but what could he do? As my father would say: 'the fish was caught in his net.' "

Thor chuckled while Billie asked: "What do we know about the couple they were having dinner with?"

"The Shareefs? Both Harvard grads, the husband Malik had a Ph.D. in psychology, his wife Habiba an MBA. He was from Oakland, she from L.A. They were squeaky-clean, no enemies, no bad habits, not even an outstanding parking ticket. All they were trying to do was get their toy company off the ground."

"What was the name of their company?" Billie asked.

"Beautiful You Dollworks."

"That's not the same black toy company in L.A. that went out of business a few years ago?"

"You're thinking of Shindana, which started in the aftermath of the

Watts riots and closed in the mid-eighties. And that was despite some funding from Mattel."

"Which has gone on to dominate the black doll market. How did the Shareefs think they could compete with that?"

"Habiba Shareef told me they weren't initially planning on selling their ethnic dolls to the general public like Mattel, just special-edition collectibles until they could build their reputation. She and her husband believed they had a good shot at it, if they could raise enough capital. Sad thing was their dream was just about to come true—they had just signed a multimillion-dollar joint venture deal between Beautiful You and CZ Toys. They were celebrating with the Zuccaris when Malik got shot along with Zuccari and his family. He died a month later from complications related to the open-heart surgery they had to perform on him."

"What about their deal with CZ Toys?" Thor asked.

"In limbo, along with Chuck Zuccari. He's been in a coma since the shooting."

I fell silent, painfully aware of how a bullet can end a life, or worse.

"A black toymaker like Shareef's not a high-profiler," Billie noted after a moment. "How'd we end up with the case instead of it being assigned to Central Bureau?"

"We were catching it from two sides. With Zuccari's Republican connections, the governor's office was on our tails from the get-go. And the head of the L.A. Tourism Bureau sits on the Police Commission, so he put a lot of pressure on the chief to get the case wrapped up before it affected what little convention business the city's had since the riots."

"And I'm assuming Zuccari's family had alibis for the night of the shooting?" Billie said.

"Every last one of them. Checked and rechecked."

Thor squinted into the distance. "What about the Black Muslim angle? I remember Steve running that by me last summer."

In response to Billie's questioning look, I explained: "There was a theory floating around the office that the shooting was connected to the Nation of Islam."

"Like I said, Black Muslims," Thor added.

"Not all black Muslims are in the Nation of Islam," Billie broke in. "The majority of African-American Muslims adhere to the more traditional forms of Islam, ever since Elijah Muhammad's son Wallace D. split from the Nation in the seventies."

"Thank you for the world religion lesson, Detective," Thor said. "How do you know so much about these whatever-you-call-them Muslims?"

"There are a number of Islamic centers in the Southwest Division," Billie replied, her tone equally scornful. "You should visit one sometime. It might open your eyes."

Shaking his head, Thor said, "You seen one, you seen 'em all, I say," clearly playing to the peanut gallery.

Billie rolled her eyes heavenward, then asked me if there was any truth to the rumors.

"Malik had grown up in the Nation, up in Oakland, his wife down here. But by her own admission, they'd been away from the Nation since grad school."

"Did he convert to one of the other branches of Islam?" Billie asked. "A number of former Nation members did."

"I think they're Sunnis. Is that important?"

"Maybe. It would certainly create some serious ethical considerations in the way he'd approach a business deal with CZ Toys. And I have no idea what kind of prohibitions there'd be for Shareef doing business with a company with Nazi connections. Talk about your strange bedfellows!"

"Just remember, we could find no evidence that the Nazi rumor has ever surfaced in this country."

"Still, if someone sent Zuccari that article," Thor argued, "one of these Muslim groups could have known about it, too."

"And what?" Billie interrupted. "Shot Shareef and Zuccari to teach them the errors of their ways? Wouldn't that be a little extreme?"

"Don't dismiss it so quickly," Thor warned. "That Nation of Islam tip was highly credible!"

"No one said it wasn't, Thor," I replied carefully. "It just turned out to be a dead end. Then Engalla popped up."

The phone on Thor's desk jangled. "Continue."

"A few weeks after the shooting, Engalla quit CZ Toys, just before his internship ended. The company's V.P. of Human Resources called to say it was the first time that'd ever happened with one of the kids from the UC Irvine program."

Thor's phone stopped ringing and then started up again. "Go on," he insisted, waving his hand at the phone as if shooing away a bothersome pigeon.

"And when the HR Department called the following week to say Engalla hadn't picked up his last paycheck, we decided we'd better interview the boy. That's when we discovered he'd moved out of his apartment and left no forwarding address."

Thor's phone kept ringing. "I'd better take this." Thor listened to the voice on the other end, his face softening as he turned away and called the name of a favorite daughter. "Sweetheart, I'm in a meeting."

"Maybe Engalla took his last paycheck with him," Billie whispered. "That twenty-seven thousand the Highway Patrol found in his car would be an awfully big payday for a kid working a summer internship. What department was he in?"

"Finance."

"So he could have had access."

Something his daughter said seemed to upset Thor, who, his face turning ashen, cursed softly and assured her he'd be there as soon as he could.

"And Engalla never returned to campus?" Billie asked.

"Never did."

Thor hung up and apologized for the interruption. "Are you okay?" I asked, noting that the color was still drained from his face.

"I'm fine. Engalla's a Filipino name, right?"

"Yeah, why?"

"You look for him in the Flip community over near Temple?"

Hearing what sounded like a slur come from Thor's lips reminded me of some of the more racist and sexist comments that had been circulating around the department. "We put out BOLOs with all our divisions to be on the lookout for him and put him on all the interstate and national databases, in case he showed up in another jurisdiction. His parents live up north, in Daly City, so the local PD even surveilled their house for a couple of months as a courtesy, but he never surfaced."

"Maybe his parents are migrant workers," Thor suggested. "That might account for him turning up in the Central Valley. They got a bunch of 'em there."

I didn't remember that coming up in our investigation, but I said I'd check the file. "Gena conducted those interviews."

Billie's spine stiffened. "Did you only look in Filipino neighborhoods? Isn't it a big assumption to think he'd only go there?"

Thor sighed heavily and rolled his eyes. "Spare me the PC lecture, Truesdale!"

"I know what Billie means, Thor," I broke in. "I raised that question myself when we heard Engalla had disappeared. But we found out the kid hadn't made many friends down in Orange County, spent his time in that last year either working or volunteering at a Filipino cultural center up here, so it was a logical conclusion."

"What was he doing at the cultural center?" Billie asked.

"Tutoring neighborhood kids in math is what I remember, but you should verify that against the first sixty-dayer in the case file." Sixty-dayers were reports on ongoing cases that one of the investigating detectives completed every two months to recap the investigation and demonstrate to the higher-ups we were doing our jobs. Gena Cortez had completed the first two on the Smiley Face shootings, and I had written the last one after she went out on medical leave.

Thor threw a pen on his desk. "Whaddya wanna bet the boy embezzled that cash they found in his car? If Chuck Zuccari found out about it, it would provide a motive for Engalla shooting him."

"But if Zuccari knew, wouldn't someone else in the company have had to tell him?" Billie asked. "I mean CEOs don't go around checking the books themselves, do they?"

"No one at the company reported any money missing, either when Engalla first disappeared or afterward. And it's not like they didn't know how to contact us if something came up—we interviewed all of Engalla's supervisors, plus Zuccari's son and Alma."

"How many supervisors did he have?"

"Three. He was on some kind of financial internship, as I recall, that rotated through Internal Auditing, Accounts Payable, and maybe the controller's office."

Thor raised a bushy eyebrow. "You would think, among that group, that someone would have discovered any missing funds by now."

"Yeah, but we haven't heard anything from the company or the Zuccari family in months."

"Bet you will now," he predicted, sighing as he ran a hand over his gray hair. Although Thor had been threatening for years to retire to Oregon to be closer to his daughter and her family, he always seemed to stick around for one more notch in his famed belt of killers apprehended and called to account. In fact, he'd parlayed that fame into more than one consulting gig, the first of which had earned him the Norse god nickname, bestowed by a television producer who'd used Thor's old case files to create an Emmy-winning detective series in the early eighties. Presiding over the successful resurrection and closing of a case that had stopped people from frequenting downtown restaurants and nightspots for almost a year would be particularly sweet nectar for this god.

Maybe even lead to another television series.

"I'm calling the Zuccari family as soon as we finish this meeting, just to bring them up to speed," Thor was saying. He asked me for their home numbers.

"I can look through my old notebook. But it might be faster to call Firestone. He was lead—"

"I'm not bothering Steve at home for some numbers you should have at your fingertips! Where's the goddamn case file?"

"Lieutenant Stobaugh had me send the files over to Central Records after I filled that last sixty-dayer," I snapped back, not sure whether Thor was annoyed that I didn't know the family's numbers by heart or still pissed that I'd helped set Steve Firestone up on a sexual harassment beef that had gotten him suspended.

"Who rode the paper?"

"Gena Cortez, who's—"

"Still on medical leave." His face contorted at the mention of the name of my former partner—and the principal accuser of his passing-for-white protégé Firestone.

"I can call her, if you want."

Thor's look was withering. "Not with both of you scheduled to give testimony at Steve's hearing in a couple of weeks."

The rustling of my colleagues in the bullpen ceased, letting me know they were still eavesdropping. My mouth went dry, and I had to remind myself to breathe. "Where'd you hear that? No one's given me a date."

Thor reached for one of his LAPD coffee mugs, this one commemorating the department's one-hundred-and-twenty-fifth anniversary. "I have my sources."

In that moment, if I could have dropped through the floor, I would have.

Billie shot me a sympathetic look. She knew how much I dreaded testifying against my former supervisor, even if the asshole deserved every punishment the Board of Rights could impose. "Why don't I retrieve the files from Central Records and debrief with Detective Cortez? It'll be a good way for me to get up to speed."

"Fine. Justice, call CZ Toys' headquarters, see if Zuccari's family is available to talk." Thor gave me another smug look. "Unless you've got a problem doing a little spadework."

Billie and I stared at each other, aware of the emphasis he'd put on the word "spade." What possessed me to think Thor was turning a deaf ear to the outrageous comments of his colleagues? He was probably as much a part of generating them as everyone else.

"What is it, Justice?" he prodded. "You got a problem working under a male supervisor?"

Thor's inflection told me he was clearly playing to the peanut gallery, letting them know that he was still one of them and he wasn't going to let me off easy about Firestone. "Not at all," I replied, loud enough for them to hear me, too. "Besides, I'm the one who knows the case best."

"And I'm the one running it now." Thor took another sip of his coffee. "Lieutenant Stobaugh put me on this case because he thought we needed some fresh eyes. If that's a problem for you, maybe it *would* be better if you stayed here and rode the paper."

I heard a couple of guys at the nearby desks snicker. Billie sucked in her cheeks and studied her notes. While given to bluntness in his working relationships, I thought Thor and I had made peace after the Park case.

Guess you thought wrong, my little voice mocked.

"No problem. When do you want to go down there?"

"Soon as Detective Truesdale gets back with the file."

Billie checked her watch. "I can be back with it at one."

"How's three?" Thor said to me. "That'll give us a couple of hours to review it."

I shook my head. "We should leave here by two, avoid the traffic heading south."

"Fine," Thor agreed, sipping his coffee, "if being there later conflicts with your *busy* schedule."

Was I imagining it, or had he intentionally mangled the pronunciation of the word *busy,* making it sound like the initials for Behavioral Sciences Services? Did he know I had been ordered in to see a BSS shrink, and would that knowledge make my life on the job more miserable than usual?

"Not at all." *You asshole.* "Not at all."

5

Behind the Orange Curtain

As I drove the unmarked through traffic to the I-5 interchange and headed south, I was reminded of my childhood, when riding south along the stretch of I-5 known as the Santa Ana Freeway was a magical journey, the long drive from my parents' house through fragrant orange groves and dairy land culminating in our arrival at my brother's and my personal kingdom—Disneyland. Behind that orange curtain, I could be Sleeping Beauty awaiting her Prince Charming or Becky chasing Indians with Tom Sawyer on our own private island, while Perris played out his big-game hunting fantasies on the Jungle River Cruise. We were too young to know that while the Magic Kingdom welcomed children like us (and our parents' money), the reality was that colored girls and boys couldn't be Becky Sharp, a big-game hunter, or any other "cast member" until a good decade after the park opened.

"And those first jobs were shoeshine boys and tap dancers!" my father, Matt, always reminded us. As I drove that road now with Thor, I wondered whether it was facts or fantasies that drove Nilo Engalla south from the Bay Area to behind Orange County's mythical curtain.

A quick scan of the case file Billie had retrieved hadn't provided many clues. The interviews Gena Cortez had conducted with Nilo Engalla's parents, José and Rhea, had revealed that the boy was the only child of a union organizer father and an accountant mother. He'd grown up and attended public schools in Daly City, south of San Francisco, as part of a close-knit Filipino community. The boy's only act of rebellion, it appeared, was going to UC Irvine instead of Berkeley, his mother's alma mater. His parents had told Gena there were relatives in a province not far from Manila and in Northern California, but Gena's subsequent notes and interviews confirmed that Engalla had neither left the country nor contacted any family members since his disappearance last summer.

"The parents were probably lying," Thor pointed out when I recapped the file for him. "Filipinos can lie you around the block and you'd never know it. And before you drive the car off the road, I'm not saying this to be racist."

They never do. "Then why *are* you saying it?"

"Years ago, we arrested a Filipino suspect at the scene of a crime, covered in blood, knife in hand. The little bastard beat the machine. The polygraph examiner said it wasn't the first time it'd happened with Filipinos, either."

"And how do Filipinos allegedly do that?"

"Not allegedly." Thor looked past me toward The Citadel, a recently opened outlet mall on the site of a historic tire factory. "The examiner's theory is that Filipinos attach no cultural shame to lying. Saving face at any cost, especially with outsiders, is what matters most. So, when necessary, they'll lie. And, true to form, our guy had no discernible physiological response to the key questions we were asking."

I knew there were some suspects—particularly among psychopaths and sociopaths, who lack the guilty conscience that motivates most people—who could beat a polygraph machine, but to make that assumption about an entire ethnic group sounded racist to me. Did Thor and that examiner have similar "theories" for every ethnic group not their own? I shook off the possibility and focused on the case at hand. "Regardless, that's why we asked the Daly City PD to surveil the parents' house, just in case the boy showed up there."

Thor patted my shoulder. "No need to be so defensive, Justice. Nobody's saying you weren't doing your job. With Steve supervising, I'm sure you covered all the bases."

I must have bristled at hearing Firestone's name, because Thor then asked how long Steve and I had worked together. I exhaled and kept my mind on the road ahead. "Long enough."

"Two and a half years altogether, am I right? I worked with the man for seven years before he was promoted to D-three and you transferred in. Steve Firestone is aces far as I'm concerned—always eager to learn something new, always willing to go the extra mile on a case."

I took in a breath, waiting for the other shoe to drop.

I didn't have to wait long. "It's a shame what this whole sexual harassment charge has done to him. He's started drinking again, you know."

I bit my tongue and remembered my vow: *Go along to get along.*

"Jessica's left him for good," Thor went on, "and giving him one hell of a custody battle over the kids. All because some coochie-coochie split tail he was banging on the side got pissed off when he and his wife reconciled."

That was it for me. I was tired of seeing red; whether from biting my tongue or from Thor's comments didn't matter. "You should have your polygraph examiner administer a test to Firestone, if *that's* what he's telling you! Firestone started hitting the bottle when Jessica first left him last *spring*, Thor. I know because he showed up at my house, stinking of beer and trying to make a pass at me. If I hadn't threatened to kick his ass, he would have done me the same way he did Gena Cortez!"

"Come on, Justice! Steve was just kidding around. You know how he is."

I realized this conversation was going nowhere fast and might even be engineered by the crafty senior detective to get me to reveal what I might say at Firestone's upcoming hearing. Thoroughly annoyed at Thor and myself, I clamped my mouth shut and concentrated on the traffic while leaving him to leaf through his notebook. Several minutes passed in awkward silence. Finally, in an effort to put Firestone behind us, I said: "How's your daughter—what's her—?"

"Julia."

"—yes, Julia—liking Oregon?"

"Salem's okay," he replied, lips drawn tight as he read through his notebook. "Her daughter Kate's just having a little trouble adjusting to her new middle school. I promised Julia that my wife and I'd go up there this weekend and have a little talk with her."

"Middle school can be quite a transition. All those different classes, and the heightened social scene."

"Yeah, the social scene." I could sense Thor's restlessness in the seat beside me, as if he were making up his mind about something. "I want your opinion on something, as a woman, not a cop, okay?"

"Okay," I said, not sure where this was headed.

"Some boys at Kate's school found out she had, uh, you know, had her first, she'd . . ." His gaze fell on his notes as if the missing phrase was there.

"Gotten her period?"

He nodded, relief suffusing his face. I was sure mine was flushing. This was not a conversation I wanted to have with a man my father's age.

"They decorated her locker with those, you know . . . those sanitary things. That's what Julia was calling about yesterday, crying and arguing with Kate because she wants to come back to L.A. to live with her grandmother and me." He sat back in his seat. "Damn near broke my heart. I'm just wondering if I said the right things."

Moved by the emotion in the old detective's voice, I told myself I should just shut up, pretend I had no opinion at all.

Chicken!

Oh, all right. "What did you tell her?"

"That she couldn't let a bunch of losers shame Kate into short-changing her education!"

"Sounds like good advice to me."

"My wife and I are hoping to go up there this weekend. But until we do, I told Julia to take Kate up to the school and file a complaint with the principal. Can't let a bunch of bullies ruin your daughter's life, I told her."

"I think that was the right call. It's nice that you stood up for Kate. It'll teach her not to be afraid."

"She's had a rough go of it. Heart defect when she was a baby, then her dad and mom divorced a couple of years ago. I feel like I'm all she's got sometimes, so I gotta stand up for her."

His comment lingered in the air for a bit. "I'd do the same thing for my niece or my sisters," I said gently. "Same goes for my sisters in blue."

If looks could kill, Thor had just put me six feet under. He slapped his notebook shut, hunkered down in his seat, and covered his eyes with his right hand. "Let me know when we get there," he muttered.

The headquarters for CZ Toys was located in one of Irvine's numerous office developments, clusters of reflective glass buildings that had been spreading like the plague since the city's incorporation in 1971. We checked in with a guard in the granite-floored lobby and made our way into an elevator that was decorated with posters for the company's latest line of interactive toys.

The lobby on the top floor was a plush affair, adorned on one wall with oil paintings of what must have been the company's earlier headquarters in the mountains of Germany and the flatlands of New Jersey, and the other with full-length portraits of Carlo Zuccari and his son Chuck, the current CEO and a chip off the old man's block, down to the piercing blue eyes and ramrod-straight bearing. Seeing the two men together, at about the same time in their lives, made me wonder again if the rumors of the father's ties to the Nazis were true, and how much like the father was the son.

The receptionist on the top floor directed us down a long hallway to the boardroom where we were to meet the Zuccari family. Someone had gone to the trouble of laying out the latest in chi-chi waters, lattes, frappés, and fancy cookies, artfully arranged on silver trays. Yet as trendy as the spread before us was, the room itself was a throwback to an earlier time, down to the dark paneling and high-backed leather chairs surrounding a mahogany conference table with a raised shelf.

On the buildings' outside I could see the logos of everything from accounting firms to insurance companies, all of which I bet paid handsomely to be first among equals in this particular circle of corporate hell.

Our Dante was the sixtyish Barbara McIntyre, Chuck Zuccari's helmet-haired assistant, whom I'd met when we first caught the case. Greeting us as she briskly entered the room, she shook hands with Thor, took his card, and made sure we had everything we needed. A squawk-box conversation could be heard coming from the adjoining office, which belonged to Chuck Zuccari. "Ms. Zuccari is just finishing up an overseas call," she informed us after we were seated. "Is there a new development, Detective Justice?"

"Will she be long?"

"Not too much longer, I suspect."

"Has Ms. Zuccari recovered from her injuries?"

Mrs. McIntyre turned a bright red. "I'm sorry, Alma is not employed by the company," she explained in a clipped voice. "I was referring to Gabby."

"Who?"

"Pardon me. Gabriella, Chuck's daughter. The board named her interim president and chief executive officer last December."

"I'm impressed. How old is she?"

"Thirty-four, four years younger than Mr. Zuccari when he moved the company to California."

And five years younger than me. "Impressive. So now you're her executive assistant?"

Mrs. McIntyre smoothed the sleeves of her jacket and crossed her arms. "Until we can find a replacement."

Thor shot me a look. "Has Ms. Zuccari worked for the company long?" he asked.

"She was executive vice president of European marketing until she was called back from Paris at Thanksgiving, once the board realized Mr. Zuccari couldn't . . ." Mrs. McIntyre swallowed hard and dropped her head, unable to continue.

There was a pained silence until I inquired about Mr. Zuccari's condition. Mrs. McIntyre cleared her throat. "There's been no change. When you called about wanting to speak with the family, I took the liberty of contacting the current Mrs. Zuccari, too."

I noticed the coldness in her voice, how she emphasized the word *current* in referring to Alma. "Will Mrs. Zuccari be joining us?"

"She's down at the hospital with Chuck and their baby. She wondered if you could meet her there when you're finished."

McIntyre offered me a slip of paper on which she'd written the name and address of a hospital in South Orange County. She then excused herself and glided to the outer door, closing it softly behind her. I opened a Perrier and took a seat closer to Gabriella's closed door, thinking I might overhear something useful. Thor wandered over to an oversized glass display case at the other end of the room to study a selection of the company's vintage toys. He still hadn't spoken to me directly since our little set-to in the car.

"It's amazing how long CZ Toys has been in business," I tried.

No response.

"I remember the first of their toys I ever had—a talking Gabby doll. Maybe the doll was named after Zuccari's daughter. You heard how Mrs. McIntyre called her Gabby?"

"My daughter Julia had one of these Gabby dolls." Thor was peering at a doll about fifteen inches high, with brown ringlets and chubby cheeks, wearing a blue-and-white gingham checked dress and black patent leather shoes.

"Me, too."

He continued to gaze at the doll. "Chatty Patty—"

"You mean Chatty Cathy."

"Cathy, Patty, Catty, *whatever* the hell she was called, had just come out and by Christmas of that year, every little girl had to have a talking doll."

"I remember that Christmas." It was the year after our rambunctious family had moved to View Park, into a stately house architect Paul Williams had designed for my parents.

"But the damn things were scarce as hen's teeth," Thor went on. "I couldn't find one until the night before Christmas. The store had run out of Chatty what's-her-name, so I brought home a Gabby doll instead. Boy, was that ever the wrong thing to do! My little girl cried and cried because Santa didn't bring her the right doll."

"Santa brought me a Gabby doll that year, too." I didn't tell him I was so disappointed in her skin color that my father helped me dye her brown, with disastrous results.

Thor turned away from the display case. "That squeaking little voice drove me nuts! Always begging for a bedtime story." His voice dropped to a whisper. "I heard that damned line so many times, I would pull the string after Julia went to sleep and tell it stories about the homicide cases I was working!"

"Maybe you would have preferred the phrase Mattel included in a couple of their Chatty Cathy prototypes." The female speaking had emerged from Chuck Zuccari's old office, accompanied by Robert Merritt, whom I recognized as the head of the company's legal department. The woman was tall and lean in that gym-addicted way usually seen in women with too much money and time on their hands. Her heavily made-up cheeks were sunken; her shoulder-length highlighted brown hair was pulled into a ponytail that bore little resemblance to her curly-headed namesake in that display case. As if to accentuate their differences, this Gabby wore a black satin bustier decorated with studs under a black skirted suit that shrieked couture, and a diamond-studded Rolex worn on her right wrist that I was sure cost more than a month of my salary.

I could see Thor sizing up the thirty or so feet from where he stood to the door Merritt and Gabriella Zuccari had entered when they ruined his punch line. Was he thinking the same thing I was—*how in the hell did she hear what he'd just whispered?* "What phrase was that?" he asked, surreptitiously glancing around the room.

"Now remember," she cautioned, a twinkle in her brown eyes, "these were the days when male sales reps sold to male toy store buyers."

Thor's smile faded as he looked warily from the advancing executives to me.

"The phrase was 'Put me down, you bastard!' My dad said it helped

Mattel move tens of thousands of units. They outsold us five to one that Christmas."

Although Thor laughed, he had turned a bright red. I stifled a smile, pleased to see another female get the veteran detective's goat.

Gabriella approached the spot where I was sitting and stuck out her acrylic-nailed hand, the diamonds in her watch winking at me in the overhead lights. "You must be Detective Justice. Mrs. McIntyre tells me you have some news for us."

I shook her hand and introduced her and Merritt to Thor, who, recovered by then, explained his supervisory role in the case. "Then perhaps I should be asking you that question," Gabriella said, tossing her ponytail and giving him a brilliant smile as she pumped his hand in turn.

Thor's eyes drifted to Gabriella's exposed chest, then shifted quickly to her face. "There *have* been some developments," he muttered, and sat across from me.

"Then we need to hear them," Merritt said. A conservatively groomed man in his early sixties, Merritt was the typical corporate attorney and as different from Gabriella as night and day. Merritt had been a thorn in the side of our investigation from the beginning, always trying to block us from talking to employees, insisting that he or one of his staff be in the room during every interview. I knew he was only doing his job, but I couldn't stop thinking that Robert Merritt was more of a hindrance than a help in solving the crime, even the kind of man who would push his own agenda, regardless of anyone else's needs.

Merritt sat at one end of the table while Gabriella took the seat at the other. With her supermodel affectations and garish outfit, she was a little out of place in this traditional conference room, as if she were playacting the role of mistress of the universe, even if her domain extended only to dolls and model cars and things that go beep in the night. God only knew what a corporate veteran like Merritt thought of her.

"Did you find the gangbanger who shot my dad?"

"Will your brother be joining us?" I asked.

"He'd better." She checked her watch and frowned, causing an ugly crease to form between her eyes. "We've got a big conference call in fifteen minutes. My sixth for the day."

It was not quite four. "That's quite a schedule," Thor observed.

"I don't know how my dad did it. And the day's just getting started at our Asian manufacturing plants." She cast a petulant look in Merritt's direction. "I won't leave here before ten tonight."

"It must be quite a challenge," Thor went on, "taking the reins from your father at so young an age."

Merritt checked his cufflinks and smoothed his rep tie before saying, "Pending the results of the search, the board has placed its complete confidence in Ms. Zuccari's abilities."

Gabriella's lips twitched into a smile. "Which I have every intention of earning."

The mood in the conference room had turned tense, unlike the playful vibe I'd gotten when Gabriella had first entered the room. "Still, there can't be too many women at your level," I added, hoping to relax her a bit with the compliment.

Instead, her voice grew strident. "A woman was named president and COO of Mattel last year. And there are a few others outside of the toy industry—CEOs of apparel companies and that specialty produce company in Los Alamitos."

"Frieda's?"

"That's the one. But you could still fit all of us into an elevator and have space left over." She checked her watch again, tapping its face impatiently with one French-tipped nail. "Where is Mario, anyway?" she asked Merritt.

"Finalizing the schedule for your meetings in New York," the attorney murmured, eyes back on his cufflinks.

Gabriella turned back to me. "How long have you been a detective?" she asked, clearly stalling for time.

"On the department since 'seventy-nine, made detective in 'eighty-two, and worked homicide for the last eight years."

"Are there many female homicide detectives in the LAPD?"

"More females than in your corporate CEO elevator, but probably not enough to field a decent football team."

This time it was Merritt who glanced at his watch. "Perhaps we should . . ."

Thor cleared his throat. "Let's not monopolize these good people's time." He went on to give her the highlights of how Nilo Engalla had been found, and the cash discovered in the former intern's car.

Gabriella listened with a look of growing surprise on her face. "And so you suspect this Engalla kid killed Mr. Shareef and shot my dad and Alma?"

"He's been your chief suspect since he disappeared last summer, hasn't he?" Merritt asked.

"It's a little premature to make that assumption without more information, Mr. Merritt, which is why we're here," Thor said smoothly.

"What has he told you?" Gabriella asked. "Will you be putting him in a lineup, see if Alma or Mrs. Shareef recognizes him?"

"We need a few questions answered before we do that," Thor replied. "Have there been any large sums of money missing from the company's accounts?"

Gabriella looked to Merritt, who shook his head slightly, his mouth pulled down at the corners. "None that I'm aware of."

"Although we haven't received a final report from our external auditors," Merritt hastened to add.

"When do you think that will be?" Thor asked.

"What was that about the auditors?" A man, a head shorter than Gabriella but curly-haired and more olive-complected, entered the conference room from Gabriella's office. Mario Zuccari, as stern and proper as I'd remembered from last summer, had lost a few pounds since our first interview. It was understandable.

When I'd met him in July, Mario had been grief-stricken over his father's shooting but clearly anticipating being named his successor. And as I gathered background information on him I understood why. He had all the tickets—summer job on the company's warehouse floor at fourteen, took a year off from school to help his father with the relocation to Orange County, eventually earned a bachelor's degree and an MBA from Stanford. He'd been Chuck Zuccari's right hand ever since, taking on operating assignments in the company's Latin American and Asian divisions before becoming, at thirty-five, executive vice president and chief financial officer, a position he'd held for the past five years. I wondered how he felt about his hair-tossing, couture-wearing sister getting tapped to run the company instead of him, even if only temporarily.

Mario introduced himself to Thor and nodded hello to me across the table. "When should we be receiving the auditor's report?" Gabriella repeated.

"We're just resolving some loose ends, so maybe three or four weeks," Mario replied. "Why?"

"They want to know if the auditors discovered any cash discrepancies."

Mario unbuttoned his navy suit jacket before sitting down next to Gabriella, revealing a tiny navy blue cross at the bottom of his dark red tie. "My sister forgets that our revenues were almost two hundred million last year. How would you expect the auditors to find a missing twenty-seven thousand?"

Thor and I exchanged a look. "We didn't say how much money was found on Mr. Engalla," he said.

Merritt frowned while Mario's eyebrows shot up. "I'm sorry, did I get the figure wrong? I thought that's what they said on the news this morning."

I caught the way Thor pursed his lips and knew he was as annoyed about the media's revelations of key information about Engalla as I was. "Perhaps you can have your Finance Department look into it," he said to Gabriella.

"I'm the company's chief financial officer, and the Finance Department reports to *me*," Mario replied, his words clipped. "And unfortunately, my people don't have time to drop everything to look into this. They're deeply involved in our upcoming meeting with analysts in New York."

"And there's the annual shareholders' meeting in April," Merritt reminded him.

"You're aware this could lead us to who killed Mr. Shareef and shot your father?"

Mario glared at Thor, mottled color rising to his cheeks. Before he could reply, Gabriella reached over and encircled his wrist. "Maybe we could get the Internal Audit Department to check into it."

Mario disentangled himself from her grasp. "It's certainly more important than that other matter the Audit Committee asked them to investigate," he conceded. "But that request would have to come directly from the board."

Gabriella glanced down the table at Merritt. "We can speak to Mother about it," she said, her tone making it more of a question than a statement.

Mario frowned as he put the tip of a pen in his mouth. With his close-cut sandy curls, he looked a little like that doll in the case. Or an Airedale worrying a chew toy.

"Both of your parents sit on the board?" Thor asked Gabriella.

"Before the shooting," Merritt broke in, "it was just Mr. Zuccari. But afterward, the family felt it needed representation, given its sizeable block of voting stock. So the other directors decided that Gabriella and Mario's mother should fill Mr. Zuccari's seat temporarily and be put forward to the stockholders as chair of the board."

"That must have happened after our interviews last summer," I noted.

"It was the end of last year," he agreed. "But Mrs. Lippincott's appointment isn't official until after the shareholders' vote in April."

Mario cleared his throat. "Gabby, on second thought, having our internal auditing staff look into possible missing cash is not such a good idea. A few of them worked with Nilo and might try and protect him."

"Then what's your solution, Mario?" she snapped back, annoyed—whether at her brother's change of heart or his using her nickname, I couldn't be sure.

Before he could answer, Thor said, "Perhaps we should speak to Mrs. Lippincott."

"I hardly think that's necessary," Merritt objected.

Still irritated, Gabriella waved away Thor's suggestion. "I'll take care of it, Detective. Don't worry, we'll get you what you need."

A look passed between the siblings that reminded me of when Perris and I locked horns. Mario broke the stare-down by turning to Thor. "Didn't the news say the money was found in Nilo's car at the scene of the accident?"

The corners of Thor's mouth pulled downward again. "Why do you ask?"

"Point is, you don't know who it belonged to." Mario Zuccari looked from one to the other of us. "The money might have been someone else's who was riding with him and not have come from CZ Toys at all. Or Nilo could have gotten it some other way."

Thor tilted his patrician head slightly to the left and considered Mario as if he were an interesting toy in the case behind him. "What way did you have in mind, Mr. Zuccari?"

Mario's face reddened again under the scrutiny. "I was just suggesting that you might be better served to talk directly to Nilo," he said stiffly, "rather than disrupt our company's operations."

"The police don't need us to tell them how to investigate their case," Merritt said with an apologetic smile to us. "Other than checking for any missing funds, what else can we do for you, Detective Thorfinsen?"

Ignoring the attorney, Thor asked Mario what he could tell us about Nilo Engalla. "Was he a good employee?"

"His supervisors said his work was acceptable, but they only had him working on special projects. Can't give these kids too much responsibility."

I wondered whether Mario's last comment was a slur against Nilo's inexperience or his ethnicity.

"Who were his supervisors?" Thor asked.

Mario resorted to his fingers. "Natalie Johnson in Accounts Payable, Felton Carruthers in the controller's office, and Howard Hebson in Internal Auditing. And given that Nilo worked with Hebson and his people in Internal Auditing, I don't think we should ask them to look into whether he might have embezzled that money they found on him."

"You said that before." Thor referred to the notes he'd been taking. "You've mentioned external auditors and an internal audit department. What's the difference?"

Gabriella sat back and gestured to Mario for an explanation. His color calmed down a bit and he cleared his throat again. "An external audit is designed to determine if the financial statements prepared by management fairly present the financial position of the company. The board's Audit Committee selects an independent accounting firm—"

"Like Price Waterhouse or one of those Big Eight firms," Gabriella explained.

"My sister gets her audit information from watching the Academy Awards." Mario's sculptured lips twisted into something between a smile and a sneer. "Financial professionals know that mergers have reduced the Big Eight significantly."

Gabriella rolled her eyes and reached for a bottle of Perrier.

"We use Shuttleworth and Bezney, which is a regional firm and a bit more hands-on than the 'sincere blue suit' outfits."

"What specifically do they do?" Thor asked.

"Audit our balance sheet and the related statements of operation and changes in net assets. They also focus on how we book revenues and inventory, cash and cash equivalents, accounts receivable from our distributors and customers, accounts payable from our suppliers, major contracts from vendors, that kind of thing."

"And how are they different from this internal audit department you mentioned that supervised Nilo?" Thor pressed.

Gabriella checked her watch and shook her right hand as if to hurry her brother along.

"Our internal audit department conducts special focus reviews and process improvement in areas like financial accounting, operations, and information processing. In short, it provides an added layer of control we deem appropriate for the company."

Thor nodded as he made a note. "That's a lot of work to be sure you're stating your profits accurately."

"Or losses."

Mario Zuccari frowned and looked my way. "What did you say?"

"Profits or losses."

A veil dropped over his blue eyes, but I could tell CZ Toys' chief financial officer was pissed that I would even suggest the possibility. "That goes without saying."

"Although last year was tremendous for us," Merritt hastened to add.

"The last *two* years, actually," Mario corrected.

I murmured something suitably complimentary, prompting Mario to reply: "Seventeen cents net income per share was what we projected this year, but we're coming in closer to twenty."

Thor made another note. "So there would have been nothing last summer of a financial nature that might have worried Mr. Zuccari?"

"Nothing that we know of," Merritt replied, and looked down the table at Gabriella, who shrugged. Next to her, Mario was drawing ovals on his notepad.

"Gabriella was out of the country during that time, Detective," Mario explained, looking up from his handiwork. "But, as two of this company's key executives, Robert and I can assure you that in July, as we were going into our third quarter, we'd been tracking ahead of our projections, and the stock price was up. What was there to worry about?"

"What about the letter he received?" Thor asked.

Merritt seemed to pale at the question. "What letter?" Gabriella asked sharply.

"Dad got a crank letter from some woman a while back is all, Gabby," Mario said as he frowned at his notepad.

"And that's all it was, Gabriella," Merritt said, his color returning. "Nothing that need concern you, my dear."

Gabriella shrugged, checked her watch again, and began to push her chair away from the table. "Then if there's nothing else—"

"There is one more thing." Thor closed his notebook with a soft thud. "We'll need to interview Ms. Johnson, Mr. Carruthers, and Mr. Hebson as well as Mr. Engalla's coworkers in those departments."

"That was done months ago!" Merritt objected.

We think it would be useful to speak with everyone who knew or worked with him again. And we'd like to talk to one of the auditors from Shuttleworth and Bezney, as well."

"Certainly," Gabriella agreed, a look of surprise on her face. "My brother can arrange that, can't you, Mario?"

Mario nodded, although his jaw was set in a manner that said he'd rather be doing anything else besides carrying out his little sister's wishes.

"Good. Detective Justice and I can be back here tomorrow morning—say at ten?"

"Gabby," Mario whispered, leaning close, "I'm flying out with you tomorrow to meet with the analysts, remember?"

"Perhaps you should stay here and work with the detectives."

Mario whispered something else to his sister that I couldn't make out. She mulled it over for a moment, then nodded. "Mario's right," she said to us, "I'm going to need him in New York."

Merritt said: "I'll stay here and oversee the interviews, Gabriella, not to worry."

Gabriella's assistant appeared at the door. "I've got Mr. Agnafilo over in Laguna on the line."

Gabriella rose and walked around the table to shake our hands. "Mrs. McIntyre is at your service. She or Mr. Merritt will know how to get in touch with us in New York, should you need to speak with me or Mario directly."

Gabriella strode out of the office, Mario close on her heels. Merritt lingered behind. "Thank you for your discretion about that letter," he murmured to Thor. "Mr. Zuccari would have been mortified if some wild-eyed story about his father had gotten back to his family or out to the press. He's always been a stickler about appearances."

"That I can see," Thor said, looking about the elegantly appointed office. "Did you try to find out who wrote it?"

Merritt started stacking up his papers. "Not really. Chuck was adamant that we not give it any more attention than it deserved, but we still took certain precautions."

"The outside PR firm and the extra security," I reminded Thor.

Merritt nodded. "We wanted to be prepared for any eventuality, but as Mario said, it turned out to be nothing."

Thor nodded thoughtfully. "Do you know where the letter is now, Mr. Merritt?"

The attorney gave an elaborate shrug. "I think it irritated Chuck so much, he eventually destroyed it."

"And you didn't keep a copy?"

"Mr. Zuccari never let any of us *see* the damned thing," he said, with an embarrassed chuckle, "never mind copying it!"

"But you were concerned enough to hire the PR firm and the extra security personnel?" Thor pressed. "Why, if it was so insignificant?"

"Just being prudent. The PR consultant helped us craft a response in case the rumors got to the press. And as for the security, Mr. Zuccari was worried some Jewish survivors' group might try and accost him— you know, act out in some way like those god-awful PETA people. So, we had our security chief add an extra guard in the lobby and a private detail to keep an eye on Mr. Zuccari's residence. He was pretty annoyed by that. God knows what he'd say about the guys at the hospital."

"Was that necessary?" I asked.

"Mario thought so." Merritt stood up a little straighter. "Enough to hire two private contractors, through our security department after the shooting."

"Ex-cops?" Thor asked.

Merritt shook his head and pursed his lips. "Given the attempt, Mario felt Mr. Zuccari needed something a little *earthier*, if you will."

Thor and I exchanged a look. "Did Mr. Zuccari say there was a specific threat in the letter?" Thor pressed.

"To be perfectly honest with you, I thought Chuck was going a little overboard," Merritt said as he walked to the door. "From what he told me, that letter was just a bunch of innuendos from a bitter, disgruntled woman."

After the door closed, I said to Thor: "What's Gabriella playing at?" I was about to say more when Thor put a finger to his lips and moved across the room to sit next to me.

His note read: *I think the room is bugged. Maybe mics in the table somewhere.*

I ducked under the conference table to inspect the fabric-covered shelf running around it, which was full of plugs and dials. And discreetly placed microphones.

"I don't think Mario told his sister anything about Engalla." I wrote on the page he'd started.

Thor nodded emphatic agreement. "I need to make some calls," he said aloud as he resumed writing. "Give me that number for Alma Zuccari. I'll call and tell her we're on our way. You make the arrangements for tomorrow."

And get the lowdown on the family, his message read.

6

Hell in Heels

t wasn't until I was at the wheel, steering us deeper behind the Orange Curtain, that I felt I could talk to Thor freely. "Mrs. McIntyre was so full up, she was about to burst." I filled Thor in on the son's background history with the company, and the initial impressions I had of his expectations about the job, which McIntyre had confirmed. "But Gabriella's mother went to bat for her baby girl when the board brought her in as the interim chair. She convinced them Gabriella would be better suited to serve as interim CEO than Mario. McIntire said they literally had to remove the son from his father's office, he was so sure he was getting the job."

"That's pretty ugly," Thor said as he started writing in his notebook. "What's the mother's full name?"

"Renata Lippincott."

"Remarried, you said?"

"To some big-time venture capitalist down in Newport Beach."

Thor grunted. "Why would the board of directors let Zuccari's ex-wife chair and his daughter run the company when he intended his son to get the nod? You see how that lawyer and Mario keep information from Gabriella? They can't respect her!"

"Not to mention how Merritt was tiptoeing around explaining the change in leadership to us. The board was probably afraid to stand up to the family's block of voting stock."

Thor shook his head, still unsatisfied. "But getting the ex-wife outta there if the poor guy ever comes to could be messier than the divorce!"

"No joke. But McIntyre said Renata was a major factor in growing the business for some thirty-odd years. She was the senior vice president of new product development up until the divorce. CZ Toys is as much her company as Zuccari's."

"Then why would she side with Gabriella over Mario as CEO, if that's what her ex-husband thought was in the best interest of the company?"

"Maybe because Mario was the one who introduced his father to Alma at that toy convention, according to Mrs. McIntyre."

"Ouch!" Thor grimaced. "That's a little messy."

"It gets worse. A couple of months after Mario introduced them, Chuck decided to leave his wife of thirty years without so much as a thank-you note for raising his children. He forced her to step down from the board and then invoked some ancient prenup agreement when it came time for the divorce settlement. If she hadn't had her own separate stock in the company, she'd have been up shit creek. Mrs. Lippincott's wanted nothing to do with either of them since."

Thor grunted. "Hell hath no fury. When did all this happen?"

"Four years ago now. Even Mrs. McIntyre is sympathetic to the ex-wife's cause, which I can't blame her for. For all Merritt's talk about Zuccari caring about appearances, he could cut them low when he wanted to."

"But then again," Thor pointed out, "McIntyre and the ex are probably close to the same age." Out of the corner of my eye, I could see Thor turn to face me. "Why didn't any of this come out in your initial investigation? You were the one who interviewed the son and the other company execs, right?"

It was a legitimate question. "When Chuck Zuccari was shot, all signs pointed to a drive-by. Then we were chasing down background on the father's Nazi connections and after that the Nation of Islam lead. By the time we got back around to CZ Toys, Engalla's disappearance was our top priority, not what was going on in the executive suite."

"But Chuck's messy divorce—"

"Not a breath of any of it in our interviews. All we knew was that wife number two was with her new husband and daughter in Europe when Chuck was shot. And they were in the Hamptons when Engalla went missing over the summer, so there seemed no reason to interview her on either matter."

"You should always talk to the exes, regardless of their whereabouts at the time of the crime," Thor chided. "You never know what kind of grudges they could be carrying."

He was right, of course, and I started to tell him that the decision for how far we'd ultimately gone in digging into the family's business had been dictated by his boy Firestone, who had us running around in circles after Nazi haters and Muslim baiters. But what would be the point? He'd never think Steve Firestone did anything other than walk on water and talk to God.

"So when do you want to interview Lippincott?" I fished a card out of my pocket and handed it over. "Courtesy of Mrs. McIntyre."

Thor wrote down the information. "Today, if we can. Did McIntyre give up anything else about the daughter?"

"Only that Gabriella's job as EVP of European marketing was little more than an opportunity for her to get a front-row seat at all of the major designers' spring and fall shows. That's not exactly how Mrs. McIntyre put it, but the inference was clear enough."

Thor shook his head in disgust.

"And check this out—the reason I never talked to Gabriella during our initial investigation was because she and her mother were buying up everything at the Versace show in Paris when her father got shot. At the time, all the family said was that she was in Europe, but this time McIntyre spilled the beans."

"That's because McIntyre's got no loyalty to her now."

"Told me Gabriella didn't come back to the States until a week after the shooting, reportedly delayed by negotiations with Versace to design an exclusive designer collection for one of their fashion dolls. She claimed her father would have wanted her to carry on, but I could tell McIntyre wasn't buying it."

"That Gabriella's hell on heels. Did McIntyre say how Mario's taking all of this?"

"Understandably disappointed about not getting the interim CEO job, but she says Mario's ultimately going to do what's best for the company."

"Not to mention what's best for that stock he's holding."

"You want me to come back down and help with the interviews?" I asked.

"Yeah, but I've put in a call to Financial Crimes to get one of their people down here. Let them talk cash and cash equivalents with the bean counters."

It was a good call on Thor's part to involve the department's Financial Crimes unit, something that had not occurred to me. If I could get past his attitude, maybe I could learn something new from Thor on this case, too.

Rush hour traffic delayed us almost an hour in getting to South Orange County and the hospital where Chuck Zuccari was being treated. Maybe being warehoused was a better word, because the second-floor nursing unit on which he was being kept seemed deserted, save for two thick-necked security guards stationed at the entrance to Two South.

"Sorry sir; no visitors allowed," said the larger one, a white male about six-one with a chestnut-brown buzz cut and massive arms, which he crossed over his broad, navy blazer–clad chest.

Which had zero effect on me or Thor, who stepped within inches of those bulging biceps. "This is police business, son," he explained, showing his badge.

"Not unless you gots some ID," said Mr. Universe's sidekick, a sawed-off piece of work who was about five feet tall by five feet wide with a tear tattooed in the corner of one eye.

"What's your name, son?" Thor asked.

"I ain't telling you *shit* unless I see that ID, old man!" Five by Five snapped, his singsong voice betraying his cholo roots.

"We're sorta new at this," Mr. Universe explained.

"New to polite society," Thor scoffed, taking in Five by Five's ill-fitting black suit jacket and scuffed shoes.

"Sorry, sir." Mr. Universe's smile was apologetic even as he stood his ground. "But we got our instructions."

They checked our IDs, grudgingly told us their names—Jeff Leykis and Luis Ybarra—and let us pass onto the unit. "I see what Merritt meant," I whispered to Thor. "What's a company like CZ Toys doing with a couple of roughnecks like them?"

"Good question. I'll have to run them through our databases, see what comes back."

At the nursing unit sat a redheaded nurse, one eye on the green squiggles of a makeshift telemetry monitor while she wrote in a chart and talked to another white woman, this one silver-haired and wearing a conservative navy pantsuit. Who saw us approach and stepped forward to greet us. "I'm Avis Gipson, chief nursing officer for the hospital." She took our cards and shook our hands. "We were told to expect you."

"Too bad everyone didn't get the memo," I muttered as I turned to watch Chuck Zuccari's sorry excuse for a security team resume their positions.

"There was no memo," she replied briskly. "Mrs. McIntyre called."

"She checks up on Mr. Zuccari regularly," the younger nurse added.

Gipson agreed. "The company has been very involved, and very helpful, in Mr. Zuccari's care."

"What's going on with the setup here?" Thor wondered aloud.

"There was some concern about another possible attack on Mr. Zuccari," Gipson explained. "So when he was discharged from critical care in August, it was arranged for him to be transferred here, where his private security team can better monitor the situation."

It was an odd move to protect a man shot some seventy miles away. Did someone really think the shooter would risk coming to South Orange County to finish off a comatose witness in his hospital bed, or was this just a case of special treatment for one of the rich and famous?

As if he had read my mind, Thor asked: "Who made the arrangements?"

"Administration, at the family's request."

The walls were covered in a happy floral print in pinks and blues. "Place looks like an OB unit."

"It is," Gipson replied, "or was. We lost a major OB group to another hospital last fall, so Administration mothballed this unit until the demand can catch up."

"Plus, this unit is closest to the elevator," the nurse piped up from behind her station. Her ID badge read Michaela O'Farrell, and you could hear the lilt of the Irish in her voice. "So Mrs. Zuccari can scoot upstairs and see their baby whenever she wants."

"The baby's still here?"

Nurse O'Farrell nodded. "In and out twelve times since she was transferred from Children's up in L.A."

In response to our awkward reaction, the older woman smiled. "She's quite special. Been on the brink so many times, the nurses call her Nine Lives."

"Twelve hospitalizations for the baby and how long in the hospital for Mr. Zuccari?" I made a quick calculation. "Seven months?"

Thor gave a low whistle. "I want the name of this guy's insurance company. I'm gonna have to change my coverage!"

O'Farrell chuckled, but the other woman raised an eyebrow. "No insurance, Detective Thorfinsen. CZ Toys is picking up the bill. Reopening and staffing the unit, the private security, everything."

I bet if I checked the donor wall in the lobby, I'd find CZ Toys or the Zuccari family's name on it somewhere. I couldn't imagine a hospital going to these lengths without a powerful—read monetary—inducement.

A housekeeper emerged from a utility room, mop in hand, and started swabbing the sparkling clean floor a few feet away. "Did Mr. Zuccari ever come out of that coma?" I asked.

O'Farrell shook her head. "He's deteriorated into what we call a persistent vegetative state."

Thor said, "Is that like being brain dead?"

O'Farrell shook her head, the corners of her mouth weighed down with disapproval. "That's a pejorative term for PVS. Mr. Zuccari's condition is not that severe."

"Is he awake?" Thor pressed.

"Not really. He opens his eyelids and maintains sleep-wake cycles, but his higher cerebral functioning is absent."

"So he can't talk or eat?" Thor said.

"Exactly, " O'Farrell nodded. "Other than the simplest motor functions, he's not aware of anything going on around him."

I wondered aloud whether Mr. Zuccari would be better off in a nursing home, to which Gipson pursed her lips disapprovingly. "Not everyone would agree with you on that."

Not if everyone *was being paid big bucks to keep him in this setup.* "Any chance he'll pull out of it?"

"Hard to say," O'Farrell admitted. "The chances diminish every day he's in that condition. But we're hopeful he'll improve. Miracles have been known to happen."

I asked about how Mrs. Zuccari was faring and watched the nurse's expression soften. "Alma's totally devoted to Chuck and the baby. When the baby was up in L.A., she spent mornings there, and nights down here with her husband. She still splits her time between the two of them. I don't know if the woman ever sleeps, 'cause she's never missed a day, not one."

"We understand she's here now."

O'Farrell nodded and indicated a room the housekeeper had just entered. "But they've got company."

"That's okay," Thor assured her, "she's expecting us."

Or maybe not, because we were stopped at the door by a heated discussion between Alma Zuccari and her visitor, an older version of Chuck's daughter, who stood at the head of Zuccari's bed on the far side of the room. How much older was hard to tell because her face and figure had that frozen-in-time look achieved only with careful plastic surgery, and her wardrobe was more Valentino than Versace, but the overall effect was like looking at Gabriella Zuccari fast-forwarded twenty-odd years. And if this was Gabriella's mother, she was giving no quarter—not to the hospital staff, not to Chuck Zuccari's wheelchair-bound young wife, and especially not to her ex-husband, who was elevated to a sitting position in his hospital bed, a waxen motionless prize save for his staring blue eyes and the bizarre grimace pulling at his face.

"Outrageous!" she shouted in a tone that sent the housekeeper scurrying past us into the hallway. "Do you have any idea how much all of this is costing? We're up to eight hundred thousand for that little abomination of yours and another fifteen thousand dollars a day for Chuck. My husband would not want to live like this!"

"H-h-how dare you!" The younger woman spoke hesitantly and with a whispered effort; whether from rage, deference to her husband's weakened condition, or the insult to her status as his wife I couldn't tell.

Renata Lippincott didn't hear the warning in the other woman's voice, or didn't care. "This is monstrous!" she thundered, brown eyes flashing. "How long do you intend to let him suffer like this?"

"The doctors say he's not in any pain."

"How can they say that?" the former Mrs. Zuccari shouted. "Look at him!"

"I do," came the weary reply. "Every day."

"You have no idea of the cost!" Mrs. Lippincott repeated. "Since Chuck got out of the ICU, the company's been paying another four hundred and fifty thousand a month on top of what we've already paid."

"I-I can m-multiply just fine, Renata."

"Like a rabbit." The older woman snorted and moved to the foot of the bed. "But be that as it may, one thing is for sure—you people have no sense of the value of a dollar!"

Alma Zuccari squared off her wheelchair to face her adversary. It was startling to see how much she'd changed since I'd first interviewed her months earlier. Her blond hair had grown out at the roots, revealing a wavy ridge of sandy-colored new growth, while her makeup looked as if it had been applied by a child. But even heavy foundation and concealer couldn't hide the dark blotches on her cheeks and the dark circles of exhaustion rimming her blue eyes. She looked more like fifty-eight than thirty-eight.

"Look who's talking! CZ Toys spent three times more last year on that little boondoggle retreat in Montecito than they did to care for Chuck and the baby." Was Alma's tone conveying her contempt for the other woman, or her pain? "And I know about that jet they keep in Europe for that Madison Avenue Barbie—"

"You deceitful little bitch!" Lippincott spat. "Stay the hell out of the company's business, or you'll be sorry!"

"If CZ Toys . . . can support you," Alma gasped, "they can support us in a time like this."

The argument sent the younger woman into a coughing fit, but Lippincott kept right on talking. "Not if I have anything to do with it. Gabby and I are running the company now, Alma, so the gravy train you've been riding is about to come to an abrupt halt!"

Chuck Zuccari suddenly stirred in his bed. His legs flailed underneath the light covers, and his wrists twisted against the restraints, even though his blue eyes were completely blank and his face was still frozen in that grotesque grin. "Evil bitch!" Alma rasped, and turned to her husband. "We've been trying to keep him calm since he developed an infection. Now you've upset him!"

Lippincott backed away from the bed, a stricken look on her face. "I-I thought . . . that nurse said he couldn't hear me!"

Thor stepped into the room, positioning himself between the women. "I'm sorry to interrupt you ladies," he said, facing the current wife and motioning for me to handle the ex, "but would you be Alma Zuccari?"

Alma coughed and nodded her head furiously. Releasing her husband's rigid hand, she tried to reach beyond a photograph and several greeting cards for a cup on the bed stand.

While Thor assisted her, I offered my card to the Valentino-clad shrew. "And you must be Renata Lippincott."

"Who are you?" Lippincott stared at my outstretched hand as if it were leprous.

Thor handed her his card as well. "There's been a development since last summer's shooting, and we need to speak with Mrs. Zuccari."

Chuck Zuccari's bizarre movements had subsided, allowing Alma to recover her own breath. "If you'll excuse us, Renata."

Zuccari's ex-wife read our cards, her eyebrows inching up as high as her face-lift would allow. "If you've found out who shot Chuck, I need to know."

"If you could wait in the lobby downstairs, ma'am, we'll be right with you," Thor replied.

"Evidently you don't know who I am," she said, pulling her jacket together and standing a little straighter.

Hell on heels, Senior? I wanted to say, reminded of her daughter.

"As the chair of CZ Toys' board of directors, I have a right to know who shot the CEO of our company!"

"We'll meet you in the lobby." I grabbed Madame Chair by the elbow, not caring if I was a little rough. "Or, if the lobby isn't grand enough, perhaps you'd prefer our offices downtown."

"You expect me to come to downtown *Los Angeles*?" I figured the mere thought of leaving Orange County would be enough to get her moving, but Lippincott couldn't resist a parting shot at her marital successor. "This bedside vigil you're keeping is quite touching, honey, but I'm onto your game. You've bled poor Chuck and our company dry enough."

"You and your narrow-ass daughter beat me to the trough on that one!" the younger woman snapped. Then she took a deep breath as if counting to ten. "Just go, Renata. Talk to Chuck's lawyer if you've got any other complaints. I'm sure you have the number."

Lippincott looked as if she wanted to slap the taste out Alma's mouth. I tightened my grip on her arm. "I'll be waiting in my car, Detective," she said to Thor, intentionally ignoring me. "It's the black Bentley parked near the emergency entrance."

"I'm sure we won't miss it."

I hustled Lippincott to the elevator and made sure she was on her way down before rejoining Thor and Alma. Standing near the door, I wished I had some sage to burn out the nasty vibe left in the room.

"I doubt if I'll be able to help you, Detective Thorfinsen," Alma was saying. "Although I was facing south, Chuck and Malik were blocking my view of the street, so I never saw the car coming. The last thing I remember was Chuck turning around pushing me as we were waiting for the valet to bring our car."

"Which way did he push you?" Thor asked. "Toward the building or the street?"

"I don't remember," she said, her voice snappish. "I told Detective Justice before: that's about when my memory of that night runs out. Does it matter?"

Thor ignored the question and made a note. "And you remember nothing after that?"

"Not until I woke up in the hospital a couple of days later."

"And since then?"

Frustration clouded her face. "Nothing! The doctors call it post-traumatic stress disorder."

So far, her statement was consistent with my earlier interviews, but Thor was undeterred. He murmured sympathetically as he pulled out his notebook and started making a sketch. "If the Oviatt Building is here, where were you standing, Mrs. Zuccari?"

Alma shot me an irritable glance. "D-didn't we cover this when you talked to me last year?"

Curious why she was growing so agitated, I had pulled out my notebook as well and had started making quick notes. "Yes, ma'am, we did, but Detective Thorfinsen—"

"We've put fresh eyes on the case, Mrs. Zuccari," he interrupted, "to see if we can uncover anything new that will help us nail these lowlifes who shot your husband."

"And my daughter." Alma's shoulders began to tremble as her eyes filled with tears. "Don't forget my daughter. She didn't deserve what they did to her."

Chuck Zuccari stirred again, his head lolling toward us, his fixed smile in mute agreement. I averted my eyes from the disturbing sight, and my gaze fell on the bedside table. Get-well cards from friends and well-wishers were crowded around a color photograph of a relaxed and smiling Chuck Zuccari, posing with Alma and his son at what I assumed was a toy convention, given the colorful outfit Alma was wearing and the display in the background. Zuccari looked radically different from the portrait I'd seen in the company's offices or in magazines when we were doing background on the family. In the portrait and the photos, he was somber, almost morose. Here Zuccari was happy, almost giddy. Had Alma Gordone, with her flashing eyes and ready smile, really transformed her stiff, navy-suited husband? Could the fierce love and devotion she displayed now bring him back to life?

Wondering why the photo was here, I realized that it was all Alma Zuccari had left of her life before. In the photo, surrounded by dolls and a giant mock-up of a handheld gaming device, the unlikely couple looked as if they had a limitless future ahead of them, like the photo of Keith and me at that long-ago Fourth of July barbecue.

Before and After was the way I had come to measure my life, the space between them an abyss I'd struggled for years to cross. I knew firsthand how happiness could be destroyed and our souls sent to hell in an instant by a loved one taking the wrong flight, driving a different route to work, or getting caught standing in the wrong place at the wrong time. Through my career in law enforcement I'd managed to climb out of my personal hell and, in the process, find meaning in my life. And while I couldn't get Alma Zuccari a job in the LAPD, maybe I could give her a glimpse of a better After.

"We'll catch who did this to your family," I promised her.

"Tell that to my husband and child."

Chuck Zuccari's face still bore that senseless smile. Maybe it was a change of light in the room, or a cloud moving by the window outside, but for just an instant I could have sworn I saw a flicker of something in his staring blue eyes.

As Thor and I exited the nursing unit we were intercepted by a third security guard, this one better dressed and more polished than Leykis and Ybarra. "I'm Pete Collins." He smiled, revealing a set of orthodontist-perfect teeth as he handed each of us a card. "Head of security for CZ Toys. Mrs. McIntyre called to say you were down here."

With his sun-streaked hair, even tan, and muscles rippling beneath his jacket, I could imagine Pete Collins catching waves in Newport or Huntington Beach faster than running a security operation for a corporation. Maybe he had driven from one of those beaches to meet us. My little voice told me to check his shoes for sand, but I knew that would be tacky.

"I see you've got pretty tight security on your boss," Thor was saying.

Collins flicked an unreadable glance at his colleagues, then turned that dazzling smile back on us. "Mario Zuccari thought we should bring in outside reinforcements as long as whoever did this is on the loose."

I voiced the doubts I'd had earlier about the likelihood of a repeat attack on Mr. Zuccari or his family. But my challenge didn't seem to ruffle Collins's professional feathers in the least. "I admit it may seem extreme, Detective, but I'd rather we err on the side of caution when it comes to something like this. Mr. Zuccari and his family are much beloved by the company and the toy industry. So we've got to take every precaution to protect them, even if it seems to outsiders like we're going overboard."

From what I'd seen and heard today, it was debatable how "much beloved" Chuck Zuccari really was.

Collins asked whether we needed assistance on the interviews Mrs. McIntyre was scheduling for tomorrow morning. "Robert Merritt, your legal counsel, has offered as well, but we don't think we're going to need any help right now," Thor replied.

"But we'll call you if something comes up," I added.

Mrs. McIntyre had also told Collins about Nilo Engalla's reappearance. "Has he said anything about why he took off like that?"

"Not yet." Thor pulled out his cell phone. "Which reminds me—"

"Can't use no cell phones in the hospital," Ybarra warned, stubby fingers pointing.

"Interferes with the equipment," Leykis added, his smile a sharky version of his associate's.

"The hospital's given us an office on the unit," Collins said, "if you'd like to use the phone in there."

Instead of joining them, I told Thor I needed to make a pit stop. "If I'm not in the lobby by the time you're done, go ahead without me."

Behind Collins's retreating back, Thor made a face and mouthed: *You owe me for this.*

Once Thor had rounded the corner with Collins, I told Leykis and Ybarra where I was headed and was directed to the fifth floor. I walked along the corridor, pausing at the first window on the left. Inside lay half a dozen babies in cute knitted blue and pink caps. Family and friends were clustered in front of various bassinettes, fingers pressed eagerly against the windows or filming the momentous occasion with video cameras. I could imagine Alma Zuccari passing this happy fishbowl every day, each trip adding darker and darker circles under her once-bright blue eyes.

I passed a windowed door and paused to count twelve domed Plexiglas incubators arranged in precise rows, some covered with fanciful baby quilts, others open as nurses hovered, checking monitors, conferring in tight circles with doctors, or encouraging a reluctant mother and father to stroke their baby. I saw an IV taped to one baby's kicking foot. Another baby jerked spasmodically, a tiny hand hitting a little Beanie Baby bear positioned near its head. A pink-clad angel with a tube snaking down her tiny throat made me want to retch on her behalf. How many times had Alma Zuccari crossed this strange threshold to visit her precious child.

Finally I tore myself away and found the pediatric wing. A white-coated young doctor looked my way and, with a frown that told me he knew I didn't belong, demanded to know my business. When I produced ID and told him who I wanted to see, he led me to a room close to the nurses' station. To enter it, I had to squeeze by a couple of monitors stationed outside the door like Chuck Zuccari's security guards. Inside, even with the light on over the bed, it was hard to find the baby among the welter of tubes and contraptions, all working to keep heart and lungs and other organs functioning.

After a while, my eyes adjusted to the chaos. "What's wrong with her?"

"Right now she's having some gastric problems related to her last surgery."

I could feel my throat closing and the walls moving in. "Will she make it?"

"She might get over the gastric problems, but she had some bleeding in her brain early on," the resident conceded. "It's a common problem in these micropreemies."

"So . . ."

"Brain damage is a distinct possibility."

My vision wavering a bit, I stepped back and examined the label at the foot of the bed. CARLA ISABELLA ZUCCARI, it read. I repeated the promise I'd made to her mother that I'd get whoever was responsible for this.

Her tiny chest fluttered and fell in an unfathomable response.

7

Unforgiven

t was nearly eight by the time I arrived at Aubrey's hillside home, bone-tired and ready to climb back into the cocoon of steam where I had begun this day. I had pulled off my jacket at the door and was about to remove my weapon and holster when I heard voices coming from the den downstairs. It took a moment before I remembered it was our turn to host Justice Family Film Night.

I tiptoed down the front staircase to find most of the usual suspects in attendance. My father had planted himself in one of the leather armchairs by the television, my mother was sitting on the sofa talking to Uncle Syl and Grandmama Cile, and my sister-in-law Louise and Aubrey were descending the back stairs with bowls of popcorn. But my brother Perris was nowhere in sight.

Spotting me, my uncle called out: "There's my Baby Girl! You're just in time."

Everyone shouted out a greeting except Aubrey, who was concentrating on positioning the bowls on the coffee table. That finished, he moved to give me a perfunctory hug. "It wasn't right to keep your family waiting dinner for you," he whispered in my ear; then for everyone to hear, "You want something to eat?"

Beast ran to my side and leaned into me to be petted. At least my boxer's affection was genuine. "We picked up something on the drive back," I muttered, hoping my stomach wouldn't growl and make me a liar.

Staccato explosions were coming from the kitchen. "That's the popcorn," Aubrey explained, and followed the sound up the front stairs.

"You missed a good dinner, Baby Girl." Uncle Syl smacked his lips. "I didn't know Aubrey could rattle pots like that."

"Go up there and see if some'a them buffalo wing appetizers are left over," Grandmama Cile added. "Although I never knowed buffaloes had wings!"

My grandmother chuckled at her own joke, while my mother and Uncle Syl exchanged long-suffering looks. "Aubrey mentioned you went back to work on the Malik Shareef case," my father said as I was on my way to the bedroom.

I closed the door between us. "Why wouldn't I?"

My quick response threw him a bit. "It's just that . . . you've been through a lot lately."

I rolled my eyes, dropped my purse, shed my weapon and clothes. Put on my favorite jeans, and decided on a sweatshirt from Sting's Nothing But the Sun tour to go with it. Checked out my appearance in the mirror, reminded myself to try and get some sun, and reentered the den with a suitable smile. "Don't worry, Daddy. I'm not lead on the case. They put Larry Thorfinsen in charge."

"Didn't you tell me he was retirin'?" my father said.

"I thought he was, but I'm beginning to think now that'll only happen if they carry him out feet first."

"Some people would say that about you," my mother mumbled around a mouthful of popcorn.

"Joymarie!" my father snapped in warning.

Before I could launch a retort, Uncle Syl popped up to give me a hug. "Now, Baby Girl, I know you like Sting, but you shouldn't wear that sweatshirt with the tour dates on them. Tells people how old your clothes are!"

I disentangled myself from his embrace. The twinkle in my uncle's eye said, *Forget it, she's not worth it.* I retreated to the bar in a neutral corner and grabbed a glass. "You keep promising me you're going to make a lounging outfit for me, Uncle Syl, but I haven't seen it yet."

While my uncle and I debated the virtues of silk versus cotton knit, I poured myself a Lagavulin, hoping its heavy aroma and smoky bite would blunt the effect of my mother's barbed observations. My father cleared his throat. "How'd it feel to be back?"

His tone made me wonder if Chief Youngblood, aka Uncle Henry, had ratted me out about my visit to Chinatown, but there was no way I could find out, with my family waiting expectantly for my response and Aubrey appearing from the back stairs with another bowl of popcorn. "Weird," I decided on, sitting near my father on the carpeted floor. "I'm not used to having so many live victims, or sort of alive."

Plopping down next to me, Aubrey listened while I described the condition of Chuck Zuccari, his wife, and his infant daughter. "When I was working the ER," he said, "we used to see a lot of gunshot victims who ended up that way. You get to the point you know which ones will end up in the vegetable bin."

"Aubrey!" my mother exclaimed, her hands over her ears. "That's a terrible thing to say!"

"No worse than cops calling dead bodies DBs or floaters," Louise reminded her from the armchair where she had settled. "Perris still slips up and says that kind of stuff when we're watching the news."

At the sound of her favorite child's name, my mother had uncovered her ears. "After all these years?" she asked incredulously.

"He says it puts some space between him and the ugliness."

"Speaking of ugliness, where is my darling brother? Afraid I'll kick his butt for pilfering Keith's files?"

"Leave her alone, Charlotte," my mother cautioned. "She didn't have anything to do with those files."

"That's true." I turned to my mother, glad she'd provided me with an opening. " 'Cause the way I heard it, you were the one locked up in Keith's office with Perris and the files that Sunday, just before he stole them."

Cutting her eyes in Aubrey's direction, Joymarie's face turned a mottled red, just like Mario Zuccari's when he was put on the spot by Thor. "W-we were just talking . . ."

"Come on, Mother! I might have been born at night, but it wasn't last night!"

Her eyes darted to my father, who placed a restraining hand on my shoulder and whispered: "Ease up now, Char. We don't need to dredge up the distant past tonight."

"Distant past? We're only talking about a week ago!"

"I was trying to talk some sense into him!" my mother insisted.

"Get real, Mother! You and Perris have been after me to get rid of the files on Keith and Erica's murders for years."

Her mouth was working, but little sound came out.

"And since I wouldn't do it, you took matters into your own hands!" I blinked back the rage stinging my eyes. "You were supposed to be helping me finish packing up the house for the movers, not aiding and abetting my brother in robbing me blind!"

"Come on, everyone." Uncle Syl's tone was cajoling. "Let's not ruin our first Justice Family Film Night at Aubrey's lovely home. He might not ask us back!"

"I just want an answer to my question!"

Despite the coolness of the evening, a prickly discomfort filled the room. Aubrey got up to load the tape while my father watched, as fascinated as if he were performing a tracheotomy. Grandmama Cile flipped through one of Aubrey's emergency medicine journals and showed an article to Uncle Syl, who pretended to read it without his glasses. My mother chewed the inside of her cheek while Louise fingered the fringe on a throw pillow.

It was Louise who broke the silence. "Look, Char, I don't know why Perris borrowed those files, but—"

"*Borrowed*? Let me find my dictionary so you can look up that word."

"Why don't you call and confront him instead of me?" she snapped back. "He's at home with the twins, nursing a cold."

Before I could press her, my father squeezed my shoulder hard. "She can do that later." He turned to Aubrey, who was moving back to his spot next to me. "What's on the bill tonight, son?"

"*Unforgiven*," he replied, glancing at me, concern knitting his brow. I nodded a go-ahead while, remote in hand, he cued up the tape in the VCR.

The irony of the title made me chuckle and take a long sip of Scotch, but Grandmama Cile groaned in response. "Not the one where they cast poor Audrey Hepburn as an Indian?"

"That's *The Unforgiven*, Mom," my father told her. "And the correct term is Native American, not Indian."

" 'Fore you know it, Indians will have gone through as many name changes as black folks!" my grandmother tsked. "As for that Audrey Hepburn movie, I always thought it was a little strange."

Uncle Syl dismissed my grandmother's criticism with a wave of his hand. "Girlfriend still looked *fabulous!*"

"You talk like you designed the costumes yourself," my grandmother teased.

From inside my glass, my family's faces were distorted, their pasted-on smiles and gestures almost comical as they tried to steer the conversation away from the elephant in the middle of the room.

"To answer your question, Grandmama Cile," Aubrey said over the hubbub, "this is the one with Clint Eastwood and Morgan Freeman."

"How'd you get a tape so soon?" Uncle Syl wanted to know.

"My next-door neighbor is a member of the Academy, so he let me borrow his screening copy."

"Didn't he have *Malcolm X?*" I said, just to be contrary.

My grandmother grunted. "I loves me some Denzel!"

"You know, a sister by the name of Ruth Carter is nominated for best costume design on that one," Uncle Syl said to me, with obvious pride in his voice.

A murmur of appreciation flowed through the room. Through my family's not-so-subtle maneuvering, the moment had passed to confront the problem of Perris. Maybe it was just as well. I grabbed a handful of popcorn from the bowl on the coffee table and handed the rest to my father as a peace offering. "I've been so busy I haven't had time to see any of the nominated movies, Uncle Syl."

Aubrey kissed my ear and whispered: "I've been trying to get you to go."

I could feel another argument tickling the back of my throat, which I doused with a swallow of Scotch. Aubrey knew I'd been preoccupied the past few months, between the job and the months I'd spent working with Perris and my Police Protective League rep to fight that last suspension, so why was he rubbing it in?

"I'm so glad Morgan Freeman's in this one," Louise whispered over the opening prologue. "He's such a great actor."

My mother sighed. "Thank heaven he's not playing a pimp or a chauffeur this time. I'm tired of seeing our actors in those stereotypical roles."

"He don't fare much better in this one," Grandmama replied. "I hear he gets . . ."

"*Mom!*" my father pleaded.

"I'm just trying to prepare you," she said innocently. "My missionary group saw this one over the holidays, and hated it!"

"Hush, Cile," my uncle exclaimed, snickering at her imitation of the movie critics on *In Living Color*. "You'll spoil it for the rest of us!"

The general hue and cry subsided as we watched a prostitute get brutally slashed by a drunken john. The excuse the brothel owner gave for the crime—"Just hard-workin' boys that was foolish"—drew derisive whoops from the room. "Why white men think they can just use women any way they want is beyond me!" my mother said, her voice quavering with anger. "It's one of the reasons I've told my children to be careful who they lay down with. It's like Mother Justice says: You lie down with dogs, you get up with fleas!"

"Joymarie!" my father warned his wife again. "We don't need to get into that right now."

But for once, Mother and I were in agreement. The scene was an uncomfortable reminder of Steve Firestone, Larry Thorfinsen, and every other jackass I worked with who thought they could get away with perpetrating everything from tasteless jokes to sexual assault against their female colleagues. And the only thing that stood between them and their next target was me, and Gena, and the other good women in the department who stood up to them, told the truth and damn the consequences.

Don't forget Perris. He takes a lot of those good women's cases. I sat with that thought for a few minutes. Finally, I tapped Aubrey's shoulder. "Can we talk for a minute?"

"I want to watch the movie."

I pulled Aubrey by the hand into the bedroom and closed the door. He sat on the edge of the bed, leaned back on his elbows, and waited. "Sorry about earlier," I began, moving toward him.

He crossed his leg, effectively blocking my approach, and just stared.

I stopped in my tracks, feeling the sting. "You know, getting home late." I decided it was better not to mention forgetting about Film Night, my argument with my family, or anything else. "I didn't expect to end up behind the Orange Curtain this afternoon."

"You've got a bad habit of not showing up to *your* family's events that's got to stop."

"What do you mean?"

"Last time it was brunch when you were working that political consultant's murder."

"You know how it is when I'm working a case!"

"The time before that it was—"

"Look, I didn't call you in here to fight. I just wanted to apologize and, you know, tell you what was going on with me."

Aubrey tilted his head the way Beast does sometimes and said: "So what *is* going on with you, Char?"

I had longed to tell him about my therapy, about how angry I was at being cornered by some soft-gutted shrink, about my ambivalence at being back on the job, about how deeply Perris's antics hurt me. But something about Aubrey's tone made me bite my tongue, suddenly unsure of what his reaction would be. Or that I could handle it.

"Nothing that can't wait. Go watch your movie."

Aubrey was already on his feet. "Good. I want to see what happens to Morgan."

"You go ahead. I'm going to slip into my office and sort through my notes for tomorrow."

"That's not being fair to your family, Char! They came here to see you, not me."

"They came to eat good food and see a movie, both of which they're doing. Besides, they know how it is when I'm on a case. *You're* the one who seems to have a problem."

But instead of returning to the den, Aubrey stood in front of me and held my arms. "That's bullshit, Char! Given the kind of work I do, I know better than most that work can get in the way. You just can't let it eat up your life and drive you crazy!"

I squirmed out of his grasp and shook myself. I'd be damned if I told him about Chinatown now. "You don't have to be concerned for my sanity, Aubrey."

"Fine." Before I knew it, he was at the door, his hand on the doorknob. "I'll see you out there in a few?"

Aubrey Scott was as tall and good-looking as I'd remembered from the days of my schoolgirl crush, back when he and Perris were high school seniors and I was a sophomore. But I knew that was a fairy tale of long, long ago, and there was a lot I didn't know about the very real man standing before me.

"In a few," I said.

*U*nforgiven got a split decision: three thumbs up, three down. My father—who just couldn't break ranks with Spike Lee—spoke for the defense. "*Malcolm X* is the best movie Spike's ever made," he argued as they all trooped upstairs. "He deserves that Oscar!"

Amazingly, my mother disagreed. "It's also the best movie Clint Eastwood's ever made. For one thing, he didn't let them call Morgan a nigger in a couple of scenes, like you know they would have if it had been some other director. And they didn't lynch him either!"

"That's one of the things that bothered me," my uncle admitted as he helped Cile into her coat. "It wasn't real."

"It's nice not to have to suffer through watching a black man degraded like that," Louise said, her dreadlocks swaying as she shrugged into a leather jacket. "But you noticed Morgan's character was still the only good guy who got killed!"

"Frankly, I appreciated the way the movie dealt with the violence," I said, although I had left the room during a couple of scenes on the pretense of checking the office for messages.

"Me, too," my mother agreed, surprising me again. "It wasn't pret-tied up. And that one line William Munny says after the guy got shot in the outhouse really got me."

" 'Hell of a thing, killing a man,' " I quoted. " 'Takes away all he's got an' all he's ever gonna have.' " In response to everyone's surprised looks, I explained: "When you interview people in your job, you get used to remembering what they say."

My father gave me a hug. "Lets you know there's a price to be paid on all sides, doesn't it?" He kissed my cheek before dashing into the night to retrieve the car.

Aubrey had gone inside to clean up the kitchen, and the others were waiting at the curb, but Louise still lingered at the door. "Char, I—"

I put my arm around her and hugged her close. "I'm sorry I went off on you like that, Louise. I know you can't control my brother any more than my father can control Joymarie."

But my little joke was lost on my sister-in-love, so intent was she on what she had to say. "I don't know what's gotten into Perris," she whis-pered. "You know he's started drinking again, heavily."

"Yeah, Aubrey told me about what happened." Two Sundays ago, Perris had gotten what Aubrey termed "tore up from the floor up" at a brunch I had missed because of the Vicki Park case. Perris's behavior must have been particularly difficult for Louise, whom he'd met at an AA meeting after he had injured himself in a drunk driving accident and she had lost her job as a management consultant because of her drinking.

In the ten years since, they had gotten their lives together, married, and had two great kids. Along the way, Louise had given up her career to raise the kids while becoming the unofficial president of the Perris Justice Fan Club. But over the past few months, I'd noticed her thin-lipped disapproval of my brother's little transgressions—a celebratory glass of champagne last spring, the Chardonnay at Thanksgiving. Plus there were the ones she hadn't seen—the beers he'd have after shoot-ing hoops with Aubrey and his buddies, the sips of Glenlivet he'd sneaked out of my glass at The Townhouse, a black bar in Ladera Heights where we met to strategize my testimony before the Board of Rights.

But Louise had to have seen the effects of those clandestine drinking sessions and known what was going on. Spouses always do. Yet, regardless of what she knew or when she knew it, Louise remained fiercely loyal to her husband, so for her to admit that his drinking was a problem let me know how concerned she was, and how far it had progressed.

"And he's been calling some of his old contacts in the LAPD, having these long conversations late at night."

"About what?"

"I don't know," Louise muttered as she worried a cuticle between her teeth.

A few feet ahead, I could hear my mother saying something to Uncle Syl about what she would wear for a senior golf tournament my parents were playing at Chester Washington on Friday, and some reception at a local bank they were all attending the following night.

"When I walk into the room," Louise went on, "he hangs up the phone. And when I ask him what's going on, he says it's nothing to be worried about."

I put myself between her and the others. "How do you know he's been calling cops?"

"Maybe he wasn't." Louise's dark face was thrown into relief by the light coming from the living room windows. "But whoever it is, he talks to them in a shorthand kind of way. I just assumed they were cops, but it might have been his frat brothers or something."

Some uglier possibilities came to mind, but I bit back my suspicions to concentrate on what she was saying.

"Last night, I'm pretty sure he was shut up in the den with the files—"

"The ones he took from my house?"

She nodded. "And he was on the phone for the longest. But when I asked him if he was talking to one of his Omega buddies, he just said something about Qs I didn't understand."

Perris belonged to one of the older black fraternities, Omega Psi Phi, whose members were commonly called Qs. But I couldn't understand what the connection was between a fraternity and my late husband's files on a black militant group, unless Perris was talking about Q-Dog, one of the members of the Black Freedom Militia. Then there was the kid I'd met at a reception during the riots named Quarles, but I was with Aubrey that night, not Perris.

What about Querida Strange, the girl Perris had the hots for in high school? I was just wondering if they could have run into each other when Louise said: "Talk to him, Char. He'll listen to you."

"I don't know, Louise." Suddenly I wasn't sure I wanted to get into the middle of Perris's late-night tête-à-têtes.

"It's a short list of people he'd open up to; you know that."

And I knew every name on it. "I'll think about it."

"Thanks. But if you talk to him, don't let on that I've said anything."

I promised, giving her another hug and a kiss before sending her into the night.

Inside, I bypassed the kitchen, where Aubrey was loading the dishwasher, and tiptoed downstairs to my office. Converted from a guest bedroom, my little office was a bit of my old house transplanted to the hills. My favorite Betye Saar collage hung above my desk, and my collection of black dolls sat on shelves across the opposite wall. My hand-dyed Gabby doll was there, as well as the Black Chatty Cathy I got when I was nine and a Colored Francie doll that my Uncle Syl gave me, outfitted in a sequined dress he'd made himself. All served as bookends for my collection of texts on criminology and policing, including the indispensable *Techniques of Crime Scene Investigation*. Yet, the kind of crime I feared my brother was perpetrating seemed as far from the cases contained in Barry Fisher's classic as honky-tonk was from Beethoven's fifth.

I picked up the phone and punched in Perris's number. He answered on the third ring and slurred out a hello. When I didn't answer, he said "Fuck off!" and slammed down the phone.

Unless he'd OD'd on flu medication, Perris was tore up from that floor up again. My heart pumping pure dread, I rummaged through my desk drawer until I found my phone book and dialed a number I used to know by heart. "Hey, can we meet for breakfast?" I said, dispensing with the formalities. "I need some advice."

8

Moving On, Moving Fast

He **picked the** place—John O'Groats, a popular breakfast spot on Pico frequented by the Mommy-and-me crowd, local businessmen, a lot of golfers, and very few cops. And he was definitely no longer the latter, if the pastel cardigan and designer polo shirt he wore with his khakis were any indication. He'd even shaved off his mustache, which made him look a good ten years younger than I knew him to be.

He ambled toward me, his height and bearing still more reminiscent of John Wayne than John Q. Public, and extended a pale mitt of a hand in my direction. "I hope this is okay."

"Come on, now, Burt." I brushed his hand aside and embraced his midsection. "You know me better than that."

"This place has got the best biscuits in town," he explained, a little embarrassed at my show of affection.

"Not to mention it's close to a golf course, which it looks like you've been visiting a bit lately."

"What makes you say that?"

"One, I've never seen you wear a cardigan in all the time I've known you. Two, I bought that same cardigan for my father at a golf shop last Christmas, and three, the tan face and pale right hand are a dead giveaway."

He nodded approvingly. "Good to see you're keeping your skills up, Charlotte."

"I was taught by the best."

Almost thirteen years earlier, Sergeant Burt Rivers had been my training officer, back when I was a boot in Southwest, a rough-and-tumble division separated from this Westside location by a few miles and more money than you could shake a stick at. Burt had taught me how to deal with drunk drivers and domestic disputes, how to search a hooker and do field interviews when no one wanted to talk to a cop. Last time I'd seen him was during the Rodney King riots, when Cinque Lewis's body was discovered behind a taco stand. It was Burt who'd ID'd the murderer of my husband and child, who'd recognized Lewis from his days as leader of the Southwest-based Black Freedom Militia.

I'd called Burt because he was on my short list of people I'd go to when I was in trouble. And more importantly, he was on Perris's short list as well. They'd been coworkers and good friends until Perris left the force after being shot and went over to the other side of the law-and-order aisle—a fact that Burt mentioned almost every day we rode together. Perris's defection to the ranks of criminal attorneys rankled the department and Burt. Which I was painfully reminded of when I saw the two of them circling each other like roosters in a cockfight the night they found Lewis's body. But I remembered the caring underneath the sparring that night, at least on Burt's part, which I was hoping I could tap into to help understand what in the hell was going on with my brother now.

We selected a table by the window and ordered. I was aware that while I was ordering, Burt was looking me over as carefully as a mother hen inspecting one of her chicks. "You don't look any the worse for wear," he concluded after the server left.

I mustered a smile. "Should I?"

"I hear you've been through the wars lately."

"Heard from whom?"

A part of me hoped, for once, that Perris had talked out of school, which would make having this conversation that much easier, but all Burt would say was "I still have my sources."

The phrase made me uneasy, but I shrugged off my reaction to give him a brief outline of the Koreatown case I'd worked last week, and the Smiley Face shootings that were occupying my attention now. "But what about you? How's life off the job treating you? I was surprised to hear you were even eligible for retirement."

"Fifty-two and twenty-three. You do the math." Burt had opted out of the LAPD, availing himself of a formula that allowed an officer to retire if his age plus years of service equaled seventy-five or more. But at Burt's age, cops left the department only if they had hit the Lotto—or were forced out under the new "pick the low-hanging fruit" initiative of weeding out the worst LAPD troublemakers, starting with the Christopher Commission's infamous List of Forty-Four.

The current chief had achieved only moderate success with his plan, but neither it nor a lottery win had made Burt trade in his shield for a five-iron. "I was just burned out," he admitted. "Too many morning shifts, too little sleep, and no end in sight. So I got off the hamster wheel and started helping out my wife at our flower shop."

"You and Angie own a flower shop?"

Burt hiked up his shoulders. "It's just a fifty percent interest. We put some money into Angie's brother's flower shop after he died. Used a chunk of my retirement to do it, so I'm working a couple of afternoons a week, keeping an eye on my investment for me and my sister-in-law."

I pulled out my notebook and asked for the name. "God knows I want your retirement to be a success."

"Tip-Top Florists, over in Culver City."

I had the strange yet familiar sensation of hairs rising on my neck, usually a sign of my sixth sense working overtime, warning me that something was amiss. Burt must have seen the look in my eye because he asked if I was okay. "You look like you saw a ghost."

I flipped my notebook shut. "What? No, I-I just can't imagine you arranging flowers is all."

"I do deliveries mostly. That and the golfing pass the time until I get my ticket back from BSIS."

"You're getting your P.I. license?"

"Why not? There's a guy retired out of Hollywood Division who's had his own agency for over fifteen years!"

"I'm not being critical, Burt. I'm just surprised is all."

"I've got more than enough hours to qualify. But until the paperwork comes through, I'm doing a little consulting on the side."

"Consulting? Who with?"

"Companies from here to San Diego would jump at having an ex-LAPD cop evaluate their security procedures."

Pete Collins and his roughneck staff's handling of Chuck Zuccari's security flashed through my mind. "I think you'll run rings around most of them. You'll probably be bored."

"It'll be different, that's for sure. But the pay is a hell of a lot better than working as a cop, and the hours ain't bad either."

"There are some benefits to being on the department," I argued.

"I do miss some of the funny shit that happened on the street," Burt admitted a bit wistfully. "Remember the Leimert Park Lothario? Dude's wife is working double shifts in the emergency room at California Hospital, trying to get enough money for a down payment on a house in Baldwin Hills, while her husband the hairdresser is running the women through their apartment, two and three a night, giving them a little more than a shampoo and a trim."

"And then the wife comes home sick one night and finds him doing the horizontal bop with a hostess from some neighborhood club."

Burt nodded. "Popped him two times in the ass with a twenty-five she kept in her purse."

"What was it she said when we arrived on the scene?"

" 'Don't take him to the hospital,' " Burt piped in a high-voiced imitation; " 'they'll save his sorry ass and I want him to suffer!' "

I pointed in his direction. "And you talked her into giving up her weapon."

"Whole time, she kept repeating, 'Suffer, baby, suffer!' "

"That *was* funny," I agreed, feeling a rush of adrenaline even at the memory of that night. "Scary, but funny. I learned a lot from you on that call."

Burt's face grew somber. "It was Romper Room compared to what

I was seeing on the streets those last few years. The gangs and drugs made the job too unpredictable, and too dangerous, even for a veteran like me."

"And you never considered going behind a desk full-time?" I said, repeating something Dr. P. had suggested to me. "I remember a rumor going around back in the day that you turned down a promotion and a desk job at Parker Center to stay on the street."

Burt ducked his head. "Nah, I'm not cut out to push paper," he scoffed, his tan not quite concealing the flushing of his skin. "Although one of the shrinks over at BSS tried to talk me into it."

I could feel my adrenaline surge again, every nerve coming alive. "You've been to Chinatown?"

"How many times!" He grimaced as the server brought our drinks.

"You've been more than *once*?"

"The first time was when my second partner got shot on the job. Then I had to shoot a kid high on crack who attacked me with a knife a couple of years ago and got sent back again. The last time was right after the riots. Every time I thought I'd never be back on the street. That last time, I was right."

"You retired how long after Rodney King?"

Burt grinned, his eyes getting lost in a mass of crow's feet. "My last session in Chinatown was July twentieth last year, and I retired August thirty-first."

I couldn't have been more surprised if the sky had cracked open and rained elephants. Burt caught my expression and leaned forward. "What—were you there about then?"

I scanned the room for familiar faces. "I wouldn't want it to get around . . ."

"Who the hell am I gonna tell?"

"Well, for a man who 'still has his sources' . . ."

His look was mischievous. "I got you to spill your guts with that one, didn't I?"

I relaxed a little, even though I knew I'd been played. "You old dog!"

"How many sessions?"

"Four after the riots. And you?"

"Eight," he said matter-of-factly. "I was surprised they kept me that long, there were so many of us back then."

"No one I know went to BSS after the riots!"

"Grow up, Charlotte!" Burt shook his head and emptied the first of two creams into his coffee. "There were plenty who did, but they'd never admit it. No cop worth his badge wants people to think he's crazy."

"You ain't said nothing but a word there."

"But you know what my shrink said? 'If you *think* you're crazy, there's a good chance you're not. It's the ones who think they're normal and everyone else is nuts that you've got to worry about.' "

Steve Firestone and the way he had manipulated me and Gena came to mind. "Amen to that."

"It's why I finally had to get out. There was just too much denial, and I'm not talking about a river—or rivers—in Egypt, get it?"

Burt's deep laughter drew the attention of the few early birds at the counter. "I'm seeing one of them right now."

"One of what?"

"A BSS shrink!" I hissed.

"Is it Dr. Betty?"

"I saw her the last time, but she's not available now."

"Probably speaking at a conference or teaching a class somewhere." At my surprised look, he said: "Don't you know who Betty Frasier is? When did you graduate the Academy?"

"May of 'seventy-nine."

"Then you should have run into her. Dr. Betty was deep into the POWER Program with the boots."

"I was involved in the program, but I don't remember her being connected to it." A lawsuit filed by Fanchon Blake, a female LAPD sergeant, in the early seventies had been settled a few years before I came on the department. As a result of *Blake v. City of Los Angeles*, the LAPD was under a consent decree to hire and promote more women and minorities. A number of us, from the diminutive Billie Truesdale to some of my other black and Latino sisters and brothers in blue, would have never gotten on the LAPD if it hadn't been for Sergeant Blake. And couldn't have stayed on the job if not for Positive Orientation for a Winning Response, aka the POWER Program. "I wish I had known that when I was seeing her."

"Dr. Betty's not one to toot her own horn."

"You seem to know a lot about her."

"I was one of the first mentors she identified to work with the new crop of female boots. Why do you think they paired me with you?"

"I had no idea."

"You weren't supposed to. I caught a lot of flak for it, though. Some of the old-timers said I was part of"—he looked around to see if we were being overheard—"the Pussy Posse."

That sounded about right for the Neanderthals I knew in Southwest. "But you never let on."

"Why should I? I was closer in age to you than the gray hairs who were riding my ass, so I felt like we were on the same side. Anyways, you young ladies—er, females—had enough to worry about."

I swallowed a bit of my omelet, trying to decide how to proceed. "I appreciate you telling me about Chinatown. Doesn't make me feel like such a freak."

He saluted me with his mug. "Or at least you're a freak in good company."

I pushed my food around on my plate a bit longer, hoping Burt wouldn't notice I'd stopped eating. "I wish BSS had been around when Perris got shot. Maybe it would have helped him stay on the job."

Burt shifted in his chair, took another sip of coffee. "I doubt it."

"Well, he sure needed someone to talk to back then. Still does, far as I'm concerned."

"Is he in trouble again?"

I looked away, suddenly not sure if I should even be having this conversation.

"What's this all about, Charlotte? I get the feeling there's something you're not telling me."

It took a while for Burt to drag it out of me, asking a few clarifying questions here and there, his cop instincts leading him to zero in on the stunt Perris had pulled at my house. "Which files were these?"

"Some of my husband's gang files, the ones about the Black Freedom Militia."

Burt set down his mug, sloshing liquid over the side and across the table. "Damn!" he exclaimed.

I handed him my napkin to wipe up the mess. "The day it happened, Aubrey wondered if there was something in those files that could pertain to one of Perris's current cases. I thought I'd ask you, since you used to ride with him."

"I don't know anything about Perris's current cases!"

"You know what I mean."

He shook his head sadly. "I wouldn't know where to begin, Charlotte."

"Has he been in touch with you?"

Burt shrugged as he finished off his second biscuit. "I talked to him a few times after I saw him that night during the riots, but not about anything specific."

So maybe one of my other suspicions about Perris was correct. Maybe he wasn't reliving the old days with cops or his frat brothers but tipping out on his wife. "What did you talk about?"

He bristled a bit at the question. "Nothing much."

"Did you talk about Q-Dog?"

"Who the hell is that?" he snapped.

"One of the members of the old Black Freedom Militia. Louise thought she heard items talking about some Q on the phone one night, so I thought maybe—"

"It was personal, okay?"

"I'm not trying to pry, Burt, I'm just trying to figure out if my brother is in trouble again. I'm afraid any night the phone will ring and I'll have to bail him out of jail on a DUI, or worse."

Burt sat staring at his half-empty cup, remaining in that position even after our server poured him a refill. Then, as if she had pulled a string, he began doctoring his coffee, eyes averted. "I don't think Perris has ever forgiven himself for what happened to your husband and daughter."

Burt's observation sparked a memory, of how Perris had sat in my kitchen table about a month after they were killed, drunk on Keith's

Rémy Martin, crying over him and our baby as hard as I had if not harder. "Perris got shot the day it happened! No one blamed him for that!"

"Yeah, but he was on his way to your house that day, remember?"

"How could I forget?" When Cinque Lewis heard about Keith's research into gangs, and how his girlfriend, Sojourner Truth, had given him information about the Black Freedom Militia, he'd made threats against Keith, Erica, and me, which the LAPD took very seriously. A patrol car was stationed outside our house, and an officer was assigned to escort Keith and me everywhere we went on campus. Perris was on his way over to our house to start his voluntary shift when he got shot—a shooting that was never solved and that I believed contributed to his leaving the department. "But that's no excuse for taking those files without my permission. Or for him looking for answers in a bottle."

"Or the end of a coke spoon," Burt agreed, stirring his coffee.

Recalling how I'd lost my young family made the pain of that day feel fresher and closer than my breath, which had suddenly grown sour at the thought I might lose Perris all over again. "Burt, those files were all I had left of my husband's work, of what was important to him. Perris had no right to steal them."

"You were what was important to Keith, Charlotte. Don't you think he would want you to move on? After all, it's been almost fifteen years!"

An eerie feeling came over me, as if someone was walking over my grave. "How can you say that? You never met Keith!"

Burt's tan glowed with embarrassment. "I just know what I'd want Angie to do if I got killed, and what I've always told her, is all I'm trying to say. Perris tells me you're living with someone. Would he want to have Keith thrown up in his face all the time?"

How *did* Aubrey feel about that argument last night? We hadn't made love afterward, or any other night in the last week or so since Perris had taken those files. Was my obsession with getting back a piece of my past jeopardizing my future?

But even while I was wondering, the little voice in my head was shrieking: *But you only moved in with Aubrey the beginning of this year!*

Which meant Burt had spoken to Perris not just right after the riots in the spring, but sometime in the last two months. And, if my instincts were right, they had talked about my cases, my personal life, and God knows what else. The question was—why?

"Aubrey's a good guy," I said carefully, praying my response hadn't been noticeably slow in coming. "He's been a friend of Perris's since they were kids, you know."

Burt put his hand over mine, causing my stomach to churn. "I'm sure Perris only wants you to be happy, Charlotte. He wouldn't want you to start up a new relationship with all of that old baggage along for the ride."

The hairs on the back of my neck were screaming at me to get the hell out of there. I glanced at my watch and put a twenty on the table as I stood up. "I'm sure that's all it is. Maybe it's better Perris keeps the damned files. Why be reminded of the past when I've got such a bright future?"

Burt's cheerful smile exposed a few too many teeth. "I couldn't agree more."

I made myself pat him on the shoulder. "Thanks, Burt. This has been very helpful."

Before I could leave, Burt grabbed my hand and pressed a card into it. "Here's my number at the shop. I'm there Tuesday and Thursday afternoons, if you ever need anything."

I glanced at the card, its logo of a top hat filled with a floral bouquet sending chills straight through me. I let the card drop to the bottom of my purse. "Thanks."

"You want me to speak to Perris? Maybe I can talk some sense into him."

"My family's tried, Burt, so I don't know what more you could do." I made sure I was looking him in the eye when I said: "Unless you can get him to give back those files."

His gaze flickered only for an instant, but it was long enough to tell me what I needed to know. "Damn!" I exclaimed, making a show of checking my watch again. "It's ten after eight. I've got to get out of here. I've got interviews down in Irvine."

We said our good-byes on Pico, Burt moving east in the direction of the golf course and I hurrying to my car. I headed west, a direction that would lead me to the freeway and Orange County, checking my rearview mirror all the while, just in case Burt was watching me. When I was certain he was out of sight, I doubled back and sped east on Pico toward my real destination, my head crammed with memories and a dimly outlined objective.

My old house in the Fairfax District was a couple of miles east of John O'Groats, in an area a lot of black folks consider the Westside but most whites think is a half step above the ghetto. But for me the old Spanish Colonial–style homes and independently owned businesses in my 'hood were every bit as desirable as those on the white folks' Westside—a John O'Groats there versus a Maurice's Snak 'n' Chat here, the latter owned by a black woman whose tacky decor, down-home cooking, and sharp tongue drew celebrities like Keenan Ivory Wayans and Johnny Carson, and tourists by the busload.

But, as my real estate agent reminded me, O'Groats and the Westside had one advantage over my neighborhood that could not be denied: *location, location, location.* So it wasn't surprising that the FOR SALE sign, which had been in front of my house for a few weeks, had attracted no offers, nor did I expect it to any time soon, given how slowly properties were moving anywhere near the riot zone. And although my neighborhood had suffered only a fraction of the devastation of most others, there were gaping holes where my favorite Indian restaurant and a handful of other businesses had been—absences that hurt as much as losing a member of the family.

It was eight-twenty when I arrived at my house. I knew I'd have to move fast to make it to the office before driving to Irvine for our interviews at ten. I waved a quick hello to Mrs. Franklin, who was just getting into her car, opened my front door, and scooped up a pile of junk mail that had fallen on the floor. My footsteps echoed in the living room, which held only a sofa and coffee table. On the coffee table were a photograph of the Justice clan and some dried-up flowers that someone in my family had bought when they spruced up the place for that first broker's open house. As I hurried outside to toss the flowers in a trash can, I was reminded of the time after Keith and Erica's funeral, when I hadn't had the energy to dispose of the floral arrangements that had been sent by our friends and families, Keith's colleagues at the university, and the members of my grandmother's church. After a couple of weeks they had dried and rotted so badly that at the instigation of my mother, her housekeeper had been dispatched to throw them away.

She had also been instructed by my mother to save the little cards that came with the arrangements, for the time when I would feel up to sending acknowledgment cards. To the chagrin of my Emily Post–loving mother, I could never bring myself to do it but relegated the cards to a file with the other funeral arrangements. That file and some others were stashed in a box that was awaiting transport to Aubrey's garage.

Maybe I was just being paranoid, but I'd been a detective long enough to know when someone was hiding something, and Burt Rivers showed all the telltale signs—flushed face, inability to look me in the eye, the way he hesitated when I suggested he get Perris to return those files. Or maybe I just wanted to take the onus off my brother, who, despite being a royal pain in the ass, I'd always believed had my best interests at heart.

The few remaining boxes in Keith's office seemed to be in the same location where I'd left them when I'd gone through them that Sunday. Which meant that Perris, who had access to my parents' copy of my house key, must have found what he was looking for the first time around. But he'd never think to look for the bit of evidence I was seeking because he would not have known of its existence or understood the significance it might have.

I found the box labeled PERSONAL and, inside, the file that contained Keith's obituary and other mementos from the funeral. The sympathy cards and ribbons from the floral arrangements brought back the memory of the two closed caskets, side by side in the funeral home, the damage done to those dear bodies making them too difficult to restore for viewing. Perris had held my hand at the funeral home when I was making the arrangements, had ended up picking the caskets, viewing their bodies, and even determining with the funeral director that the caskets would remain closed. How could my brother have done all that and then betrayed their memories with this theft? Had it all been an act? And if so, what was he covering up?

I pawed through the envelope until I found the cards that came with the bouquets.

OUR HEARTFELT SYMPATHIES, the first card read, signed by the criminology department at the university. The chair of the department, a craggy old coot who smelled of Old Spice and cigar smoke, had made a point of letting me know at the repast that they'd sent it and a donation to the university faculty fund in Keith's name.

That arrangement had come from Edelweiss, a floral shop in Santa Monica. Allen A.M.E.'s Missionary Society, my grandmother's group, had sent an arrangement from a black florist on La Brea, the card reading: NO MATTER THE CHALLENGE, THE LORD IS YOUR STRENGTH AND YOUR SHIELD. And while you could put what I really knew of the Bible onto the head of a pin, that little paraphrase of Scripture had brought me comfort, as had a handwritten copy of the Twenty-eighth Psalm from which it was taken that Grandmama Cile gave me before the service.

Then I found it. SO SORRY FOR YOUR LOSS, it read and was signed simply, A FRIEND. No one had come forward to claim the enormous spray of white roses and gladiola that the card accompanied, and I was too overwhelmed by grief to bother figuring out who had sent it. And by the time I'd joined the department a year later, had uttered that inadequate phrase myself a hundred times when interviewing the families of victims in the years since, the card had been long forgotten. But Burt's slip of the lip plus that little card, its envelope yellowed with age, brought it all back.

The arrangement was from Tip-Top Florists in Culver City, the silhouetted logo on the envelope identical with the one on the card Burt gave me. Too bad Burt's brother-in-law wasn't around to tell me who had sent it. But even if he was alive, I doubted if he'd remember, or tell me if he did.

But I remembered. Remembered Burt had never met Keith, had never taken part in surveilling our house when Cinque Lewis threatened our lives, or had met him anywhere else that I knew of. But somehow Burt *knew* Keith would have wanted me to "move on" and had the nerve to tell me so, knew what my brother's wishes were for me, too.

"I'll move on," I promised Burt's card. "Just not the way you think."

9

Coffee and Cream

I **practically flew downtown**, my mind racing ahead of my speeding car. A dozen memories flickered in front of me, including a conversation I'd had with my godfather, Chief Youngblood, just over a week earlier.

We had just closed the Vicki Park investigation, and he had called to get the names of my partners who'd helped crack the case. Then he switched hats and urged me to cut Perris some slack. "Your brother's got a lot of demons he's wrestling with," he counseled, "just like the rest of us." But I was so busy deflecting what I assumed were criticisms about the way I'd handled my cases that I'd overlooked the parts that came back to me now.

Uncle Henry had also said that night that he had a good idea about what was bugging Perris, but he had never explained what he meant. I thought about dropping by his office to see if he would elaborate now, but I decided to hold off until I could present him with something more than missing files, a floral card, and vague suspicions about my brother and Burt Rivers.

Arriving at my desk on the third floor of the PAB, I saw a note from Thor: MEET US IN BIG MAC'S OFFICE ASAP. Concerned I was missing a strategy session for our interviews at CZ Toys, I rummaged through my mail until I found a copy of the letter of commendation Billie told me Chief Youngblood had written about our work on the Park case. I stuck a Post-it note on it and folded it together with a form I grabbed from a stack on top of the file cabinets. Shoving the whole thing into an interdepartmental envelope, I hurried to the ladies' room and locked myself into a stall at the far end of the room.

Years before, I had cobbled together scraps of information on Keith and Erica's murders and the hunt for Cinque Lewis into some files, wheedling information from my Uncle Henry, then a lieutenant in the Southwest Division, where the Black Freedom Militia was headquartered, and later from the detectives who had investigated the case. When Lewis turned up dead last year during the riots, I had pulled the murder book on Keith and Erica, seeing for the first time as complete a file on the investigation as was available. And while I recalled nothing there that linked Burt Rivers to my husband, Keith, or Perris and Burt to his or Erica's murder, there was something in my files that had turned my brother into a thief—something he didn't want me to know.

But there were gaps in the information I had, and in Keith and Erica's murder book, identified by numerous blacked-out pages and the words "confidential" stamped across them. Those pages came from PDID, the department's Public Disorder Intelligence Division, which investigated black nationalist and other high-profile targets, and the BFM, with its revolutionary slogans and "death to the pig" demonstrations, was one of them. Problem was, no one below the rank of deputy chief could access PDID files.

Which was why I was hiding out in the ladies' room.

A few minutes later, I was done, the paperwork completed in nondescript block letters, Deputy Chief Henry Youngblood's tight scrawl carefully copied into the blank for the requesting officer, and a Post-it note attached requesting that the PDID file on the BFM be delivered to Detective Justice in RHD. Maybe these files would give me the answers I sought, maybe not, but I was tired of people trying to pull the okey-doke on me, pretending to be concerned about me when they were just covering their own asses. Satisfied, I dropped the envelope in the outgoing mail, stashed my purse, and knocked on Big Mac's door.

I was surprised to see Captain MacIverson Armstrong in the office so early. Or at all, truth be told. Our commanding officer had coasted so long on his thirty-plus-year reputation in RHD—a rep that had earned him the nickname Big Mac—that I'd taken to calling him something else: Captain MIA. But MIA was there that day, his patrician features grim as he sat in an old leather chair at the head of his conference table. To his right was my boss, Lieutenant Kenneth Stobaugh, jittery as one of the racehorses in the engravings that lined MIA's walls. To MIA's immediate left sat Billie and next to her Thor, both of whom looked as if they wanted to jump down the table at two men who sat at the other end, their backs to the door.

"Ah, here she is now. Detective Justice, we were just talking about you." MIA motioned me forward and explained how I was one of the original detectives investigating the Smiley Face shootings.

Wondering who was talking about me, I walked around the table to sit next to Stobaugh and to get a better look at our mystery guests. Seated directly across from me was Jackie Perkins, a young detective I knew from Financial Crimes assigned to help out on the interviews down in Irvine. Jackie's blond bob bounced in greeting, but the other two sat immobile in suits so crisply tailored it could mean only one thing.

MIA nodded at Perkins to continue. "As I was saying, when I got the assignment, I called the local SEC office and got copies of their last few ten-K and ten-Q reports faxed over." She adjusted her cat's-eye glasses, her gray pupils large behind the lenses, and licked at her lips. "An hour after I made the request, I got a call from Special Agent Taft."

An olive-drab suit, draped over the broad shoulders of a man the color of black coffee, took up the story from there. "The Securities and Exchange Commission knew the FBI and U.S. Attorney's office were in the middle of a joint investigation of some of the officers of CZ Toys and called us when your request came through."

MIA's lips curled inward as he glanced at us. "What are you looking at them for?"

"A number of charges are in the works."

Although the look on MIA's face made clear that he wasn't satisfied with his answer, Taft did not elaborate. "What are we talking—

embezzlement?" I demanded, thinking of the argument I'd overheard between Renata and Alma at the hospital.

"If the SEC is in the loop, I would think you're investigating possible securities violations, too," Perkins added.

Taft's full lips parted enough for him to say: "Perhaps. And maybe other charges, as well."

Thor consulted his notes from our interview at CZ Toys. "So should we assume the company's better-than-expected earnings are bogus?"

"That's what we're in the middle of ascertaining." Taft spoke again while the other guy made a note. "So you people stomping around asking questions is not what we need at the moment."

" '*You people!*' " Color rising to his cheeks, Lieutenant Stobaugh snorted like the black people at the NAACP convention where Ross Perot first uttered the phrase, but this time the shoe was on the other foot. "I'm sure ticking and tying numbers makes your and Mr. Wunderlich's boats float, but you forget this is a murder investigation we're working, not some kind of corporate paper chase!"

Stobaugh's outburst made both men seem to swell in their suits, a reaction that was not lost on MIA. "You're not suggesting we back off of a murder investigation for this?" he demanded.

"If so, you boys are a little late." Thor tapped at some pages on the table before him. "CZ Toys has already confirmed our interviews today with a half dozen of their financial people plus their external auditors. We're due down there in a little over an hour."

Wunderlich, the paler side of the coffee-and-cream team, finally spoke up. "Hey, we understand this is a little awkward for you." This one's flattened Brooklyn accent, which made *you* sound like *youze*, was at odds with his Brooks Brothers–style suit and oversized Mont Blanc pen. "But it was our understanding that the shooting last summer—"

"Which, need I remind you, resulted in the death of one of the victims," Billie snapped.

"—was the work of the Nation of Islam," Taft finished, cutting off the smart remark I could see forming on his colleague's lips.

The FBI agent's dark skin and melodious baritone reminded me of an actor in a Michelle Pfeiffer movie my girlfriend Katrina had swooned over a few months before, but what he was saying just didn't add up. "Those theories didn't—"

"Hold up, Justice." Thor leaned forward. "You say that, Agent Taft, like you have some evidence of the Nation's involvement."

Taft turned up his palms as if to say *That's why we're here.*

Thor nodded triumphantly at Billie and me. "I told you it was a plausible theory!"

Billie sat stone-faced, but Kenneth Stobaugh looked as if he was having trouble controlling his excitement. "For God's sake, man," our lieutenant exclaimed. "If you and Wunderlich have something, put your cards on the table!"

"The FBI tries not to interfere in local law enforcement's investigations," Taft demurred.

"I'm sorry, but this doesn't add up for me."

All eyes shifted toward me, including Special Agent Taft's, which I noticed were the color of dark chocolate. "I'm sorry, ma'am," he said evenly. "I don't know what you mean."

"It's Detective Justice," I reminded him, annoyed by the tingling sensation his gaze was causing along my spine. "And since you and Agent Wunderlich—"

"That's Assistant U.S. Attorney Wunderlich," the other guy corrected, his voice condescending.

"Sorry, since you and the AUSA here seem to know so much about the Nation of Islam being behind the Smiley Face shootings, why didn't you come to us sooner? You'd have saved us a lot of time, energy, and effort if you'd just told us what you had."

"Frankly," Wunderlich replied, his voice testy now, "we believe your murder investigation and our investigation of CZ Toys are unrelated. And, given our understanding that you were already pursuing the Nation, it was decided that we should continue our own investigation as quietly as possible."

"Where did you get all of this 'understanding' about our investigation?" Stobaugh wanted to know.

"From our contacts within Justice." Agent Wunderlich wasn't talking about members of the Justice Family Nut House but about the Department of Justice, which had recently indicted Sergeant Koon and his band of merry ass-kickers on civil rights violations after they were acquitted of the criminal charges in the Rodney King beating. The civil trial against them was just a few weeks old, but with a new U.S. Attorney General in place and reportedly watching the proceedings closely, it was a new day in the DOJ and, it seemed, a new set of eyes watching over our shoulders.

Billie leaned forward. "What did your contacts within Justice think when they heard about—"

"Our request for the ten-Ks and ten-Qs?" I interrupted, hoping to forestall Billie mentioning Nilo Engalla's reappearance up north.

Wunderlich looked from Billie to me to Taft. "That we needed to come forward with what we know about Malik Shareef and his dealings with certain elements within the Nation of Islam."

"Which was not a priority," Billie added, "until you thought we were getting too close to *your* investigation."

"That's your interpretation, Detective Truesdale." Wunderlich's smile was strained. "That's not the way we'd characterize our intentions at all."

Billie rolled her eyes and sucked her teeth in reply.

Taft raised his hands in a truce-like gesture. "Look, folks, we came here in the spirit of cooperation. We had to get clearance from our bosses at the Bureau and DOJ to even be talking to you about either the Nation of Islam or CZ Toys!"

"Which we fully appreciate," MIA assured him. "And I'm sure you appreciate that my detectives have to go where the case takes them, even if it's in the path of your investigation. As Lieutenant Stobaugh said, we've got a murder to solve."

Wunderlich's face had turned red, his mouth twisted in an ugly grimace. He was just about to explode when Taft leaned over and whispered something to him, which made him reconsider and nod reluctantly. "Perhaps we could put you in touch with our informant," Taft offered.

"Who's that?" Thor asked.

"Christopher Deinhart," Wunderlich said grudgingly.

"Of Shuttleworth and Bezney?" Thor consulted his list. "We've got him down here as the manager for the CZ Toys audit. We're seeing him and his audit partner this afternoon."

"Deinhart was arrested last December in Santa Ana on a DUI and possession of cocaine charges," Wunderlich told us. "Once he gets in front of the DA, he starts trying to bargain. Swears he's got information about accounting irregularities at CZ Toys that he wants to trade for the DA making the charges go away. The locals didn't know what to make of him, so they called us."

"Is his information any good?" Thor asked.

"It might be. When the audit staff was testing the depreciation on some of the company's scheduled assets, they discovered some personal usage that concerned them."

"Like the corporate jet Gabriella Zuccari uses to attend the Paris fashion shows?"

Wunderlich stared at me. "Where did you—"

"We have our sources, same as you," Thor replied, warning me to keep quiet with a stern look. "But if what you're talking about is the company's practice, how's that illegal?"

"It isn't necessarily," Perkins piped up from her spot next to Thor, "unless management fails to appropriately disclose it. Which I'm assuming they haven't, or you wouldn't be talking to Mr. Deinhart."

Wunderlich's lips firmly held his response in check.

"Let me ask you this, then," Perkins pressed. "Have Shuttleworth and Bezney filed an eight-K?"

Thin-lipped silence from Wunderlich. "It's a matter of public record, Vern," Taft reminded him.

"No, they haven't," the other man replied tersely.

Nodding, Perkins explained to us: "Anytime an auditor resigns a publicly traded company, they have to file a Form Eight-K with the SEC." She turned back to Wunderlich. "Which means, since they haven't, you could also be looking at Shuttleworth and Bezney for not busting the company's chops for the accounting violations."

"I really can't comment on that," Wunderlich said, the same pained expression on his face.

Perkins sat back in her chair, a look of triumph on her face, but I couldn't figure why she should be so smug. We were still no closer to being able to get past these two puffed-up suits to talk to the company's staff than we were when I walked into MIA's office.

Thor must have been feeling the same frustration as I. "Since we already know about the jet," he said, "why don't you want us to interview the Shuttleworth and Bezney folks this afternoon as planned?"

"Mr. Deinhart took a considerable risk in coming to us," Taft explained carefully. "He could lose his job if you go in there asking a bunch of questions about CZ Toys' accounting practices and his partner tags him as the leak."

"And you could lose your only entree into the company as well as Shuttleworth and Bezney," Perkins added.

Wunderlich had to agree. "So you see," he said, his voice more congenial, "we can't afford to spook Mr. Deinhart by having a bunch of cops storming CZ Toys before we can gather enough evidence to present to a grand jury."

"Besides," Taft assured us, "there's plenty of evidence on the Nation to keep you busy on the Shareef murder."

"We don't need to be kept busy," Stobaugh shot back. "We need to solve a murder!"

Billie's head bobbed in agreement. "Just because the FBI's had a hard-on for the Nation of Islam since the sixties doesn't mean we should take your word for it that they're responsible for Shareef's death," she argued, "or that we shouldn't be permitted to conduct a thorough investigation, no matter which sacred cows get sacrificed in the process!"

"I resent your inference, Detective!" Taft snapped, pointing a finger in Billie's direction.

Stobaugh pointed back. "And I resent you coming here, teasing us with some mealy-mouthed information about the Nation of Islam—"

I nudged Stobaugh's elbow and muttered: "Which we have yet to hear."

Stobaugh nodded in agreement. "—while trying to tell our people how to investigate a homicide!"

Wunderlich's gaze, cold with contempt, shifted to MIA. "Captain Armstrong, given the current climate, I would think you would want to cooperate with the DOJ in any way you can. And if you don't see it that way," he went on, "I'm sure the chief or the president of the police commission certainly will."

The threat to go over his head made MIA's gaze flicker as coldly as Wunderlich's, but his lips were pulled into a tight smile. "I think I have a solution that will satisfy everyone," he said, a forced joviality making his voice sound too loud for the room. "Thor, call the folks down at CZ Toys; tell them there's been a development on another front and you'll get back to them later."

"But—"

"Then you and Detective Perkins can meet independently with Agent Wunderlich and Mr. Deinhart, hear what he has to tell you. Then decide if you still need to meet with the CZ Toys staff."

"You might want to hold off on meeting with Deinhart until tomorrow," Agent Taft advised. "You don't want his partners to get suspicious when the meeting at the company gets canceled and he disappears."

"Good thinking," MIA said, shifting his attention to Wunderlich. "And we need a full debriefing on what you've got on the Nation."

Wunderlich gestured to his colleague. "Special Agent Taft is on point on that one."

"Maybe Detective Justice and I could talk," he said, his dark face warming up with a smile.

I turned to Thor. "Don't you want me to stay on CZ Toys?"

Thor eyed Billie, jerking his head in Taft's direction. "Not me," she muttered, glaring at the black FBI agent as if he were a rabid dog. "I'm still catching up on the case file."

Thor turned back to me with an apologetic shrug.

"Then I guess it's you and me, Detective Justice," Taft said smoothly, rising from his chair. "I can brief you on what we have and then arrange for you to talk to our informant this afternoon."

"Then I guess we're done here," MIA said, rising from the table as well.

"Sorry you got the short end of the stick on this one, Charlotte," Stobaugh whispered as I gathered up my things.

"Gee, thanks," I replied, while the voice in my head mocked me for wanting back on the job so fast.

10

We Wear the Mask

Couldn't you find a conference room in Parker Center?"

"They're all being used," I said. Thor, Billie, and I had put our heads together after the meeting and agreed that no one wanted the Feds sniffing around the office, so I had taken the special agent to Teddy's, my favorite downtown coffee shop/hamburger joint. The place was almost empty, save for a couple of guys sitting at the counter, watching news of the Branch Davidians' standoff with the FBI on a television suspended from the ceiling. Helga could tell from the look on my face that I wasn't there for the pleasure of eating Teddy's legendary hamburgers, so she left a couple of menus at my booth in the back and joined her husband and the others in front of the TV.

Ignoring the menu, Taft scanned the room, eyes narrowing at a crack Teddy made about the FBI. "Who's the old guy?"

"Theodore Roosevelt. He and his wife, Helga, own the place."

Hearing the name, Taft shook his head as if to say *my people, my people.* "I would think another black man named after a president would appreciate the irony."

He smiled into my eyes and extended his hand. "It's Paul."

"What?"

It was a nice smile, enhanced by teeth so sparkling they had to be capped. "Not William Howard. Paul L. D. Taft."

"Your mother named you after a poet?"

He smiled slowly. "I'm surprised you'd pick up on that."

His hand was still out. I shook it reluctantly. "Hard to be a black kid growing up and not know Paul Laurence Dunbar's name."

"Especially among our parents' generation," he agreed, releasing my hand at last.

" 'We wear the mask that grins and lies,' " I recited. " 'It hides our cheeks and shades our eyes.' I had to recite that poem in Jack and Jill."

Taft shrugged. "My mother was more into 'When Malindy Sings' than his protest stuff."

Annoyed that I'd have something in common with this Fed, I signaled to Helga that we were ready to order. "Whatever."

Paul Taft asked for coffee, no cream, while I ordered tea. "You and that Detective Truesdale really slammed us in that meeting," he said after Helga left. "I've come to expect it from the white boys, but it packs an extra wallop coming from your own."

First it was black poetry, and now this. "Oh, so now you're trying to be my 'brother,' is that it, Special Agent Taft?"

Taft's smile returned, broader now. "As I said, the name is Paul. And this is not about me trying to be your brother, as you call it, but just straight up professionalism I'm talking about."

"You complaining about professionalism is a little like the pot calling the kettle black, don't you think?" I snorted at his arching eyebrow. "The FBI and DOJ weren't exactly forthcoming with information about the Nation of Islam's connection to the shooting."

"I thought we explained that."

"Not to my satisfaction, Paul L. D. Taft, so let me try out an alternative explanation on you."

His large hand swept out in my direction. "Be my guest."

"Someone at Justice planted information with one of our people last July about the Nation's connection to the Smiley Face shootings, but we didn't find what you wanted us to."

Taft's smiled faded a bit, and I could see the veil drop behind his eyes. "I'm listening."

"It always struck me as strange how the Nation of Islam connection kind of came out of the blue at the time. I mean, Malik Shareef and his wife had broken ties with the Nation decades ago, but we spent a lot of time running down leads on the Nation anyway. Maybe your contacts in Justice had something to do with that, too."

The smile flickered for an instant on Taft's dark face, then died. "Be that as it may, your Detective Truesdale seemed more bent about it than she needed to be."

Ooh, girl, you know you hit a nerve! Look how he's trying to change the subject.

"Is it because she hates the Bureau, or is it just men in general?"

Taft's innuendo sent a chill down my spine. Was he trying to signify some knowledge of Billie's sexuality, or was he just being snide? For the sake of her privacy, I hoped it was the latter.

"You work with her. Which do you think it is?"

I knew Billie had been raised pretty far left of center, but with the FBI's track record on COINTELPRO, not to mention the files it was rumored they kept on black folks from Thurgood Marshall to Marian Anderson, I could understand her skepticism. But Taft didn't need to know about Billie's or my feelings about the Bureau, her feelings about men, or anything else for that matter. "Maybe we should just stick to the information you have on Shareef's murder and leave Detective Truesdale out of it."

"However you want to play it." Taft watched while Helga brought our drinks and hustled back to the news program, which had moved on to report the death of a cop in Parker Center the week before. Curious to see if my name would be mentioned, I had to force myself to listen to what Taft was saying about his work on a case in northern California.

"Before I transferred back to the L.A. field office, I was pretty well hooked into the Nation of Islam community in the East Bay. Not long after the shooting down here, one of my old C.I.s called about the Shareefs."

Listening intently, I noticed how Taft was milking the mention of his confidential informant for maximum dramatic effect.

"You know Malik Shareef was raised in one of the Nation of Islam's mosques in Oakland?"

"I also know that he and his wife left the Nation in the seventies, when he entered Harvard, and adopted a traditional Muslim faith."

Taft leaned forward, his face animated. "But Malik's family stayed in the Nation. His half brother, Rashaan Muhammad, and a buddy of his, Eddie Aycox, approached him in 'eighty-six, a couple of years before Shareef and his wife's book took off. I don't know if you know of it—"

"*Beautiful You.*" When Malik was a graduate student, he replicated Kenneth Clark's landmark study used in *Brown v. Board of Education*, which showed that a majority of black girls and boys still preferred white dolls over black ones, whether it was Barbie or the latest action figure. Malik's findings, and subsequent testing over the years, became the basis for *Beautiful You*, arguably the most successful guide to black self-esteem in the past twenty years. "My sister-in-law quotes from that book all the time. She and my brother Perris loaned me their copy at the beginning of our investigation."

"Interesting," Taft murmured, a curious look on his face. "Anyway, based on their early review of Shareef's research and the manuscript for the book, Muhammad and Aycox offered to become partners with the Shareefs in a toy company that would manufacture ethnically diverse dolls."

"Which is what the Shareefs agreed to do with CZ Toys just last year, for millions."

"Exactly. But when Muhammad and Aycox became their partners, Malik Shareef was just another academic trying to get his book published by a university press. This was before it was picked up for six figures by a New York publisher and he and the wife appeared on *60 Minutes* and *Phil Donahue.*"

And the cover of *Ebony* and *Time* magazines, an occasion that was noted at the time by my race-proud father. "That young couple is going to go far," he'd predicted, passing around the article featuring the handsome Shareef and his elegantly dressed wife.

"Not so young, Daddy," my baby sister Rhodesia had corrected. "Malik Shareef's been telling the truth about black folks and self-esteem for a long time. One of his books is required reading in my 'Ethnic Issues in Psychology' class."

Needless to say, my family was devastated when Malik Shareef was shot, and furious when he died of complications some months later. "Why do we always have to lose our best and our brightest?" my father had lamented.

When I shared my family's admiration for Malik Shareef with Taft, he said: "That can go to some people's heads."

"What do you mean?"

"Were you aware that the Shareefs had formed a corporation prior to Beautiful You Dollworks?"

An uneasy feeling came over me. "That never came up in our investigation."

"That's because it was only on paper. The company never opened an office or reported any revenues. But Muhammad and Aycox contributed seventy-five thousand each into the venture, in exchange for what they thought was a forty percent equity position. You know what happened next."

I was afraid I did.

"Shareef and his wife ran the money into the ground over the next two years, doing 'research' on a line of diverse dolls that were supposed to be manufactured with Muhammad and Aycox. But, at the end of the day, not one doll came to market."

A dozen questions were swirling in my mind, like whether that kind of behavior was in keeping with the Islamic ethical beliefs Billie was talking about in our meeting and, more importantly, what did seventy-five thousand dollars represent to Shareef's half brother and his buddy. "Where'd they get the money?"

Taft sat back in his seat and crossed his arms. "I don't think that's relevant to your investigation."

"Okay, I get it, 'don't ask, don't tell.' What *can* you tell me about Muhammad and Aycox?"

"The important thing is that when that first venture went belly-up, Rashaan Muhammad and Eddie Aycox never saw a dime of their money. And the Shareefs, who had been hanging by a thread financially, came out the other side with a big house and a couple of Benzes. Then, after their book hit the best-seller lists and the media made them into stars, they formed Beautiful You Dollworks and never looked back."

"Or, let me guess, ever settled up with either Malik's half brother or Eddie Aycox."

Taft's smile was ironic. "I told you you'd know what happened next."

It was a knowledge I'd rather not possess. Just days after the shooting, I had reinterviewed Habiba Shareef at her home in Ladera Heights, one of black L.A.'s more prosperous neighborhoods. While my heart ached for Mrs. Shareef's loss, the cop in me noticed the intricate designs in her inlaid hardwood floors and her collection of vintage black dolls. But I'd assumed the money to support the Shareefs' lifestyle had come from the book or their deal with CZ Toys, not from messing over friends and family.

"At an Oakland bakery," Taft was saying, "a couple of weeks after the shooting, my informant heard Eddie Aycox spouting off about how Malik's preference for getting in bed with the blue-eyed devil cost him his life."

"Which you took as an admission of guilt as opposed to an acknowledgment of the laws of karma?"

Taft gave me a lopsided smile. "I tried to plant the seed with your superiors in RHD last summer."

Which explained Thor's earlier comments about the case and his interest in pursuing the "Black Muslim angle." "Who'd you talk to—Steve Firestone?"

"That sounds about right," Taft replied, "but I couldn't give up our informant without jeopardizing a much larger investigation."

And while Paul Taft and his colleagues were fiddling around trying to protect their precious investigation, our leads on Shareef's killers were disappearing like dust in the wind. "So when can I read this file you've developed on Muhammad and Aycox and talk to your informant?"

"Our guy's still up in Oakland," Taft said. "You think your C.O.

might approve a trip up north to talk to him? Or we could do it by phone . . ."

I signaled Helga for the check. MIA had made it clear he wanted us to pursue this lead, which meant there was no way he'd accept a phone interview with a key informant in a murder investigation. "I'll get the travel approved. Just have your informant ready."

11

Losing my Marbles

Taft couldn't arrange for us to meet his informant until Wednesday afternoon, which meant I had no excuse for missing my morning session with Pablo Wychowski at BSS. I had made the appointment for seven a.m., which meant I could go to work early and run over to Chinatown without Aubrey being any the wiser. But unlike my first visit with Dr. P., which felt like the Inquisition, I had some objectives and a plan of my own this time around.

"Can we talk about those tools you were telling me about on Monday? You know, tools to help me deal with the job."

"We'll get to that. First, I'm wondering how it felt to be back?"

I could see that this was going to be more difficult than I had thought. "Okay. But it got kind of annoying, everyone asking me that."

"Who's 'everyone'?"

"You . . . my father . . ."

Dr. P. waited, pen poised over a yellow legal pad, while I tried to come up with another name. "That doesn't sound like such a long list to me."

"Maybe not, but he and the others were inferring the same thing."

"Which was?"

"That they don't think I can handle the job anymore."

"Is that what your father said?"

I was reminded of the times I'd hung out in Matt Justice's cosmetics lab, located in a converted garage on the Nut House property, discussing some aspect of a case or his memories about L.A.'s history of violence against its citizens. "Actually, no, my father is very proud of me, and very supportive."

"How about the rest of your family? Is your mother living?"

I nodded. "Joymarie Justice is the kind of woman who thinks all of her children should be brain surgeons or attorneys." I tried to make it sound funny, but I was aware of the edge in my voice. "You could say I've been a big disappointment to her."

Dr. P.'s mustache twitched, but he did not smile. "She sounds like a very strong-willed woman."

"That's putting it politely."

"What do your siblings do?"

"My baby sister, Rhodesia, is working on her second Ph.D., but as long as she's in school my parents let her live at home. I've got another sister, Macon, but she lives up in northern California and doesn't come around much anymore."

"And what does she do?"

"Headmistress of a private school up in the Oakland Hills. Then there's my brother, Perris. He's an ex-cop who saw the light and became an attorney. He's always on my case about why I stay in the department. And then there's me, the black sheep of the family, the only one who doesn't have initials behind her name."

Dr. P. was scribbling notes on a yellow legal pad. He paused to ask: "Was your brother Perris LAPD?"

"Yeah, he was on for five years, then got out about fifteen years ago, after he was shot on the job."

"That's hard," he murmured, as if it had happened yesterday. "And you came on the department before or after he was shot?"

"Four months after." This was not the way I had expected this session to be going. I had planned to pick Dr. P.'s brain and raid his magic toolkit for techniques to help me deal with the madness on the job, showing in the process what a good little patient I was so I could get the hell out of there and back to work, I was hoping, by the end of the week. But instead of tools that were going to help me deal with the assholes on the job, we'd drifted into depths I had no intention of plumbing. "Is all this necessary?"

A frown creased Dr. P.'s soft-featured face and made his mustache twitch again. "I was just wondering how you came to policing."

Despite the coolness of the morning, Dr. P.'s office began to feel close. I peeled off my jacket and rubbed at the back of my neck. "That's too long and too boring a story."

Dr. P. put down his pen and reared back in his chair. "We've got time."

"Fine." I told him as quickly as I could about the graduate work Keith and I were doing in criminology, how theoretical it was, how isolated it made me from crimes and the people who commit them. "So I became a cop."

"Who's Keith?"

"My hus—my late husband. There isn't anything in my file about a Keith Roberts, or how he died? Surely Dr. Betty said something to you."

"You want to fill me in?"

The room began to shimmer, causing the masks on the wall to grow indistinct in the early morning light. They were replaced by Keith's face, convulsing in pain, the life pulsing out of his midsection, the light draining from his eyes. I took a deep breath and said: "There's not a lot to tell. My husband and I worked together, doing research on L.A. gangs. We got married, had a baby who was murdered with him in a drive-by the same day my brother got shot. They died, my brother lived, I went on the department, end of story."

Dr. P. sat motionless through my recitation. "How awful for you," he said quietly.

"I got over it," I said, relieved to see the masks coming back into focus.

The room was silent for a while. Eventually, Dr. P. said: "So you joined the LAPD after your husband and daughter were killed and your brother was shot."

"Is there an echo in here or what?"

"I was just wondering—"

"I passed the psychological exams, if that's what you're wondering."

"I wasn't suggesting you were unstable, Charlotte. Just that you came on despite the terrible tragedy you suffered. That's pretty remarkable."

My heart began to pound, and I held my breath for a moment to quell the rumbling of my stomach. "Coming on was actually the best thing I could have done. The pace, the variety, the ability to make things right for victims' families."

"You said something like that in our first session. Bringing closure and justice to families who will never be whole, I think you said."

"Yeah, well, it sure beats the hell out of sitting around feeling sorry for yourself." Or sitting around in places like this, picking away at words and feelings I'd rather leave be.

Dr. P. tilted his head until he caught my eye. "I can see where coming on under those circumstances must have put a tremendous burden on you to succeed," he said softly. "To fail would be like letting your family's murders go unanswered."

My eyes pricking with unexpected tears, I glanced at a bowl of marbles on the end table and managed a nod, afraid my voice would betray me.

"How long ago did this happen?"

The marbles were all sizes, from huge cat's-eyed ones to tiny swirls of milky blue and white, and every color in between. "May tenth of 'seventy-eight," I told the marbles, determined not to resort to pulling a Kleenex from a nearby box.

"And did they find the person responsible?"

"The man," I corrected, reminding myself to breathe while I explained about Cinque Lewis and his connection to Keith's research on the Black Freedom Militia. "And he wasn't found until May of last year, during the riots."

"That's a long time."

Finally, I saw an opening in the conversation and went for it like a running back for daylight. "That's how cold cases can be. Which is why I wanted back on the Smiley Face investigation, so Mrs. Shareef and the Zuccaris don't have to wait forever for some sort of resolution. Which is why I'd like to talk about some tools that will help me do my work."

Dr. P. ignored the hint, making a note on his legal pad. "You said your mother was disappointed by your decision to become a cop. Do you think it was primarily because of her aspirations for her children?"

"She's always been worried about us kids, always harping on what a dangerous world it is. But she and Perris have gone to such lengths to prove their point lately, it's a little hard to take."

"How so?"

"My brother takes a lot of criminal and civil cases where his main strategy is attacking the department. You know the drill—accusations of planted guns, tampering with evidence, sexual harassment. But this latest stunt he's pulled is beyond the pale. I'm just about finished with both him and my mother."

"You want to tell me about it?"

Surprisingly, I did. I explained about Keith's missing files on Cinque Lewis and the Black Freedom Militia, how Perris had taken them from my house with my mother's full knowledge and, I believed, encouragement. I told him about my anger at Perris, my mother, and Aubrey, and my entire family for letting me down, and about the argument last night during Justice Family Film Night. "Perris's old partner suggested he took them because he didn't want me to start my life with Aubrey carrying a lot of baggage. As if I couldn't recite every detail in those files from memory."

"Can you?"

"I was speaking theoretically."

He leaned forward. "I'll ask again—can you?"

The masks on the wall seemed to echo the question. I rubbed at my temples and fished an antacid out of my Altoids tin. "You're the mind reader, Dr. P. You tell me."

"I'm nothing of the kind, Charlotte, but to do my job I have to be a student of human behavior, just like you when you're investigating a case."

"You mean when I'm interrogating a witness. Is that what this is—an interrogation?"

"No, it's not. I'm just wondering—was there some truth to what your brother's old partner said? Before you disagree, consider this—as much as we might wish otherwise, sometimes we can get stuck on an issue, or an experience, or a person. But there comes a time when we have to examine it, and deal with it, and move on with our lives."

"Move on? If I move on any faster, I'll get jet lag! Do you realize in the past ten months, in addition to my other cases, I've solved the murder of Cinque Lewis, gotten involved with Aubrey Scott, put my house on the market, packed up, and moved in with the man? For God's sake, what more can I do?"

"That's an impressive list," Dr. P. acknowledged. "But maybe there's something you're still holding onto. Maybe that's what concerned your brother when he took those files."

"I don't need to come here and listen to you defend Perris!"

"I'm not trying to defend him, Charlotte. I'm just encouraging you to consider alternative reasons why your brother might have taken those files."

"I'm not buying it. I think it has something to do with a case he was working." I left Burt Rivers's name out of it. Given Burt's long-standing connection to Dr. Betty and BSS, I saw no need to show my hole card.

"And what if it doesn't?" he pressed.

My head was beginning to pound, and I was having trouble seeing clearly through what had become angry tears. I snatched a Kleenex from the box. "Even if what you're suggesting is true, why couldn't Perris come to me and say something? Why sneak around like some kind of a thief? He stole something very important to me. He stole . . ."

"What did he—?"

"He stole . . ."

"What?"

"It's like he stole a piece of my soul!" I could hear myself wailing, but I couldn't stop. "Something that made me who I am."

"Is that what those files represent to you? Who you are?"

"They were mine and Keith's, you know, from when we worked together! And here they were—my family—invading my space, making me move—"

"Move?"

"Move out my files and my furniture and sell the house, and . . . and . . ."

"Move in with Aubrey. Did your parents make you do that, too?"

I couldn't understand why I was crying, but I couldn't stop either. Dr. P. waited me out, giving me room to say more to incriminate myself, just the way I did with suspects. "Oh, God, you must think I don't love Aubrey, but I do!"

"I never said you don't love him."

"He's a great guy, you know? Very smart, very successful—he used to be an ER doc before he started running this big emergency medicine group—and caring, and he's great in bed. The man even cooks for me. And the sex is great."

Dr. P. nodded. "You mentioned that."

"So why am I so upset?"

"Maybe because it's all happening so fast? Maybe you don't feel you can trust him?"

"He does get up in my face about things sometimes."

"Just the kind of man your mother would want for you?"

"She *is* one of his biggest supporters."

Dr. P. leaned forward in his chair. "Charlotte, you've been through a lot of changes in the past year. You solved the murder of the man who killed your family."

I nodded, tears still flowing. "But I never had the chance to confront him!"

"I see. So perhaps a part of your anger at your brother taking those files is pent-up anger against this man, Cinque Lewis, who was a member of this gang—"

"The Black Freedom Militia."

"—whom you've never been able to confront."

"I'd never thought of it that way."

"Then there are these cases you've investigated lately. Every one of them has resulted in some sort of physical or emotional trauma to you.

And, before you say it, I know that's the nature of the job, but it all adds up, Charlotte. The bodies, the violence done to them, and the people who kill them. Pretty soon you feel like it's more than you can handle, like maybe you're about to lose it."

At that moment I felt I had already lost it, broken into a thousand pieces that were falling from my eyes and coming out of my pores. I reached for another Kleenex. "This is ridiculous! I don't usually react to things this way."

"I'm sure you don't. What cops do, like doctors or lawyers or psychologists but even more so, is put on their game face. Like these masks on my wall. They're angry or cynical or emotionless, but they're all masks to cover what's really underneath."

"But I can't function like this! I can't go out there and do my job if every little thing that goes wrong in my life reduces me to tears."

"You're a highly skilled professional, Charlotte, so I think there's little chance of that happening. But what if it did? What's the worst that could happen?"

"I can't imagine. Guess I'd be crying all the time."

"And what would happen then?"

"I'd just be crying. I don't know what else you want me to say." But even as I said it, I could think of one more thing: *Everyone would know I'm faking it.*

Dr. P. studied me for a moment before saying: "Stress manifests itself in different ways. You may not break down in tears, but your reflexes may be off a beat; your cop's intuition may falter. Sometimes cops end up having affairs, or drinking too much, or doing drugs to compensate for the pain."

A shudder passed through me. "So what's the solution?"

"You need to have a safe place—here, at home with Aubrey, or with members of your family—where you can be however you need to be: happy or angry or sad. You understand what I'm saying?"

"But they can't understand what the job is like! Death—it suffocates you! The pressure to close out cases, the harassment I get from the guys I work with. Aubrey has some sense of it, being a former ER doc. But even when he was working the ER, he was *saving* lives, not cleaning up the mess on the ones he couldn't."

Dr. P. nodded.

"It's not like we don't talk about the job at *all*. It's just at some point Aubrey's going to start trying to tell me what I should do, or how I should feel, trying to fix me. And that's when I turn off."

"One of the drawbacks of the male species is our propensity to fix things," Dr. P. gave me a wry smile. "Worked great out in the wild, not so great in the home."

I snorted in agreement, glad to finally be able to laugh at something this morning.

"Is it possible to hear the caring behind Aubrey's words when he's trying to 'fix' you? Maybe see him as a sounding board instead of your judge and jury?"

"A sounding board instead of the Board of Rights."

Dr. P. smiled at my cop humor. "In a manner of speaking."

"Maybe. I can try."

He noticed I was checking my watch. "We've still got a few more minutes, if there's something else you want to discuss."

"When are we going to talk about tools? You said you'd show me some tools to help me cope."

"Okay, Charlotte," he replied, smiling and moving to the bowl of marbles on the end table. He grabbed a big handful and encouraged me to do the same. "Now hold them as tight as you can."

I tried, but they began to dig into my palm, slipping out of my grasp and onto the carpeted floor.

So were his. "When we try to control, to hold on so tight to these marbles, or to our emotions, they seep out, hitting the floor, making us feel like we're—"

"I get it. Losing our marbles."

"Exactly. Now loosen your grip on them. See how they nestle in your hand? Imagine they're your feelings about the job, your boyfriend, your family. Let those feelings nestle somewhere in you, Charlotte. Make room for them instead of wrapping your mind around them so tightly. Soon those feelings begin to feel more natural, even the angry ones—just marbles in your hand, nothing more and nothing less."

He rose from his chair and deposited his marbles back in the bowl. "That's all we have time for today. See you next Monday?"

I dumped my marbles into the bowl except for a little yellow one, the color of egg yolks, swirled with white, which I put in my jacket pocket. "See you next Monday."

12

A Smile and a Gun

By five that evening, Paul Taft and I were inching across the Bay Bridge in a Crown Vic signed out from the FBI motor pool. We had spent the afternoon interviewing Taft's old informant, Verdelle Shabazz, at the Bureau's Golden Gate Avenue field offices, and we were on our way to an Oakland bakery where Malik Shareef's half brother, Rashaan Muhammad, worked.

Fog rolling across the lower deck was obscuring the path ahead, as were the circumspect answers Taft was giving me. "Tell me again—why are we talking to Muhammad when Shabazz said it was Eddie Aycox who made the blue-eyed devil comment?"

"One, because Aycox is slick as eel shit, and he's a jailhouse lawyer to boot, so you're only going to get one shot at him before he demands representation. Interviewing Muhammad first will help you get your ducks in a row before you make a run at Aycox."

"Slick how?"

Taft was silent. To my right, cranes at the Port of Oakland were suspended over shipping containers like ravenous insects. "Look, I'm not traipsing all over the Bay Area without knowing what I'm getting into here!"

"Okay, okay!" Taft exclaimed. "But this is not for general consumption, understand?"

Should I activate the Cone of Silence? I wanted to ask. "Just spit it out, will you?"

"Eddie Aycox used to own a bunch of vending machines down in Mobile, Alabama. Cigarette, snacks and candy, soda, you name it. You know how that kind of business is—cash only, difficult as hell to trace the income, half of the machines stocked with goods that fell off of the back of a truck somewhere—"

"Sounds like a money launderer's heaven."

"Very good, Detective," Taft nodded approvingly. "Fourteen years ago, the Birmingham and Mobile offices collaborated on hooking up Aycox and three of his associates for laundering money for a group of Jamaican drug dealers. The U.S. Attorney froze all of their assets they could find, but we suspected they might have missed some of them. After Aycox was paroled, the Mobile office was watching him pretty closely when he fell in with Muhammad and got permission from his parole officer to move to California to take a job."

A jailhouse convert to the Nation of Islam, Aycox had met Rashaan Muhammad and Verdelle Shabazz at a Saviour's Day Rally, where he had repented his association with drugs and alcohol. Aycox had joined Muhammad in Oakland soon thereafter, and the two of them had begun a nonprofit business development firm in the black community, which catered to small start-ups, until they latched onto the Shareefs. If Aycox was angry enough at Malik Shareef to contract to have him killed, Shabazz contended, Muhammad would have known about it.

It was an assessment Taft accepted without question, but I wasn't convinced. There was something about Verdelle Shabazz that made the hairs stand up on my neck. A medium-complected, average-looking brother whose only distinguishing characteristics were patches of acne scars on his cheeks, Shabazz certainly had that bow-tie-wearing, clean-cut look you would expect from men in the Nation, but on him it looked a little too clean, a little too square. Moreover, he had seemed way too comfortable sitting in the FBI's interview room, as if he'd been there many times before. The question was—was he telling the truth, or just saying what Taft and I wanted to hear so he could get paid?

Once we were downtown, we circled the one-way streets at Seventeenth, Webster, Eighteenth, and Franklin a couple of times to get the lay of the land. I had to admit that Shabazz's assessment of this Muslim bakery seemed solid, judging by the diverse appearance of the young men and women I saw either working behind the counter or coming and going from the establishment. Shabazz had said that although the place where Muhammad worked was famous for giving all kinds of down-and-out brothers and sisters a second chance, it was and probably always would be family owned. "From entrepreneur to shift supervisor at a Muslim bakery in a few short years. That would be enough to make Muhammad a bona fide BBM."

Taft had pulled up on the opposite side of the street, a few doors away from the bakery, and was shifting the car into park. "Pardon?"

"BBM—bitter black man."

"I gotta remember that one." Taft chuckled, but his eyes were on the bakery, which was bustling with last-minute customers emerging with pink boxes and brown paper bags. "You heard what Shabazz said: Muhammad's failed investment in the Shareefs bankrupted him. He was lucky the owners of the bakery gave him a job."

"I wonder if he'd see it that way." According to a copy of the driver's license that Taft had gotten from the DMV, Rashaan Muhammad was forty-seven, way too old for a black man to be starting over. Five-eight and two-ten, Muhammad had glared morosely at the camera, his deep-set brown eyes little pinpricks behind the oversized black eyeglasses that covered a third of his face. With a faded kente-cloth bow tie and his suit jacket just visible in the photo, he reminded me of a slightly threadbare Muslim version of Heavy D. But other than his beat-down appearance, I was damned if I saw anything in that photo that made me think Rashaan Muhammad would withhold information about the death of his brother. "Has Verdelle Shabazz been a reliable informant?"

"What kind of question is that?"

Not a good one, judging by the challenge in Taft's voice. "Has he ever steered you wrong?"

"Not in the four years he's been working with the northern California field offices."

"How'd he end up being an FBI informant in the first place?" I pressed, unnerved to find Taft watching my lips as I spoke.

Then his eyes were back on the bakery. "How about I tell you over dinner later? Art's Crab Shack's not far from here. They have the best—"

"You'd better tell me now." I could feel the anger rising at the back of my throat and a different kind of heat growing elsewhere in my body. I fingered the marble in my pocket that I'd lifted from my session with Dr. P., letting its smoothness center my mind. "I've made plans for dinner."

"Too bad. Seeing that sister of yours?" In response to my startled look, he explained: "I overheard you on the phone at the office."

During a break in the Shabazz interview, I had slipped out and called my younger sister Macon, aka Fugitive from Justice. Macon had stopped communicating with the family since Thanksgiving a couple of years before, for reasons my father didn't know and my mother was unwilling to say. When I wrote a message in her last birthday card asking what was up, she'd written back that she was willing to talk about it, but not on Justice Family turf. So while she seemed surprised by my unexpected call, she'd needed little coaxing to agree to meet for dinner that night.

It felt weird knowing Taft had overheard my conversation. "Maybe some other time," I muttered uneasily.

He glanced my way and smiled. "I'm going to take you up on that, Detective."

"Do you smile *all* the time?"

"Is it bothering you?"

"It just strikes me as a little excessive for someone in law enforcement."

"I take my inspiration from Al Capone."

"How's that?"

"Capone once said: 'You can go a long way with a smile.' " Taft demonstrated with another dazzler, then patted the breast pocket of his jacket. Capone also said: 'You can go a lot farther with a smile and a gun.' I've been following his advice ever since."

I could feel the corners of my mouth creep up. "Now you've given me one to remember."

"Besides, I only smile when I see something I like."

I concentrated on the foot traffic going into the barbershop just ahead of us on the left. Taft leaned over until he caught my eye. "Are you blushing, Detective Justice?"

"Don't flatter yourself."

"You're too young to be having hot flashes. What are you, thirty-five?"

"Can we just stick to business?" I said, smiling inwardly at the compliment.

"Whatever you say. I like a woman who takes charge." A few moments passed in blessed silence, then: "I'm forty-eight myself. Been with the Bureau since 'seventy-three."

"What made you apply?" I asked, grateful he'd stopped flirting.

"I'd been on the NYPD for a few years and had just gotten my master's in Criminal Justice from John Jay when—"

"That's funny, I've got a master's in criminology, too."

Taft gave me a surprised look. "Really? What were you going to do with it?"

"Research, maybe teach after I got the Ph.D., which I never did."

"Me, I was thinking of a command position in the NYPD, but a recruiter from the FBI was on campus, so I listened to what he had to say. I think they were as surprised to see me as I was to be there."

"Do they really transfer agents around a lot?"

"Oh, yeah. I've been in four cities since Quantico."

"From what you were saying yesterday, you've been in L.A. twice now? When was the first time?"

" 'Seventy-three to 'seventy-eight."

"Then you probably remember a case involving Cinque Lewis and the Black Freedom Militia. He killed a father and child in a drive-by, then disappeared."

Taft shook his head, the corners of his mouth twitching downward.

"I'm surprised you wouldn't have heard of it. Lewis disappeared afterward, wasn't found until just last year during the riots. The Feds were looking for him in five states back in the day."

"Sorry," he murmured. "There were so many cases like that in those days. The Panthers, the Symbionese Liberation Army assassinating Marcus Foster up here, tracking down that Weathermen gang. Those were some crazy times in the Bureau."

"I'm sure." It was disappointing to think that the murder of Keith and Erica, an event so central in my life, didn't even merit a footnote in this FBI agent's memory bank. "Maybe you knew my brother."

Taft's gaze went back out the window. "I doubt it. I didn't run into too many locals the time I was there."

"What was your assignment?"

"A little of this and that," he replied, "which was why I put in for a transfer after five years to Birmingham. I was there for nine years, then San Francisco for five before transferring back to L.A. in January."

"That's a lot of moving around."

Taft was watching my lips again. "I think I'm going to like being in L.A. a whole lot better this time around."

I ignored the comment, but I couldn't ignore the tingling sensation Taft's words were creating in my body. "I can't imagine being in Birmingham, Alabama, for nine years. My parents used to call it Bombingham, after those little girls were killed."

He turned away, his eyes back on the bakery. "Your parents weren't the only ones."

I followed his gaze, noticed the lettering on the window, which proclaimed A TASTE OF THE HEREAFTER, and the people moving about inside. "I remember the day it happened." It was September 15, 1963, less than a month after the March on Washington, and Reverend King's words of hope were still ringing in our ears. I'd just started the sixth grade when twenty-one children were injured and four black girls, ages eleven to fourteen, were killed in the bombing of the Sixteenth Street Baptist Church in Birmingham. I remember being afraid to go to Sunday School, afraid the Ku Klux Klan would bomb our church in Los Angeles with Perris, little Macon, and me in it. I remember my parents and Grandmama Cile holding our hands as we walked into Allen A.M.E. the following Sunday and found the altar covered in flower arrangements bearing the names of Cynthia Wesley, Addie Mae Collins, Denise McNair, and Carole Robertson, as if they were lost members of our own congregation. What might they have become, our minister asked in his sermon, had they not been cut down by hate? It was the same question I'd asked, some thirty years later, about my own daughter. "Did you work on the team that arrested that KKK guy?"

Taft shook his head. "I was transferred to Birmingham the year after Chambliss was convicted for Denise McNair's murder. And I left Birmingham right before Gary Tucker confessed. It was a hard time to be in the Bureau, even harder to be black and in Birmingham."

"These days, I feel the same way about being on the LAPD."

"Yours is a completely different situation."

"It doesn't feel like it sometimes."

"I'm telling you, if our new AG has anything to say about it, those good old boys in the LAPD are going down."

"Kicking and screaming every step of the way. Makes me wonder if I should try and ride it out."

"It'll get better," he assured me. "It has to."

"From your lips to God's ear."

"Have you considered going federal? If you're interested, I'd be willing to make a couple of calls."

"Why, thank you, Special Agent Taft. I appreciate the thought, but—"

"I thought we were past the formalities," he broke in with a smile.

"I actually know a black female in the Bureau, but I think she was fairly young when she joined. Aren't I a little long in the tooth to be starting over with the Bureau?"

"You wouldn't be starting over. With your experience, you'd proba-bly get a plum assignment. And a black woman, too?" He snorted. "The Bureau needs black females worse than the LAPD does!"

We fell into a more comfortable silence this time, until I asked him if moving around that much was hard on his family.

"That's why I don't have one." He raised a bare left hand for me to see for myself. "I mean, I have a mother in San Jose, but that's about it."

As big a flirt as he appeared to be, I was sure there were some ex-wives or ex-girlfriends in the picture somewhere. "Why don't you drive down and see your mom after this? San Jose's—what—an hour south of here?"

"I'd rather have dinner with you."

You gotta give him high marks for persistence. "Can I ask you a question?"

"I'm a Scorpio."

I almost punched his arm. "Were there many black agents when you joined the Bureau?"

"Damn," he laughed. "You say that like it was back in the days of Bonnie and Clyde! A few. Not enough, especially given the number of investigations we do in our communities."

"You ever investigate this bakery?"

A smile played on his lips as he murmured: "You don't give up, do you, Charlotte?"

I smiled back. "It's another thing we have in common."

He leaned over and whispered: "I'll tell all over a nightcap. Instead of going back tonight, why don't we check into the Marriott over on—"

I tapped him, hard, on the shoulder. "Heads up. Here comes Muhammad."

Four high school–aged girls in plaid uniforms emerged from the bakery, shoving quarters of bean pie in their mouths. Behind them shuffled Rashaan Muhammad, a Windbreaker bulking up his already ample frame and a baseball cap pulled low on his brow.

"Brother looks like he's trying to be *incognegro*," I deadpanned. "You think Shabazz tipped him?"

"No way."

"How can you be so certain?"

Taft had to tear his eyes away from Muhammad, whom he'd been watching intently. "Huh? Uh—I left one of the agents at the office to babysit him, with strict instructions to hold him incommunicado until I called in with the all clear. You see me make a call?"

The girls turned right toward Webster, while Muhammad turned left as he made his way toward Franklin. Taft guided the Crown Vic around the block again, ending up on Franklin, where we tailed the big man from a discreet distance. He settled in at a bus stop while Taft circled that block as well. "Just in case he suspects something," he explained.

A couple of minutes later, we pulled up alongside the bus bench where Muhammad was still waiting, the window on my side rolled down. "*Asalaam aleikum*, my brother!" Taft called. "Can we talk with you for a minute?"

Muhammad's welcoming smile and response died on his lips as he checked out the car, then looked at the other passengers scattered around the bench. "You talkin' to me?"

Taft's smile, however, remained bright. "You are Brother Muhammad, right? Brother over at the mosque thought you might be able to help us out."

Muhammad frowned behind his thick glasses while his stained sneakers tapped out an anxious syncopation on the concrete. "Who'd you say referred you?"

I started to say Brother Shabazz, but was silenced by Taft's hand over mine. "We want to discuss a business proposition with you," he told Muhammad. "Won't take more than thirty minutes of your time."

Muhammad rolled a big shoulder. "I 'ont know. I gotta get over to my mother's."

"Just give us a call and we'll set it up for tomorrow. But we're only in town until noon."

"Lemme get your number and I'll think about it," he said, and started for the car.

Taft looked at me and winked. "Hand me that notepad in the glove compartment."

I leaned forward to get the pad while Taft reached into his breast pocket for a pen. As I looked back to hand him the pad I leaned back quickly, hoping my movement would keep Muhammad from seeing Taft's holster.

It didn't. Muhammad took off, lumbering down the side street faster than I would have thought possible for a man of his size. Taft cursed and slammed the car into gear but was hemmed in by a minivan in the lane to our left and a Q-tip in front of us, an old man slowing as he looked for an address.

I already had the door open and was scrambling out of my seat. "I'll run him down on foot; you back me up with the car." I could hear Taft shouting something, but I was already tearing down the street, my holster banging against my side.

At a driveway a few doors up, I noticed that Muhammad had lost his eyeglasses. But he was still barreling down the driveway at full speed, his poor vision probably making him unaware that the driveway emptied into a large parking lot hemmed in by buildings on all sides. I scooped up his broken eyeglasses and was about a third of the way down the driveway when I heard a car skidding behind me. I squeezed between a couple of Dumpsters as Taft sped by, stopping just short of Muhammad, who was pounding on the back door of one of the buildings.

The door opened from the inside, and Muhammad was about to shove aside the old woman who had opened it when Taft drew his weapon. I was right behind him with my nine. "Stop right there, nigger!"

As much as I hated Taft's language, it had the desired effect. Muhammad froze like a cockroach when the lights are turned on. Seeing the situation, the woman screamed something in Chinese and quickly closed the door.

"Put your hands where I can see them!" Taft ordered.

"Don't be stupid, Mr. Muhammad," I called. "No sudden moves!"

Muhammad was sputtering and gasping, trying to catch his breath. "What you want with me?"

"Why'd you run, nigger?" Taft shouted, his voice bouncing off the walls of the building surrounding us.

"I ain't no fool! I saw that gun!"

"Easy, Agent Taft, I've got him!" I'd seen cases go wrong like this. A sudden flick of movement, a twitch, and someone is dead, leaving ruined lives and careers in their wake. So I shouted as much to encourage Taft to calm down as to let him know that I had my weapon drawn and was prepared to fire if necessary.

But instead of a nod of gratitude, Taft gave me a dirty look as he holstered his weapon. "Who the hell are you?" Muhammad asked.

In one swift movement, Taft slammed Muhammad's face into the door and pulled out his cuffs. "Special Agent Taft, FBI."

Muhammad yelped in pain. Taft cuffed one of his wrists roughly, then the other, and spun him around. "L-l-lemme see some ID!" Muhammad stuttered. He squinted at the badge Taft waved under his nose. "I can't read that damn thing!"

Taft popped him in the back of the head. "Mind your manners! You Muslim brothers are usually more polite than that."

Muhammad tried to bat away Taft's hand. "You saw that?" Taft asked me. "This nigger is trying to assault an agent of the U.S. government!"

"I ain't no nigger," Muhammad whispered fiercely.

Taft's smile wasn't nice at all this time. "Get in the car, Mr. Muhammad." He pushed the big man into the back of the Crown Vic and made him crouch behind the seats. He adjusted his seat back, virtually pinning Muhammad into position, then threw the keys at me. "Let's get out of here before Mama-san calls the cops."

"Where?" I asked, tension making my voice shrill in my head. "Back to the office?"

Taft was already in the shotgun seat, facing the back. "Too much traffic over there," he said, which I took to mean Verdelle Shabazz. "I've got another idea."

Taft called out directions over his shoulder, his weapon trained on Muhammad through the front seat. Soon we'd left downtown and were in the Oakland Hills, at the edge of a heavily wooded park off Joaquin Miller Road that offered sunset views of downtown Oakland and the Bay beyond.

Taft directed me up Sanborn and past a ranger station with an Oakland PD cruiser parked in front. "Why are we here?"

"Keep driving." I could just make out the glint of Taft's teeth in the growing darkness. "It's a nice night for a walk."

I tried to let the queasy feeling in my stomach nestle as comfortably as that marble in my pocket, but it was no use. "I'm not feeling this, Paul," I warned, remembering to soften it by using his first name.

He flashed me a nicer smile. "Don't worry. I'll keep you out of it."

He instructed me to pull into a deserted parking lot. A snuffling sound was coming from the backseat, along with the telltale smell of ammonia. "Wh-what the hell do you want with me?" Muhammad stammered.

Taft got out of the car and hauled Muhammad from the floor. He sat him up in the backseat and slapped the back of his head. "What'd I tell you about your manners?"

"Ow! What the—what you want with me, man?"

"Paul, can I speak with you for a moment?" I asked.

Taft frowned and compressed his lips. "About what?"

I was already out of the car, digging the Altoids tin out of my handbag. "In private?"

I locked Muhammad in the car and walked Taft over to a road that was blocked by a yellow metal gate. The fragrant crunch of pine needles under my feet did nothing to soothe my stomach, nor did the antacids or that little marble in my pocket.

I stopped about a hundred feet from the car. "You want to fill me in on what we're doing here?"

Taft threw his head back, looking up at the dark canopy of redwoods. "I used to hike up here on the weekends. Park's named after this wacky California writer, supposed to honor the poets and writers of the state."

I shook his arm roughly. "Paul, what in God's name is going on here?"

Taft's glance shifted sideways, to some point in the distance. He leaned close and whispered, "Charlotte, I know these little pigs-are-the-devil pieces of shit," as if someone else was listening. "He's not going to give you anything if you play it by the book."

"If this is the way you get information from people, count me out, okay? And you Feds have the nerve to be on our case about civil rights violations!"

"This has nothing to do with the Bureau."

"What?"

"I'm just assisting the LAPD in a murder investigation."

"And trying to sabotage my case! What if Muhammad conspired to kill his brother and here you are, coercing a confession out of him without even Mirandizing him? This bullshit stunt you're pulling will cause whatever information we get to be tossed out of court along with you, me, and what little is going to be left of my career!"

"You don't know these people like I do, Charlotte. If they don't want to talk, they won't."

"So, slapping Muhammad upside the head and threatening to kill him—"

"I never threatened him!"

"Well, you did *something* to make him pee in his pants like that! What do you think is going through his mind, you bringing him out to this remote location?"

"*Remember*, you drove. Besides, what can I do with the Oakland PD right here?"

I said a little prayer of thanks that they were, or who knows what might have happened. "I don't know what kind of game you're playing, but I'm out of it!"

"You'll never get ahead in law enforcement if you aren't willing to push the envelope, get creative."

"Pushing the envelope is one thing. You're about to blow the damn thing up!"

"I'm just treating him as a hostile informant."

"You're the one who's hostile, Paul. Tell you what—from now on, stay away from Mr. Muhammad, and stay away from my case, you hear me?"

"I thought you, above all people, would be open to being more creative than this."

"Just because I'm with the LAPD doesn't mean—"

"Get off it!" Taft shouted. "Don't go trying to play Miss Butter-Wouldn't-Melt-in-My-Mouth with me. Not with your pedigree and history!"

A breeze whispered through the trees, making the hairs on my neck stand at attention. "What in the hell are you talking about? Have you gotten hold of my files?"

Taft looked at me long and hard, as if doing so would make me confess to some secret I was harboring. When I didn't, he said, "Look, I'm sorry." Hands up, he backed away as if I'd drawn my weapon on him.

"I've overstepped my bounds. I misjudged the situation and I misjudged you."

"You're damn straight!"

The smile Taft mustered wasn't nearly so warm this time. "So how do you want to handle this?"

How indeed? How on earth I could deal with the nutcase standing in front of me, recover the situation with Muhammad, and still keep my job? I had the odd sensation of my mind floating away from my body, almost like I was watching myself from above. And from that vantage point I could see Muhammad, Taft, and me in a virtual stand-off that could result in someone getting dead. And I was damned sure it wasn't going to be me.

Then something Taft did gave me an idea. "I need to think for a minute," I said as I turned and walked back to the car.

"I don't know if we can salvage this." Taft was muttering to himself, his words tumbling over each other as he laid out options, but he kept coming back to one sticking point: "It's unfortunate I had to ID myself. Wouldn't've had to if you hadn't called me by name, first and last. There's no getting around that."

The way he said it let me know my instincts weren't wrong, that I was going to have to do something to bring this to an end before Taft did something to Muhammad and maybe me, too. I put my hand on his arm. "Give me the key to the cuffs, Paul."

"What for?"

"I want to have a little chat with Mr. Muhammad alone."

"You think that's a good idea?"

"Why not? When in doubt, I always fall back on the tried and true methods. I know I can get some useful information out of him without it coming back on you or me. But we can't treat him like a criminal."

Taft looked at me warily before handing over the key. "You sure you know what you're doing?"

"Don't underestimate a woman's touch," I said, giving his arm a squeeze. "And when I'm done, I'm going to call my sister and cancel that dinner. We're gonna need that drink."

Turning my back on him, I walked swiftly back to the car, putting a good ten feet between us. "It'll be fine. I'm going to give you my weapon in case he gets rambunctious, and I'll talk to him over by that picnic table. You cover us, okay?"

"And if it doesn't go well," he called out, "I'll shoot him and say he tried to escape."

Nodding my head, I pulled my weapon from its holster, but instead of handing it over I turned and pointed it at Taft, who froze. "What the fuck are you doing, Charlotte? Trying to hold me up?"

His voice had gotten louder, as if he were talking to an assailant. I glanced toward the cruiser and the ranger's station, looking for signs that someone had heard him, but saw no one.

"You wanted creative, Taft, you've got it. Toss your weapon on the ground. Don't argue, and don't try yelling to tip off the Oakland PD. Just do it!"

"Wha—?"

"Do it. *Now!*"

"Okay, okay!" He tossed his weapon in the dirt.

"Now, move back about ten yards," I ordered, advancing until I could grab his weapon and tuck it into my waistband.

"Are you sure you want to do this?" he asked, moving a step closer.

I backed him up with my weapon. "I don't want you anywhere near me or Mr. Muhammad."

"Stop and think about what you're doing, Charlotte," he reasoned, no hint of flirtatiousness in his voice. "You've drawn a weapon on a Federal agent."

"Bullshit! If you try selling that one to the FBI or LAPD, I'm sure Mr. Muhammad and I can convince them otherwise."

"That hump's not worth blowing your career over."

"Neither are you." The way I aimed at him convinced him of the strength of my convictions.

Taft took in and exhaled a breath. "Now what?"

"I'm going into that ranger station with Mr. Muhammad. And you can just drive back to the Golden Gate field office, or to L.A., or to hell, far as I'm concerned."

He shook his head sadly. "I had such hopes for you, Charlotte. I must say you've disappointed me."

I held my weapon steady, reminded myself to breathe. "Think how I feel."

"Talk to your people, honey," he whispered. "You don't want to fuck with me. I can be your best friend or worst enemy."

I forced a smile. "The feeling is mutual, Agent Taft. Now get the hell out of here before I put a cap in your ass."

13

Taft's Tip

oel Garza, the Oakland police sergeant in charge of the ranger station, was surprised by my request to use their office but took it in stride, especially after he saw the handcuffed Muhammad sitting in the middle of the parking lot and Taft's Crown Vic receding down the road, trailing an angry cloud of dust. After listening to what went down and checking my ID, he asked: "Did the agent say why he wanted to interview your guy up here?"

"I think he wanted somewhere secluded."

Garza exchanged a puzzled look with one of his officers, a beefy-armed white guy with the name RAMSTACK stenciled on his green uniform. "Park's closed from dusk to dawn," Ramstack said, "so there's not much vehicular or pedestrian traffic up here right now."

"Overall," Garza added, "it's pretty self-containing. Trail bikers getting into altercations with the joggers, that's about it. Nobody wants to be down in the flats. It's a three-ring circus—murder, drug dealing, prostitution."

And one crazy FBI agent. "Well, whatever Taft's reasons," I replied, "I'm not letting this situation go sideways on my watch."

Garza still looked suspicious. "I'd better call this in to my C.O., let him know what's up."

"Call Sergeant Word, if you want a character reference on me," I added quickly. "Richard Word. He and I were on a panel at the National Black Police convention a couple of years ago."

"I'll do that," Garza replied, making a note. "Anything else you need from us?"

"A phone."

Garza went to his car to radio in the report, and Ramstack kept an eye on Muhammad while I stepped into another room to notify Thor and Stobaugh of what had happened. Stobaugh had already left for the day, but Thor was still in the office with Detective Perkins, sorting through their notes from the interview they and Wunderlich had conducted with Shuttleworth and Bezney's audit manager.

"Before you start," I said, "I need to fill you in on what's going on up here."

"From the sound of your voice, I don't think I'm going to like it."

"You won't." I explained my misadventures with Special Agent Taft and Rashaan Muhammad, and where Malik's half brother and I were now. "Took you to some park in the hills and left you? What the hell kind of game is that asshole playing?"

"You tell me. Taft made some vague threats about how I should talk to my people and how I don't want to fuck with him, so I was thinking maybe I should ask you was there a reason you were so gung-ho about that tip he gave us."

"Not gung-ho, interested. You know as well as I do that the Black Muslims have a checkered history in this country. Do I have to remind you of the Malcolm X shooting?"

"Come on, Thor, that was damn near thirty years ago, and some people think the FBI set Malcolm up!"

"What about the hate Farrakhan and his henchmen have been spewing lately? Some of the things Wunderlich has been telling me would curl your hair!"

"If the FBI is so tough on their case, do you really think the Nation of Islam would risk killing Shareef for doing business with a white man? Don't fall for this mind game these Feds are playing with us!"

"Don't get me wrong. Regardless of what's going on within the so-called Nation, there's no way anyone in the department would go along with the kind of cowboy stunt Taft pulled up there!"

"Good, because something's very wrong with that man. On top of what he did to Muhammad, he seemed to know some stuff about me that was disturbing."

"Like what?"

"Personal information and professional, too."

There was a long pause on the line, then: "He mention Chinatown?"

I felt as if I'd been stabbed in the gut by a hot blade. "How would Taft know about that?"

I heard Thor tell Perkins to give him a moment. I heard a chair scrape, then: "I . . . uh . . . Big Mac and Stobaugh thought I needed to know about BSS, Charlotte. But it's not gone any further than me, I swear! And, I assure you, nobody here would have said anything to an outsider."

Was that what Taft meant by my pedigree and history? Was there anyone I could trust?

Go along to get along, my little voice reminded me.

How on earth was I going to do that?

Before the silence stretched on forever, I said: "Now that I think back on it, Taft never said anything specific." I reached for the marble in my pocket and tried to slow my breathing. "Just a bunch of vague innuendos. He was probably fishing, trying to get over on me."

"Don't let him," Thor said, a note of dismissal in his voice. "The Feds are notorious for trying to trip people up. I'm more concerned about how we get straight with Mr. Muhammad."

As much as I hated to admit it, so was I.

"Where is he now?" Thor asked.

"Under the watchful eye of the Oakland PD. I'll interview him, see what he can tell us about Eddie Aycox. Then I'm getting the hell out of here."

"I wouldn't waste a lot of time with him. What we learned from Deinhart might be much more relevant."

"How so?"

"Deinhart copped to a slew of accounting irregularities in effect at CZ Toys since he started on the audit three years ago."

"Like what?"

"That retreat in Montecito Alma Zuccari mentioned to Lippincott—it's really an eight-thousand-square-foot house the ex is living in. And that European jet you picked up on—eighty percent of the miles logged last year were for what the pilot's log indicates was Gabriella's personal use, not to mention hundreds of thousands in designer clothing bills she racked up that were expensed as research."

"How much are we talking here?"

"About a million a year, which the auditors were told by management would be reimbursed before they issued their report, and it always was. But last year, they found consulting fees to an overseas company with no contract, no paperwork filed with the IRS. So now the figure is up to six million."

"From one to six million over the course of a year sounds serious. Did Deinhart discuss it with anyone at the company?"

"Mario Zuccari, last February, who promised everything would be cleaned up before the auditors wrote their opinion letter. But when Zuccari's staff didn't produce the contract or issue the appropriate tax forms to the consultants, the audit partner at Shuttleworth and Bezney told Deinhart it wasn't material and deleted the comment from the letter. Deinhart thinks it's because they were afraid they'd lose the audit and consulting fees they've been pulling out of the company if they pressed too hard."

"What kind of fees are we talking about?"

"Three million a year," Thor replied, "which Perkins and Wunderlich tell me is way out of line for audit and consulting services, given the company's revenues."

"And if the auditors were getting that much, there's probably more hanky-panky going on than Deinhart was able to confirm. Now I understand why he was flipping out on drugs. Did Renata Lippincott say anything about this when you talked to her yesterday?"

"Nope, but remember how Mario was trying to convince his sister that Internal Auditing should look into the cash Engalla might have embezzled instead of some other matter the audit committee had asked about? Perkins is thinking this might have been what he was talking about."

"If Mario's diverting funds, it figures he wouldn't want the board to find out. Did Deinhart by any chance talk to Chuck Zuccari about this?"

"He says no, but Perkins and I are wondering if Zuccari found out some other way."

"If he did and took it to the board before he was shot, it would explain why they named Gabriella interim president and CEO instead of her brother."

"But not why the board would want to keep this from us," Thor countered. "This provides Mario with a motive."

"Think about it—if Mario shot his father, it means the company loses not only its CEO but its CFO as well. And if they were the brains behind the operations . . ."

"The company would take a big hit in the stock market if they were both gone." It all fit, but we had no evidence to tie Mario to the crime. "When are he and his sister due back from New York?"

A phone started ringing in the background, and Thor called out to Perkins to pick it up. "I've got a call in to Mrs. McIntyre to find out. In the meantime, I'm getting started on a search warrant for Mario's personal financial and business records. Maybe we'll find some paperwork that ties to the overseas company or deposits in his accounts that correspond to payments CZ Toys made."

"What about the Feds? You gonna bring them into it?"

"I'd rather not, but Stobaugh and Big Mac are telling me I have to."

I could hear Perkins saying something in the background and Thor tell her he'd call them right back. "That was our contact at the CHP up in Modesto. The hospital says Engalla's beginning to come around. They think we'll be able to talk to him in the morning."

"Modesto's only a couple of hours from here. I can interview him in the morning and be back by the afternoon, if you want."

"You sure? After your run-in with Taft . . ."

"It's no problem." It was true that I would much rather have gone directly back to L.A., but I knew the importance of learning what Engalla knew about CZ Toys' finances. After taking down the name of our contact at the CHP and Engalla's hospital, I asked Thor what he thought we should do about Paul Taft.

"I'll call the lieutenant and Big Mac, let them know what went down. I'll also run this by Wunderlich when I talk to him about the search warrant, see what he makes of it."

"I'd love to be a fly on the wall for *that* conversation! He's gonna be pissed you're going after the company's files."

"He'll get over it. In the meantime, try not to antagonize Mr. Muhammad any further."

"*I* wasn't the problem."

"I know. I'm just saying Wunderlich's not going to be as amenable to dealing with Taft if the department ends up being accused of violating another suspect's civil rights."

My mind was racing so fast, trying to figure out all the ways I had to protect myself, that my head hurt. "I'll do my best."

"You'll do fine," he assured me. "And, Charlotte?"

"Yeah?"

"I don't want you to think that . . . what I mean is, I haven't said anything to anyone here at the office about Chinatown . . ."

Go along to get along, my voice reminded me. "Of course not."

"I mean it, that's your personal business. But remember this— you've got nothing to be ashamed of. At least you've got enough gumption to get some help. Not everyone's that strong."

To hell with going along. I had to speak my mind. "If you're referring to your boy Firestone, God knows he needs some kind of help, the way he's been harassing females in the department."

"Steve, me, whoever. Just don't let the games people play mess with your head, you hear me?"

I was fascinated by how Thor could identify interpersonal mind games, but not the one Taft and the FBI were running on him about the Nation. But I thanked him for the vote of confidence even as I wondered how genuine his little speech was.

I emerged from the conference room to find Garza and Ramstack had set me up in the lobby of the ranger station, moving aside some paperwork on the glass-topped table and laying out a couple of sodas and some candy bars. I grabbed a soda, wishing it were a Scotch, and sat at the table where Muhammad was busy taping his glasses. Outside I could see where Garza and Ramstack had taken up positions at the front door, shooting the breeze but watchful for signs of Taft's return, leaving me alone to interview Muhammad.

Apologize is more like it, but he stopped me right after the first "I'm sorry." "My beef ain't with you, Detective Justice," he said quietly. "I 'on't think I'd be alive if you didn't pull that FBI agent offa me." He fingered the card I'd given him. "You bein' from the LAPD and all, I assume this has somethin' to do with my brother Malik, right?"

Relieved to be off the hook, I nodded and pulled out my notebook. "We have some new leads, Mr. Muhammad, but we're still trying to fill in a couple of blanks."

"Tell me what you need to know," he said, leaning forward urgently. "I'd do anything to help find who killed my brother. His murder's 'bout near killed our mother. She been closed up in her house ever since it happened."

I felt a shiver of empathy for a life thrown into limbo by grief. "What can you tell me about your brother's business dealings?"

"Malik *wudn't* a businessman. That's what's so sad about it. He was a researcher. But all that research changed how black folks see ourselves, y'know what'm sayin'?"

I thought of my sister-in-law, quoting Shareef's book like the Bible. "Yes, I do."

" 'Dr. Kinsey of the ghetto,' me and Aisha used to call him."

"Aisha is . . . ?"

"My wife. Habiba was the business head in Malik's household, always pushin' him. Habiba thought they could parlay Malik's research into a business manufacturin' dolls. Malik, he would have been just as happy teachin' his classes and writin' his textbooks."

I made a show of flipping back several pages in my notebook. "I understand you tried to help them."

Muhammad leaned over, trying to read my handwriting. "I'm surprised Habiba told you that, way they ripped us off!"

I flipped the notebook closed, not wanting to reveal that my source wasn't his sister-in-law. "Who's 'us'?"

Muhammad's eyes flashed behind his taped-together glasses. "Me and Brother Aycox—Eddie—a business associate of mine. What they did to us wudn't right, and Malik knew it! Our mother didn't raise us that way. It's that wife of his. She pushed him into it; I know she did."

"Sometimes marriage pushes people into things that they wouldn't ordinarily do."

I let him ramble a bit about how his bookish brother came to question the teaching of the Nation of Islam's leader, The Honorable Elijah Muhammad, eventually splitting from the sect and his family to attend Harvard and become a Sunni. But, ideological differences aside, the brothers had stayed in touch through the years, prompting me to ask when Malik had approached Rashaan for money.

"It was right after he finished the book, maybe seven years ago. I'd moved back to Oakland by then, and he was teachin' at some college down in L.A."

I checked my notes. At least that much of what Taft and Shabazz said was tracking with Muhammad's story.

"Malik'd heard me talk about Brother Aycox supportin' black businesses and asked me to set up a meetin'. Although Habiba did most of the talkin,' goin' on and on about needing venture capital to fulfill their dream of offering ethnically diverse dolls so children of color would change the way they see themselves." Muhammad's voice went up an octave, and he waved his hand in an unconscious imitation of his proper-talking sister-in-law. "They even named their Muslim doll after Aisha. All Habiba's high-flyin' talk sold Eddie. He decided to invest, but only if I was involved, to kind of keep everybody honest. But I had to step up with some cash, prove I wudn't in cahoots with Malik and Habiba to rook him out of his money. So, I invested seventy-five thousand altogether, every dime I could get my hands on, in SMA Enterprises."

"Which stands for . . . ?"

"Shareef Muhammad Aycox," he said, unmistakable pride in his voice. "Me and Eddie had a twenty percent share each, and Malik and Habiba split the rest."

Muhammad watched while I wrote. "But why you askin' me all these questions about Malik's business? Has that got somethin' to do with why he got shot?"

"I'm just filling in the blanks for now. Where did Mr. Aycox get the money for his share of the investment?"

"Eddie's family used to own a bunch of vendin' machines. His cousin loaned him the money."

Or accessed the funds he'd been stashing away for Aycox's use after he got out of prison. I flipped through my notebook as if searching for notes from a conversation with Habiba Shareef. "You know, your brother's wife never mentioned an SMA Enterprises in our interviews."

"That 'on't surprise me in the least bit."

"Why's that?"

"Because SMA never really got off the ground. Oh, we had articles of incorporation and all that, but when the money ran out, our forty percent of nothin' was nothin'! All we were doin' was tidin' Malik and Habiba over until they could cut a deal with the white man!"

"You're referring to Chuck Zuccari?"

"It coulda been him, or somebody else. Long as they had deep pockets, Habiba didn't care. She told us they was lookin' for what she called 'another round of financing,' but what she was really doin' was tryin' to sell their research and designs for the dolls to the highest bidder. But Mattel didn't need them, and Hasbro wouldn't return their phone calls. They ended up with CZ Toys, and the plan suddenly went from mass-produced dolls for the average kid to a rollout campaign for high-end dolls for collectors first." Muhammad snorted and rolled his eyes. "Like that many black folks collect dolls!"

I had a fleeting thought about my doll collection and my mother's and uncle's, but I held my tongue.

"Me and Eddie ended up out in the cold," Muhammad went on, "with this slick lawyer for CZ Toys tellin' us 'bout some clause in our agreement that said our equity position could be converted to a loan if a major investor wanted us bought out."

I knew just which slick lawyer Muhammad had in mind. "You're talking about Robert Merritt?"

"Yeah, that's him. Not that we've seen a dime of our money back! I ended up losing my house, my credit rating, everything!" Muhammad wiped his face and shook his head. "I couldn't believe my own blood would mess me over like that, you know?"

"I do," I murmured, thinking for a moment of my own traitorous brother. If Rashaan Muhammad were as angry with his brother as I was at Perris, we would have to consider him as a suspect as well.

Muhammad must have been reading my mind, because he said: "Hey, don't get me wrong! I wudn't even in L.A. when Malik got shot. 'Cause if you're thinking that—"

I quickly shook my head. "I can't imagine you doing anything that could result in your mother losing both of her sons."

At the mention of his mother, Muhammad's eyes glittered behind his glasses. "No, ma'am, I would never hurt my mother that way."

"But can you imagine Mr. Aycox doing something like that?"

Muhammad's eyes started blinking. "Eddie? Hurtin' Malik?"

"In the course of our investigation, we've learned Mr. Aycox has been saying some things that make us believe he may have harbored a grudge against your brother. Since you know him so well, we thought you might be able to shed some light on his comments."

"Eddie?" he repeated. "No way!"

"Our source of information is quite reliable. And, by your own admission, Mr. Aycox was very sensitive about getting rooked."

"But—"

"You're aware Mr. Aycox has a criminal record?"

"Yeah, but that was different. He didn't kill nobody!"

"Believe me, Mr. Muhammad, I wouldn't have come all the way up here without feeling confident that your friend is a legitimate suspect."

Muhammad stared out the window, shaking his head in disbelief. "What exactly did Eddie say?"

"Something about how your brother's preference for getting in bed with the blue-eyed devil cost him his life."

Muhammad snorted. "That's not a threat—that's the truth!"

"What do you mean?"

Muhammad laughed bitterly, the sound causing Officer Ramstack to peer into the lobby. "You cops are a trip! Eddie wudn't talkin' about Malik gettin' in bed with CZ Toys. He was talkin' about Malik gettin' in bed with *Mrs.* CZ Toys."

"Excuse me?"

"You heard me. They had a thing goin' on."

"How do you know that?"

"From the minute Malik and Habiba started talkin' to that company, she was all up in it. Readin' Malik's book, meetin' with him at their offices, watchin' videotapes of the interviews they'd done with the kids about the dolls—I mean *everything*. Then she started meetin' Malik over at the house when Habiba wudn't home, supposedly to talk about the names for the different dolls in the line. Hell, she even offered to write the biographies that would go into some of the packages with the dolls!"

That sounded like Renata Lippincott, back in her role of new product developer, but I was surprised she would have been that interested in the black cultural aspects of the Shareefs' line. "How did your brother react?"

"Malik just said she was havin' a black attack, but Habiba was gettin' tired of it, I know that much. And after Mrs. Zuccari got pregnant—"

"Wait a minute. You're talking about Alma, Chuck Zuccari's *current* wife?"

"Yeah, that's her name. Anyway, Habiba said to Malik: 'If that baby comes out black, you die!' Now, I 'on't really think Habiba meant it. She was just tired of seein' her husband commandeered by some rich white girl tryin' to be down with the people."

I tried to remember what Alma and Chuck's infant girl looked like, but all I recalled was the equipment surrounding her, not the kink of the baby's hair or the tint of her skin. "Why didn't Habiba tell us this when we interviewed her?"

"Once Malik got shot, he became a saint in her eyes. No way was she goin' to tell the cops, or even admit to herself, that he coulda been creepin' on her."

I sat there for a moment, trying to get my bearings. A murder investigation can turn in an instant, and it's up to the detectives working it to roll with it, even if it means careening off in new directions. But the events of this evening had me feeling totally out of synch, as if the pieces in a puzzle that was beginning to make sense had been suddenly rearranged when I wasn't looking. "Did Eddie Aycox know about Mrs. Zuccari and your brother?"

Muhammad looked embarrassed. "I might've told Eddie, you know, just in the course of lettin' him know what was happenin' with gettin' our money back."

But would that have been enough to set Aycox off? Maybe not, but it might have motivated Habiba if she was the type of woman who needed people to think she and Malik were the perfect *Ebony* cover couple. The possibilities were mind-boggling, but through the dark cloud of the headache I could feel coming on, one question overrode the others: had Paul Taft known this all along? Had he been using Eddie Aycox's slip of the lip as an excuse to dig around, see if he could find those assets he suspected Aycox was hiding? And if that was the case, I had to admit that Taft, with all his flattery and hints about jobs in the Bureau, had played *me* to do it, putting my career in jeopardy and casting more aspersions on the LAPD in the process. What on God's green earth would make a highly educated and trained law enforcement professional take those kinds of risks?

Recovering my voice, I rummaged through the paperwork on the table until I found a yellow notepad. "I'm going to need you to write out a statement of what you know about your brother and Mrs. Zuccari."

He pulled the pad toward him. "Sure. And if you 'on't believe me, you can call Eddie. He'll back me up."

At the mention of Aycox's name, I felt a sudden surge of dread. "Where is Mr. Aycox now?"

"Up in Sacramento, but he'll be back on Monday."

"Good," I said, relieved that for the moment Taft couldn't get to him. "Can you get in touch with him?"

"Sure. You want to talk to him now?"

"Just put his address and phone number down in your statement. And don't leave anything out."

14

Fugitive From Justice

t was after nine by the time my sister picked me up in front of the Joaquin Miller ranger station. I was so glad to escape the confusion of that park, to clear my head and see a familiar face, that I almost forgot I hadn't seen Macon in more than a year.

Not that I'd missed her. Sad to say, but when you have a sister who's ten years younger, it seems she'll always be a thorn in your side—a gum-snapping nuisance when you're trying to talk on the phone, a snooping machine who reads your diary and then recites the contents to your high school crush, or a babysitting chore when you'd rather be at the movies with your friends. The only thing that had kept me from sororicide was my father's theory that Macon was underfoot so much because she wanted to be like her big sister. I had another theory—Macon was the spawn of Satan, sent to earth to make my life a living hell.

It didn't help that she had adhered to our Macon, Georgia–born mother's directive of postgraduate degrees for all her children, obligingly getting not only her doctorate in education at twenty-three but becoming headmistress of an exclusive Oakland private school just three years later. But instead of basking in our mother's approval, Macon had recently dropped off her branch of the Nut House tree, becoming a no-show at Justice Family gatherings, conveniently unavailable when Mother and Daddy visited the Bay Area, communication relegated to an expensive, generic holiday card.

Just last Christmas, I'd offered to make a few discreet inquiries among my contacts in Oakland law enforcement to see if she'd seriously gone astray. But Perris argued we should leave Macon alone, while my mother said children had to eventually leave the nest and go their own way. And from the looks of it, she had, judging by her brand-new Subaru Outback, her so-short-you-could-smell-brains Afro, and the tiny gold stud adorning her right nostril.

After jumping out to give me a somewhat mechanical hug, Macon got down to business. "What are you in the mood for?"

"A drink."

She rolled her eyes. "I meant food, Char."

I scrambled into the seat beside her. "The celery from a Bloody Mary will do. Really, Macon, I don't care. As long as they've got a bar."

"Well, we love Art's Crab Shack, which has a full bar. It's only—"

"No!" I said, checking her side mirror to be sure no one was following us.

"Damn! You don't have to jump down my throat."

"Sorry. I'm just not in the mood for crab." *Or running into that crazy ass Paul Taft.*

"How about Creole?" she suggested. "T.J.'s Gingerbread House over on Fifth is pretty good. And there's an awesome doll collection upstairs you'd probably enjoy."

"No dolls, please! The last thing I want to see is something that reminds me of the case I'm working."

I could tell Macon was getting frustrated by the way she sighed. "Then how about Vietnamese—or are there Vietnamese victims on your case?"

"No, Miss Smarty Pants."

"Good. One of our favorites is over on Jefferson."

"*Our?* I didn't know you were seeing anyone."

Macon gave me a sidelong glance as she pulled onto the main road leading out of the park. "Mom didn't tell you?"

"Joymarie hasn't said a dozen words about you since that last Thanksgiving you were in L.A."

Macon snorted, her nose stud winking in the light from the approaching cars. "No surprise there." She reached into her handbag for her phone and punched in a number. "Hey, baby. We're just leaving Joaquin Miller. I suggested Le Cheval, over on Jefferson. You still want to meet us? Okay, thanks, sweetie. I love you, too."

She ended the call and handed the phone to me. "Kelly's going to call ahead for reservations and meet us there."

"Kelly, huh?" I wondered about the androgynous name, but I couldn't figure out how to ask for clarification without sounding as if I were prying into my sister's sexuality. Could this be why my mother hadn't mentioned Macon's name in over a year? How could she be so narrow-minded, especially given that her beloved brother, our Uncle Syl, was gay? But then I was forgetting that Joymarie Curry Justice's picture was in the dictionary, above the word *hypocrite*. "Where'd you two meet?"

"Jogging around Lake Merritt."

Serial rapists jog around lakes, I wanted to scream at her. "And what does Kelly do?"

"Photographer for the *Oakland Tribune*," she replied, smiling. "And a good one, too. Shared a Pulitzer a few years ago."

Was Macon being stingy with her pronouns for a reason, or was she just trying to buzz me up? "Really? I'm surprised Mother didn't tell me about this Kelly."

"And I'm surprised you didn't rent a car."

I noticed her smooth deflection of the conversation away from Kelly and Joymarie and let it go for the moment. "I should have."

"Why didn't you?"

From our vantage point in the Oakland Hills, I could see a thousand pinpricks of light from the city below, yielding to the dark velvet of the bay beyond. Paul Taft was out there somewhere. Maybe he was a few blocks behind us, hoping I'd gotten Muhammad to tell me Aycox's location and lead him there. Maybe Taft had decided to pursue Aycox on his own. Whatever he was doing, I wanted to be as far away from that man as possible. "It's a long story."

"Which, I know, is none of my business."

The petulant tone in Macon's voice made me want to tell her about
Taft, but I knew it wouldn't be wise, especially if her lover worked for
the local paper. Just imagining the headlines made my head start hurting again. "It really doesn't have anything to do with me having dinner
with you, so let's drop it."

"Fine." Macon had pulled into a parking space on Jefferson. "Le
Cheval's just across the street there. And, yes, Char, they have a full
bar."

Which was teeming with a multiculti herd of customers, spilling
out onto the sidewalk, leaning against a bronze sculpture of the restaurant's trademark horse, cramming the small bar. When I asked about
the eclectic mix of people, Macon giggled, a giddy sound I hadn't heard
since we were kids. "Kelly took photos for an article that showed that
on any given night you're liable to see everyone from pimps to politi-
cians in here."

Macon stood on tiptoe, scanning the faces in the crowd. As she
looked over my left shoulder her pecan-complected face blossomed into
a radiant smile. Whoever made my little sister smile like this was okay
with me, regardless of gender. "There's my sweetie," she beamed.

Before I could turn around, I felt strong hands on my shoulders,
and a husky voice said: "This must be my future sister-in-law."

"Charlotte. This is Kelly McDermott."

I turned to look up into a pair of smiling, deep-set eyes and a face
that told me exactly why Joymarie had never mentioned a Pulitzer
Prize or anything else about Macon's sweetie.

Kelly McDermott was a white man.

And a chivalrous one at that. After giving me a hearty hug and
leaning over to kiss my sister, he asked us what we wanted to drink,
then shouldered his way through the crowd to the bar. "Isn't he ador-
able?" she cooed.

"And tall, too." I pinched her arm. "You should have told me!"

"Told you what?" she snapped, jerking away and frowning.

"You know what I mean!"

"After the reaction I got from Mom, I decided to keep my good
news to myself for a while. You know how she can be."

I nodded in sympathy. "When she found out Aubrey and I had moved in together, it was all I could do to stop her from sending out the engagement announcements!"

"I heard you were dating Perris's old friend. How'd that happen?"

I was just catching her up on how Aubrey and I had met during the riots when we were interrupted by Kelly, balancing three drinks between the fingers of his large hands. "Glenfiddich is the best they have," he said, unloading a glass of amber bliss into my waiting hand. "If Macon had told me you were a single-malt Scotch drinker, I'd have suggested another place."

"Why so secretive, little sister?"

"Not secretive," she said, kissing Kelly lightly on the lips as she relieved him of a glass of white wine. "Just trying to respect people's boundaries."

"Well, Macon *did* tell me about your Pulitzer, Kelly. Congratulations." I clinked glasses with him, noticing that his contained a similar amber liquid. My kind of guy.

"Thanks," Kelly mumbled, his face so red that, with his copper-colored hair, he looked like a parboiled lobster.

"What was it for?"

"It was a team effort, really, for the paper's photographs of the 'eighty-nine Loma Prieta earthquake."

Kelly's name was called, and we followed our hostess to a table by the window, where she seated us and handed us oversized menus. After Kelly ordered spring rolls, lemongrass chicken, prawns with tofu, and a hot and sour catfish firepot, he picked up Macon's hand and gave it a kiss. "Your timing couldn't be better for a visit. Macon and I have decided to get married the Saturday after her birthday. We hope you can come."

"Married. Wow!" was all I could manage to say. I turned to Macon. "Is this why you've become a fugitive from Justice?"

She rolled a shoulder and gave me a noncommittal smile. "Partially."

"Have you told Joymarie and Daddy?"

Macon's half smile disappeared as she twisted her mouth and

shook her head. "Mother wouldn't come, and Daddy's not going to go against her."

"Nonsense! Daddy would be devastated if he couldn't give you away. And Mother's been itching to plan another wedding ever since Perris and Louise's. You should call them. They'll be thrilled!"

"That's what I told her," Kelly added, "and I haven't even met your parents."

"Don't worry, you will." I rose from my chair and gave each of them a hug. "Congratulations, you two. I'm so happy for you."

"Are you really, Char?"

"Of course. And Daddy and Mother will be, too!"

"I wonder." Macon looked worried for the first time that evening. "Between Mom being so negative when I first mentioned Kelly, plus all the other shit going on, I just didn't feel like dealing with the drama."

"What other shit?"

"That's why I haven't been around much lately," she explained, ignoring my question. "And why I wasn't going to tell them until after the wedding."

"You told Mother about Kelly that last time you were in L.A., didn't you? What'd she say?"

Kelly pushed back his chair. "If you two need to talk . . ."

"No, baby," Macon said, holding him down with her outstretched hand. "This is nothing you haven't heard before. You're right, Char, it was Thanksgiving. I was so excited about meeting someone I could really talk to, I was about to burst. But I knew I'd have to introduce Mom to the idea gradually. So I waited until dinner was over, then volunteered to clear and wash the dishes. You know how stressed she is until the dishes are done."

"Last year, it was five courses," I said to Kelly. "We could have used both of you to do the dishes on that one."

"When we were in the kitchen," Macon went on, "I told Mom I probably wasn't coming down for the Christmas holidays because I was going skiing with this guy I was dating and his parents. When I told her what he did, she was all excited about him working for such a well-regarded black-owned newspaper and the Pulitzer and all. Until I told her his name and she asked me if he was white."

Now it all made sense—Macon's prolonged absence, my mother's pointed comments about children going their own way, even her diatribe against white men when we were watching *Unforgiven*. All because Macon had committed the one unpardonable sin in my mother's book—crossing the color line to marry. "Who else in the family knows?"

"I assume Mom told Daddy, but I didn't say anything to him directly. I told Rho. She said Mom was either going to get over it or die with it on her mind."

Which sounded just like my baby sister Rhodesia. "Did you tell Perris?" I asked, remembering how he'd argued for leaving Macon alone.

She shook her head. "At first, I was so taken aback by Mom going off on me, I wasn't sure I could cope if anyone else started acting out. But when it got to be spring of last year and Mom was still tripping, Rho suggested I talk to Perris. We figured if anyone could get her to chill out, her Black Prince could."

I was amused, and somewhat saddened, that Rhodesia and Macon saw Perris and my mother's relationship the same way I did. And a little hurt that Macon hadn't confided in me. Maybe it was natural for my younger sisters to be tighter, given their closeness in age, but if I was honest with myself I would have to admit that I was probably too caught up in some case or departmental politics to have paid her much attention if she had called. "So what did he say?"

"We never got that far. I made the mistake of mentioning this brother up here who used to work with Perris first, and we never got around to it."

I shot a glance at Kelly. "Was this someone you were dating?"

She shook her head. "He was a parent at the school, worked for the Feds. He'd been one of the participants in a career day we had for the kids a few weeks before."

"Why mention him to Perris?"

"Because after he spoke at the assembly, he asked me if I was related to a fellow Q he knew who had twins and who worked undercover for the LAPD back in the seventies."

A chill passed through me, causing the hairs on the back of my neck to stand at attention. Louise thought some of Perris's clandestine phone calls were to an Omega, also known as Qs. "You remember his name?"

She shook her head again. "All I remember is he and his wife had moved here from the South somewhere and had twins, too."

Relief swept over me, and I could feel myself breathing again. For a minute I'd thought she was talking about Paul Taft, but he'd made a point of saying he didn't have any children, only a mother in San Jose. Besides, my brother and Louise didn't marry and have their twins until after he left the department. "Did Perris know him?"

"He said no when I told him, but he took the guy's number anyway, said he'd try to help him out."

My brother was the last person on earth who would want to help a cop, especially a Fed. "Are you sure you can't remember the guy's name? What did he look like?"

"Tall guy, older, probably about Perris's age." Macon looked to Kelly for an assist. "You'd know the name if I called it."

The hairs on my neck were pricking at my collar, and I began to feel light-headed. "Why would I know it?"

Macon said to Kelly: "The paper ran one of his poems during Black History Month, remember . . ."

Kelly frowned, eyes focused on some point in the distance. "Not *his*, exactly . . ."

Before she could say the line *"We wear the mask that grins and lies,"* the same poem I'd quoted at Teddy's, I knew she was talking about Paul Taft. Stunned, I sat trying to piece together every interaction I'd had with the FBI agent over the past two days.

In that Monday meeting with him and Frohlich, it was Taft who suggested I be the one to hear his tipster's information on the Nation of Islam, and then steered me into this trip up north.

And it was Taft who'd somehow known I was seeing my sister tonight, even though I was certain now that he hadn't been anywhere nearby when I called her from the FBI's offices.

And it was Taft who had told Macon things about Perris's alleged work in the department that our brother had never mentioned to any of us. How could Taft know all that when he told me he had never met my brother?

All I could conclude was that for some reason, Paul L. D. Taft knew Perris and had been surveilling our family for some time. But what he hadn't counted on was Macon making a lasting connection between his fishing for information about Perris last year and her fishing for a way to keep Joymarie out of her business, and then telling me about it.

Or had he? Maybe this game Taft was playing was designed to scare me, or Perris—about what I wasn't sure. But I was uneasy enough to confide in my headstrong little sister and convince her that she should take a few days off work until I could sort out what Paul Taft wanted with our family. In response to the protests she threw at me, I told her it was not only for her safety but Perris's as well.

"But why?" she insisted.

It was a question I asked myself the entire night as I kept watch in a chair in Macon's living room, my gun on the coffee table, just in case. More than once I started to call my brother, to warn him or just confront him over the phone, but I feared I'd get nothing but a drunken denial and my window of opportunity would be slammed shut forever. Besides, if Perris knew Taft and had reason to fear him, he'd be taking appropriate precautions.

But there was someone I could call who might give me a straight answer, Chief Henry Youngblood, who was not only my godfather and C.O. of the bureau under which RHD fell but had been Perris's commanding officer years before in Southwest. If Taft knew Perris professionally, Uncle Henry would have met him, too.

I caught him playing bid whist with some of the senior black command officers in the department, a ritual I knew about but had never been invited to join. "How are you doing, Goddaughter? I heard you took care of your business downtown."

"If you're talking about Chinatown, you pretty much didn't give me a choice. Can we talk for a minute?"

"Problems with the Smiley Face case?"

"Problems with Perris." Into the silence on the line, I said: "Last time we spoke, you asked me to cut him some slack. Something about his demons."

"I vaguely remember that."

"Well, one of his demons has resurfaced, and I was hoping you could tell me what it's all about." I told him about Agent Paul Taft, his and Wunderlich's appearance on our case, his lies, Macon, the whole nine. "Taft told Macon he knew Perris from when he worked undercover for the department, but he told me yesterday they'd never met. What's going on, Uncle Henry? Who is this guy and how does he seem to know that Perris worked undercover for the department when we don't?"

I could hear my godfather excuse himself from the card game and a sliding glass door open and close. A click and a long inhalation told me he'd lit a cigar, something his doctors had told him to give up. "That was a long time ago, Charlotte. And it was only for a minute."

He didn't elaborate, which I wasn't expecting, but which annoyed me just the same. "Did Perris and Taft work together?"

Uncle Henry was silent for a moment, then I heard him exhale. "How would I know? That was a *lifetime* ago, Char. Why can't you let it go?"

"Because Paul Taft won't let me." I explained what had happened in Oakland that evening. "I need you to be straight with me, Uncle Henry—does this guy circling around our family have anything to do with Perris stealing Keith's files last week?"

"That I can't tell you," he said, his voice weary.

"Can't or won't?"

"You're going to have to ask your brother."

"Don't worry. When I get back, I will."

"Maybe we can all sit down—"

"No, that's okay, Uncle Henry. I shouldn't have called you. As you said, I need to talk to Perris. This is between him and me. I'll take care of it."

"Charlotte, be careful," he warned. "I don't want to see you get hurt. Nobody does."

"Don't worry, Uncle Henry." I wedged the phone between my ear and shoulder, hefted my weapon, checked it again, and put it back on Macon's coffee table. "I can look out for myself just fine."

15

Water, Wealth, Contentment, Health

Early the next morning, I had rented a car and was on the road, bleary-eyed, heading east and south to Modesto, through the north end of California's Central Valley. Just like in L.A.'s San Fernando Valley, this settlement of the Central Valley had started out as a dream, this one born in the minds of speculators who saw in row after row of cypress trees visions of the countryside surrounding Milan or Naples—or could at least promote it that way to winter-weary East-erners. And although in college I'd read the early writers who rhap-sodized about the region, my memory of the Central Valley consisted more of boringly flat farmland than majestic cypress groves and un-ending fields of asparagus and almonds and strawberries, bisected by a highway that was little more than a conduit for Justice Family trips to Yosemite or San Francisco in the days before that monster of an inter-state, I-5, was built.

But we always approached the valley from the south, not the north as I was this morning, in a reverse commute from the East Bay. Seeing it this way was like watching a time-lapse movie in reverse, the more recently erected windmills and strip malls on the road to Tracy morph-ing into a slew of Christian schools built some ten years before, giving way to signs that proclaimed FOR SALE—DEVELOPER'S DREAM SITE on the farmland that started it all.

Thor had arranged for me to get a quick briefing from the Modesto area office of the California Highway Patrol before I interviewed Nilo Engalla. CHP officers had been the first on the scene at last Friday's tule fog collision, Detective Dale Philbrick told me. Barrel-chested and in his forties, he looked like a cross between a professional weight lifter and Chippie, the bobble-head chipmunk dressed as a CHP officer that sat on his desk.

Philbrick plucked a file from a vertical rack on his desk and reached for a notepad. MODESTO CHAMBER OF COMMERCE was printed across the top, and at the bottom a slogan: WATER, WEALTH, CONTENTMENT, HEALTH. He drew several lines to represent Highway 99, and a number of Xs crowded inside them, and proceeded to describe the fog-induced accident that had killed nine and put Engalla in the hospital. "Your guy's car was near the back of the grinder, in the median, bounced off a vehicle in the number one lane. He ended up with a collapsed lung, multiple fractures to his right leg and foot, and internal bleeding."

"No wonder he's been out of it." I made a few notes. "Where's his vehicle now?"

"At one of our evidence tows a few miles from here."

"Find anything else in his car when you inventoried it besides the money?"

Philbrick held up several pieces of paper, each encased in a plastic evidence bag. "Just a bunch of receipts, mixed in with the cash we found in a backpack."

I turned them over to examine both sides. They were for motels from the Central Valley to the far north end of the state, with one exception. "What about this paperwork from Pinoy Mailbox Services in Stockton?"

"Yeah. It appears your guy rented a box from them last September."

Two months after he quit his job at CZ Toys. "You call them yet?"

He nodded. "It's a small mom-and-pop outfit up in the Little Manila section of Stockton, 'bout thirty miles north of here. The clerk couldn't tell me much about Engalla, though. Said the owner"—he frowned, consulted his file—"woman by the name of Chona Martinez, could, but she hasn't called me back."

As I took down the owner's name and number I could hear Thor's voice, chastising: *Guess no one thought to look for him there.* "I didn't know there was a Little Manila in Stockton."

"Everybody thinks L.A. or the Bay Area when it comes to Filipinos, but we've got over thirty thousand of 'em in the Central Valley. Some of their communities, like the one in Stockton, go back some seventy years."

I reached for my Altoids tin to quell the embarrassing rumbling of my stomach. "What do you know about the vehicle Engalla was driving?"

Philbrick went back to his notes. "A five-year-old Toyota Corolla, purchased in Stockton last September and registered in the name of Rhea Carvajal, to the same address as the mail drop."

"The boy's mother is named Rhea. She must've gone down there and bought the car in her maiden name as soon as the surveillance was called off."

"Maybe she had him stashed with some relatives in the area until things cooled off."

Thor's comments about migrant workers in the Central Valley and Nilo's dad's work as a union organizer mocked me. "What do you know about the Filipino population here in Modesto?"

"We only got a couple of thousand in Stanislaus County. But that includes everyone from retired migrant workers to their gangbanging grandkids. We got three sets of Asian Crips in Modesto alone, imported mostly from L.A. Engalla coulda been hiding out with one of them."

"The migrant worker angle is more likely, given his father's background in union organizing. From everything I've heard, this kid's definitely not gang material. More like your standard advanced-placement dean's-list kind of kid."

"Dean's list or no, him popping up with all that cash got some of the folks here worried," Philbrick argued. "Especially once we realized he was wanted for the shootings down there."

"Wanted for questioning at this point," I reminded him.

"Even so, Detective, the public's on edge," he insisted. "Has been since we had those cult homicides up here three years ago."

I'd heard about the homicides in question, which the media had tried to turn into Manson Family redux. "Those doers were part of some kind of second-string Satanic cult, weren't they?"

Philbrick chuckled. " 'The Kmart of cults,' the experts called it at the trial. The ringleader and four of his cronies were convicted right about the time your Smiley Face shooting went down."

"And you think there's a connection between our guy and a case from three years ago?" I made a quick calculation to confirm my thinking. "It doesn't figure that a kid Engalla's age would've been involved. He would've been in high school up in Daly City then."

"One of the killers was in his early twenties," Philbrick pointed out.

"But surely you don't—"

"Not *me*," Philbrick corrected. "A couple of the local boys are the ones interested."

Just what we didn't need. "Looks like I'd better pay Modesto's finest a visit after I see Mr. Engalla."

Gathering up a green nylon jacket, Philbrick said: "I'll drive you over there."

"Don't trouble yourself. Just give me their address. I'll head over there after the hospital."

"Um . . . they probably won't be there," Philbrick said as he busied himself with the zipper on his jacket.

"Where are they?"

"Over at Memorial Hospital, interviewing your guy."

"They're interviewing *my* suspect? For what? The accident occurred in CHP's jurisdiction, not Modesto's. How long have they been over there?"

"They called from the hospital about a half hour before you showed up."

"Didn't anyone tell them I was on my way to interview Engalla myself?"

Philbrick couldn't look me in the eye. "I might have mentioned it to them."

I scrambled to my feet and checked my watch. It was shortly after ten now, twenty minutes since I'd arrived at the CHP's offices. Almost an hour in which the locals could screw us up with Engalla six ways from Sunday.

"What's the problem?" Philbrick asked, trying to keep up with my quickened pace.

"We're burning daylight."

ubrey has seen so many hospitals in his career that he's developed a theory that cities tell you who they are and what they think of themselves by the hospitals they build. Manhattan has its sprawling New York–Presbyterian complex, Chicago has its upscale Northwestern Medical Center on the Gold Coast, and L.A. has its Beverly Hills–adjacent Cedars-Sinai, all of which Aubrey argues serve not only the complex health needs of their populations but the ego needs of their medical staffs and donors. As Detective Philbrick escorted me over to the big nonprofit hospital in town I couldn't help thinking it fit Aubrey's model. Smaller than its big-city counterparts but no less bustling, this hospital was in the midst of a building project that seemed to have the support of the entire Central Valley, if the list of donors on the construction signage was to be believed.

The hospital's lobby was crowded with several newscasters and reporters, who were hastily setting up for what looked like a press conference. When they saw Philbrick, they scrambled to turn on their lights and get their microphones in place. "Coming through!" Philbrick shouted, shepherding me toward the elevator lobby, where we squeezed into a car filled with hospital staff and patients in wheelchairs or on gurneys.

"What the hell was that about?"

"Engalla the miracle survivor was a pretty big deal with the media up here," was all the CHP detective would say.

A big deal, too, with the nursing staff, who had tended to the young man with all the deference usually accorded to celebrities. Other than his pain, which the nurses told me was being controlled by morphine, Engalla's other complaint since regaining consciousness was a persistent loss of memory of the last few days before the accident, which the doctors were calling amnesia secondary to traumatic head injury. "It's a miracle he survived," one of the younger nurses said.

I flipped open my notebook and made a note. "He have any visitors?"

"Only the reporters," an older nurse replied, "but the Modesto police have been pretty good at heading them off at the pass."

I flipped the notebook shut and followed Philbrick down the corridor to Engalla's room, which was easy to identify with the local uniform and two plainclothes cops lingering outside the door. The uniform excused himself, and Philbrick made the introductions to Detective Art Suarez, a lanky, sport-coat-clad Latino with salt-and-pepper hair, and Detective Tom Huth, a much younger and shorter white male wearing a vintage polyester suit and heeled, pointy-toed boots, the kind my father calls cockroach killers.

Leading him a few steps away from Engalla's door, Philbrick asked Suarez: "You get anything from the kid about the money?"

"Told me he didn't know how he got it."

"That because of the amnesia?"

"That's because he's bullshitting us!" Huth whispered fiercely. "He's running drug money for one of the Asian gangs."

"Well, if he can't produce a receipt," Philbrick said, "that twenty-seven thousand and change is going into the CHP's coffers."

"Don't start spending it too soon," I warned. "It might be embezzled from the company where Engalla worked. So, I'll be taking it into custody before I leave town. Don't worry, the CHP will get a receipt."

Philbrick sighed in resignation, then straightened his tie. "We ready to do this?" he asked Huth.

"Do what?" I asked.

"The reporters downstairs are getting antsy," Suarez explained as he headed for the elevator. "Want to join us?"

"I'm going to let you all deal with the press while I concentrate on Mr. Engalla." What I didn't say was that my name or the LAPD's in the papers was about the last thing we needed at this point in the investigation.

They had put Nilo Engalla in a private room with powder-blue striped wallpaper and one of those hospital beds that takes up half the floor space. Except for one leg, which was elevated in a cast, the patient was barely visible among the IV poles, monitors, and white pillows that cushioned his broken body. Seeing him now and knowing what he'd been through made me understand why the nurses and the reporters downstairs considered his recovery a miracle, just as it was a miracle that Chuck and Alma's baby girl had survived thus far. But was there a closer connection between the two? Was Nilo Engalla responsible for that drive-by shooting last summer, and for the pain and death left in its wake?

As I approached the bed I could see he was staring out the window. "How are you feeling, Nilo?"

Engalla's attention slowly shifted toward the sound of my voice. The handsome face I'd seen in the BOLOs looked as if it had been dragged over five miles of bad road, and his eyes couldn't quite focus. "Who are you?" he asked, his voice hoarse.

I showed him my ID and pressed a card into his hand. He blinked at the card slowly. "What do you want?"

Was this kid really that out of it, or was he trying to play me? "I think you know, Nilo."

I glanced about the room. There were no flowers, no cards, no sign that anyone cared or even knew Nilo was there. "I see you haven't contacted your parents yet." When he flinched, I walked over to the window and looked down at the wisps of fog still clinging to the trees. "Jose and Rhea will be worried if they don't hear from you. And you should be worried about them, too."

"You know my parents?" he croaked.

"We know your mother bought that car you were driving in the accident," I said, keeping my voice low and steady.

He tried his best to look innocent. "I don't know what you mean . . ."

"She bought it last September, Nilo, in her maiden name right after the surveillance of your parents' house was called off. She'd sworn to one of our detectives that she hadn't spoken to you since you left CZ Toys and promised to call us if you contacted her. But your mother was lying to us, wasn't she? She knew where you were all along. She was just waiting until she could meet you down in Stockton without being followed."

"That's not why—"

"If your mother tried to help you hide from the police, or gave you that car to help you try and escape—that's called obstruction of justice. She could go to jail for that."

Engalla shook his head, his eyes glistening. "She wasn't helping me hide from the police!"

Was that an out-and-out denial, or did I detect an inflection in his voice? "Then from whom, Nilo?"

The boy's lips hardened into a thin line, and he closed his eyes against the tears. "Why won't everybody just leave us alone?"

I was afraid that if I pressed him any harder he'd ask for an attorney, so I decided on another tack. "Believe me, Nilo, I'd like nothing better than to head back to L.A. and let you get some rest. But I'm afraid the Modesto police aren't going to leave you alone until they get something they can use."

"Use?"

"Think about it, son—a potential suspect wanted by the LAPD for questioning in a major shooting is found hundreds of miles from L.A., with twenty-seven thousand dollars in cash in his car. What would you think if you were the local police? Either, one, the kid stole the money from a local business and is on the run or, two, he's dealing drugs for one of the local gangs."

Worry creased Engalla's brow, and his bottom lip began to quiver. "No way! I would never embarrass my family by doing something like that."

"From what your parents have told us, I believe you, Nilo. But those Modesto cops are on their way downstairs to hold a press conference right now, and that's what they're going to tell all those reporters unless you tell me something different."

"No!" Engalla began to twist about in the bed, as if he were trying to get away, but his traction-bound leg and other injuries held him in place and made him wince. "I don't want my parents finding out where I am and coming here. It's not safe!"

"Safe for whom?"

Engalla glanced nervously toward the door, then shook his head firmly. "I can't!"

Obviously, he was afraid of something, or someone. I moved closer to the bed. "You know, Nilo, if you're in trouble, I can help you. But you've got to help me." I gently touched his arm. "Tell me how you got that money. Did you steal it from CZ Toys?"

He shook his head, tears spilling from his eyes. "I'd never do anything like that!"

"Do you have a receipt for it?"

"A receipt?"

"That's the law—if you can't produce a receipt for cash over twenty-five thousand dollars, we have to impound it."

I could see Engalla's mind working as if he were trying to remember or trying to decide what to tell me. Finally he whispered: "The money was sent to me at Tia Chona's place."

"Your aunt is the Chona Martinez who owns Pinoy Mailbox Services?" I flipped to her name and number in the notes I'd taken while talking to Philbrick. If Nilo had conveyed his fears to his aunt, no wonder she hadn't called Philbrick back. "And she can verify all of this?"

He nodded, said, "Talk to her. She saw me open the package. But I don't want to get her into trouble!"

"Just tell me the truth about what happened, and I'll try to keep her, and your parents, from getting arrested."

He nodded eagerly and wiped at his eyes with one bandaged hand. "It was the second package I got," he began. "I let it sit for a couple of weeks, then went in with Tia Chona late one night to pick it up."

"Why all the precautions?"

"I was *scared*," he insisted. "Before the package came with the fifty thousand—"

"Wait a minute? You were originally sent *fifty* thousand dollars? Where's the rest of it?"

"I bought the car, then there were the hotels and other stuff for the last six months."

"And this was the second package you received?"

He nodded. "The first was just a note, saying I should disappear, that it wasn't safe for me at the company, but that I would be receiving enough money to help me get away. That's why I didn't go to the box to check on the money right away, and why my mother helped me buy the car, and why I've been moving around ever since—"

"Slow down, Nilo!"

"I was afraid they'd—my mother thought that they'd try and—"

"Kill you?"

Nilo looked at me, his chest heaving, but his lips were compressed tightly, as if he feared he'd said too much already.

I studied the boy, wondering if he could be lying. But Nilo Engalla was looking me in the eye, even though the effort, and our conversation, seemed to have drained what little energy he had. I had to get the rest of it out of him, and quickly, before I lost him to fatigue—or before whoever had threatened him tried to pay him a visit. "If you can't be completely honest with me, Nilo, I'm afraid I can't help you. I'm here to investigate who killed Mr. Shareef and shot Mr. Zuccari and his family."

Nilo's eyes ballooned, and he seemed to have trouble speaking. "I-I didn't know anyone died!"

"So you see, you quitting CZ Toys right after the shooting and no one seeing you since makes us think you may have been involved."

He made a weak protest, which I held off by gently pressing his arm. "Stop shaking your head and listen to me, Nilo. Seven months after you disappear, you show up here with a car and enough money to take you anywhere in America, spouting some cock-and-bull story about you and your family being threatened. Tell me why I *shouldn't* suspect you in the shooting of Chuck Zuccari and the others."

"Because Mr. Zuccari was the one who told me to leave!"

As I headed north I called Thor to fill him in on what I'd learned. "Engalla had independently discovered the bogus invoice, three months after Christopher Deinhart had brought it to the attention of Mario Zuccari and his audit partner at Shuttleworth and Bezney. Nilo was working on an assignment with Accounts Payable to calculate how much extra cash the company could generate if it changed its payment policy from thirty days to something longer. That's when he stumbled across a company called Sonrisa Safety and Security in the Philippines, which was being paid well into six figures each month, always within five days of submittal of its invoices. But, like Deinhart, Engalla couldn't find a contract or IRS paperwork filed at the company's headquarters in Irvine, nor could the divisional headquarters in Hong Kong produce any documentation."

Engalla had summarized his findings in a memo to Natalie Johnson, the manager of Accounts Payable, who'd promised to send it "upstairs for investigation." But when Engalla rotated to Internal Audit as part of his internship, neither Howard Hebson, his supervisor, nor any of his staff had seen or heard of his memo. "Engalla didn't know if the memo had been buried by Johnson or her boss, Felton Carruthers, in the controller's office, so he came in early one morning to talk to Mario Zuccari and ran into Chuck instead."

"When was this?" Thor asked.

"May of last year, two months before the shooting."

"That was three months after Deinhart confronted Mario about the same thing. What did Zuccari do?"

"Told him he wanted him to try and get more information on the vendor, reporting exclusively to him. And gave him five thousand dollars for expenses."

"So Chuck Zuccari hadn't heard any of this from Natalie Johnson or his son?"

"Apparently not."

Using his parents' business and family connections in the Philippines, Engalla had discovered that Sonrisa Safety & Security's corporate headquarters was merely a mail drop some three miles from where CZ Toys had a plant in the Laguna province. "Remember our meeting with Gabriella and Mario? They left us to take a call from some guy in Laguna. I assumed they were talking about Laguna Beach, but they were probably talking to someone at the company's plant in the Philippines."

"How'd Chuck Zuccari react to what the kid found?" Thor asked.

"He was livid, told Engalla to keep digging. Gave him another ten thousand to pay for private investigators if he needed them."

"There's something suspect about Zuccari giving an inexperienced kid that much money," Thor said. "How'd he expect Engalla to find P.I.s in the Philippines?"

"You remember Pete Collins, the surfer dude security chief? Zuccari had him source P.I. firms over there. Zuccari gave the names to Engalla, who contracted with them through an uncle and gave them their assignment. They sent their report to the uncle, who forwarded it to Nilo's box at Pinoy Mailbox Services, and his aunt forwarded them to Nilo, who then shared the results with Zuccari. That way the right hand never knew what the left hand was doing."

"Engalla and Zuccari went to a lot of trouble to cover their tracks. Was keeping Collins out of the loop Engalla's or Zuccari's idea?"

"Engalla says Zuccari, which I figure had to have been motivated by either Zuccari not wanting anyone in the company to know because he was behind the embezzlement, or because he had a good idea of who was."

"Too bad we can't ask the poor bastard," Thor murmured. "Why the hell didn't Collins say anything about these Filipino P.I. firms in the initial investigation?"

"Probably didn't put two and two together. Collins may be pretty, but he's not exactly the brightest bulb in the pack. Think about those goons he hired to watch over the Zuccaris—Leykis and Ybarra. Are they the type you'd hire to protect a corporate mover and shaker like Zuccari?"

"Thanks for reminding me. I wanted to check those two out." He was silent for a moment, writing something down. "This note that Zuccari was supposed to have sent Engalla—when did he receive it?"

"A couple of weeks after he left the company, at his box in Stockton."

"But Zuccari was in a coma by that time."

"But Nilo didn't know that. Someone must've got hold of Zuccari's files, realized what he and the kid were up to, and decided to impersonate Zuccari and pull the kid off the trail."

"Did Engalla hold onto the alleged note from Zuccari?"

"It's in an envelope at the box in Stockton, along with the private investigator's reports. Engalla put them there for safekeeping in case someone robbed his car or one of the motels where he's been hiding out. I'm headed up to Stockton to get them from the aunt now. And

I've got the cash that the CHP found in Nilo's car, too, although the Chippie didn't want to turn it loose."

"Who's watching the kid?"

"The Modesto police agreed to provide added protection for him until his folks can get him transferred to a hospital in the Bay Area."

"You think someone's out to harm him?"

"Maybe not, but the news down there widely reported him being hospitalized in Modesto, and there aren't enough of them to provide him with any anonymity. Plus, there've been reporters milling around in the hospital lobby since Saturday. Keeping him in Modesto is just asking for trouble."

"Good thinking, Justice," Thor agreed. "You gotta go with your gut on these things."

The genuine warmth in Thor's voice made me smile for the first time in what seemed like days. "Thanks."

I then gave him an update on my conversation with Rashaan Muhammad and the meaning behind Aycox's blue-eyed devil comment. Thor asked if I thought Rashaan Muhammad or Habiba Shareef should be considered as suspects.

"Him no, but you've sensitized me about these wives. So I'd like to reinterview Mrs. Shareef, see if she corroborates Muhammad's version of the facts, and see what else shakes loose."

"Take Truesdale with you. This Shareef woman may respond more positively to someone who knows about the Muslim community."

"I will." I reached for my marble and reminded myself that Thor's suggestion was a good call, not a sign that I'd messed up the first time I'd interviewed the victim's widow. "But you should still move ahead on Mario Zuccari."

"Absolutely! In fact, given what you've learned from Engalla, I'm going back to the judge for a separate search warrant to cover the company's accounts payable and internal auditing records as well as Natalie Johnson's and Felton Carruther's homes."

"It makes sense to cast the net as wide as possible. If other people in the company are involved, once they hear we hit Mario's offices, they're gonna start shredding documents right and left."

"This feels right to me, Justice." I could hear Thor making a few notes. "I think we're making some real progress here."

"At least we know the Black Muslim bill of goods Taft was selling was just that."

"I hate to admit it, but the Feds suckered us big-time on that one. Between the months you all wasted pursuing Taft's bogus Muslim lead and the Nazi rumors, you could've had this case solved by now."

Given how gung-ho he'd been on the Muslim lead, it was an amazing admission of error on the part of one of the department's legends. I wondered what it cost his pride to make it. "Has Taft surfaced yet?"

"He's gone underground. Hasn't checked into the FBI's office here in L.A. or up in San Francisco. Wunderlich prevailed on the L.A. bureau chief to send a car to his house, but other than his SUV missing, it doesn't look like he's been there either. And, what's worse, the Bureau's closed ranks. Agent in charge said they weren't going to move against a sworn agent of the Bureau based on an interpersonal beef with local law enforcement."

"They talk like they think I'm sleeping with the man!"

"It pissed me off," Thor admitted. "But I'm afraid that puts us no closer to knowing why Taft's gone off the rails, or what his next move will be."

I didn't know either, but I had a couple of ideas on how to find out.

16

The Four-One-One

By **Friday morning**, the office was in high gear. Armed with the warrants, Thor and Perkins were wrangling with Wunderlich and a team of his colleagues from Justice and the FBI over the particulars of an early afternoon visit for our combined teams to search CZ Toys' offices; the homes of Mario Zuccari, Natalie Johnson, and Felton Carruthers; and the offices of Shuttleworth & Bezney. Since coming home the night before, I'd been busy too, summarizing my notes from the interviews up north and the reports from Engalla's P.I. on CZ Toys' sham vendor so I could review my findings with the team prior to the raid.

I had just finished taking Nilo's cash to Latent Prints for processing and was logging into evidence the documents I'd obtained up north when I realized it was almost ten and I still hadn't talked to Billie about Malik Shareef and Alma Zuccari. I pulled her away from the Feds and took her into MIA's empty office to fill her in on my run-in with Special Agent Taft as well as my interest in approaching Shareef's widow. "We need to tie off that loose end ASAP, but I was hoping you could review my interview with Muhammad on your own while I handle this Taft thing."

She took the interview summary. "Sure thing, Charlotte. Whatever it takes to nail that asshole."

After she closed the door behind her, I dialed Pearline Taylor. I'd hung out (and been hung over) with Pearline one wild weekend at a black police convention three years earlier in Las Vegas. I found out that in addition to loving card games and single-malt Scotch, we were both trailblazers of sorts, me the only black female in RHD, Pearline the only one in the FBI's Sacramento office. She was such an asset to the FBI that in addition to her fieldwork she'd been charged with recruiting, but I wasn't calling to put out any feelers about a job with the Feds.

We chitchatted for a few minutes, catching up each other's plans to attend the upcoming convention, before I got down to the reason for my call. "As few of us as there are, sure, I know Taft." Pearline had put me on a speakerphone, her voice growing more distant as she closed the door. "He's been with the Bureau—what?—maybe nineteen years. What else can I tell you?"

"A lot more than that, I'm hoping." Since I'd thought of calling her yesterday, I'd been wondering how I could get Pearline to give me the four-one-one on Taft without raising her suspicions. I'd decided a sister-to-sister approach would be best. "Taft and I've crossed paths on a case I'm working down here and . . . well . . . between you and me, Pearline, he said some things to me that were highly unprofessional."

Billie came into the office, a pink message slip in her hand. I motioned her to sit down, indicating I'd be just a few minutes.

On the speakerphone, Pearline said, "Personal things?" her voice echoing sharply.

"Which are too disgusting to repeat," I said, checking with Billie to see if I was striking the right note. "But he seems nice enough otherwise, so I don't want to bust the brother's chops if he's under some kind of job or family pressure or something. Lord knows we all have enough of that."

I heard a loud snort, then Pearline picked up the receiver. "I can't tell you how disappointed I am to hear this."

"Maybe I shouldn't have brought it up."

"Shit, I'm not talking about you, Charlotte!" She was silent for a moment, then: "I'm out here busting my ass to recruit minority and female personnel to the Bureau, and Taft, and some of his frat brother cronies are sabotaging my efforts behind the scenes!"

"Don't worry, I wasn't thinking of joining the Bureau."

Billie rolled her eyes and lifted her feet off the floor as if to say, *the shit's gettin' deep in here.*

"That's not it. You know how it is when you're a minority. We're always being used as examples, and if it's a bad one, that works for some of these prejudiced white people just fine. And, unfortunately, Paul Taft's one of these dangerous brothers who thinks that just because he's wearing the badge, he's above the law."

"You've got that right," I said fervently.

She cursed again. "This has got to remain strictly confidential, okay?"

"Ditto for what I told you," I said, giving Billie a wink.

"Of course. All I know is, last fall Taft was scheduled to help me on regional recruiting visits at Berkeley, Stanford, and UC Davis, but they had to send a substitute because he got bounced out of the San Francisco office, allegedly for trying to play grabass with a civilian employee."

"Girl, no!"

"Way I heard it, he gave this female a ride home in his government-issued car and tried to put the moves on her a few blocks from her house. Her husband happened to see them as he was jogging by with their dog and knocked out four of his teeth with a five-iron!"

Taft's artificially white smile now made sense. "That must have been messy."

"It was, especially for the husband, because the Oakland PD had rolled up and arrested him for aggravated assault. Taft tried to play it off as consensual until the female started making noises about telling what she knew if Taft pressed charges, and suddenly the whole thing went away."

"What she knew about *what?*"

"That I never heard. But the fallout set affirmative action in the San Francisco office back ten years. The agent in charge of the office had to transfer Taft out of San Francisco, and his running buddy over in the DEA, Verdelle, got demoted for cutting the woman's tires so Taft could get her alone."

I felt my skin tingle. "Did you say Verdelle?"

"You working with Agent Owens, too?"

"I think I might have met him," I said carefully, "but I'm not sure if Owens was the name he gave me. Is he a medium-complected brother with acne scars on his cheeks? Real square-looking?"

"That's Verdelle."

I scribbled a note to Billie: *Taft's been playing us. His Nation of Islam informant's a DEA agent.*

"What he was doing abetting Taft in assaulting that young female I will never know," Pearline was saying. "But those two go way back—worked the Birmingham and Mobile field offices when there weren't too many of us in the South, so I guess Owens was caught between a rock and a hard place."

My hand had grown so sweaty I almost dropped the phone. Eddie Aycox's crooked vending machine business was in Mobile, Alabama. Taft and Verdelle Owens aka Shabazz had probably worked that case together, and then trailed Aycox to the West Coast, in search of his hidden assets. But the way they were approaching it—using Malik Shareef's murder as a smoke screen to trick us into delivering up Aycox—suggested that they weren't exactly on the up-and-up. And I wasn't having it.

"You need me to drop a dime on Taft from up here?" Pearline asked. "I know the agent in charge down in L.A. He's a good guy."

Not so good that he had taken my complaint seriously when Thor had presented it to him the day before. "No, that's okay. I can handle it from my end."

I never had a good feeling about that guy," Billie said after I told her what I now suspected about Paul Taft.

"He and his buddy Verdelle are up to something. I've just got to make sure Perris isn't caught up in this somehow."

"Your brother?" Billie said, her brow furrowed. "How?"

"I don't know, but he's connected to Taft—I'm almost sure of it. I was going to wait to confront him in person, but now I think I'd better call him, give him a heads-up."

"Speaking of calls," Billie said, "I almost forgot." She handed me the message slip. "This came in while you were on the phone."

It was from my godfather, Chief Youngblood, asking me to call him back ASAP. "Did he say what it was about?"

"Something about some documents he requested. He didn't sound too happy, either."

Billie left me in Stobaugh's office while I tried to decide who to call first. Uncle Henry had obviously found out I'd forged his signature on that request for the PDID files on the Black Freedom Militia, so I knew I didn't want to hear what he had to say. I dialed Perris's office instead, but his receptionist said he was tied up in a deposition in Century City, so I left a message at his cell phone number telling him about my encounter with Paul Taft and my concern for him. "I don't know what Taft has to do with you taking Keith's files, or maybe they're not related, but just watch your back and call me as soon as you can, okay?"

Back in the bullpen, Billie was talking to Thor about how we should approach Habiba Shareef. "I say we bring her in," she argued.

I disagreed. "I don't want her thinking she's a suspect and turning up with a lawyer."

"Far as I'm concerned, she *is* a suspect," Billie countered. "Based on my reading of Muhammad's statement, Mrs. Shareef could have contracted to have her husband killed because of the affair."

"We don't know that for a fact," I reminded her.

Billie flipped to the last page of Muhammad's statement. " 'If that baby comes out black, you die,' sounds like Mrs. Shareef did!"

Although I'd wondered myself if Habiba Shareef had had her husband murdered out of anger at an alleged affair, I wasn't completely sold on Billie's interpretation. "That could just be a figure of speech."

"It was," Billie said as she craned her neck. "Until her husband turned up dead."

"It may be a long shot, Justice," Thor conceded, "but something made Collins hire those two felons as muscle."

"You checked them out?"

"Leykis did two stretches for possession with intent to sell and aggravated assault, while his little sidekick, Ybarra, has some convictions from when he rolled with one of those Santa Ana gangs that would curl your hair. For Collins to turn to guys like them must mean they've got some serious concerns for the Zuccaris' safety."

"But why didn't Collins call us if he suspected Mrs. Shareef?"

"You said it yourself the other day," Thor reminded me. "Collins isn't the brightest bulb in the pack, although he is a former deputy with the Orange County Sheriff's Department."

"You're joking!"

"Worked out of Laguna Niguel for seven years before he went private. I checked him out the same time I checked out Leykis and Ybarra. He probably threw some cop talk at the family and convinced them he could handle the threat without attracting the press—or the heat from Wall Street."

I could almost understand the company's logic, but I still felt that going after Mrs. Shareef was the wrong move.

"She was the only one *not* injured that night," Thor reminded me.

"And if we bring him in and squeeze her," Billie added, "she's gonna pop, especially when we let her know we're looking at *her* for Malik's murder."

I finally relented, although, piggybacking off Thor's information about Leykis and Ybarra, I wondered aloud whether maybe we were all reading the situation incorrectly. "What if Habiba Shareef wanted Alma Zuccari dead? Alma could have uncovered something in her conversations with Malik or her subsequent review of the prototypes for the ethnic dolls that would have jeopardized their deal with CZ Toys. Maybe Habiba wanted her killed to shut her up."

"However it turns out, just interview the woman sooner rather than later," Thor cautioned. "Mario and Gabriella Zuccari got back from New York last night. Mrs. McIntyre's scheduled us for what I told her would be a brief meeting at one. I want to serve him the warrants and have you two in place to search his residence by no later than two."

But when I called Mrs. Shareef's office, I was told she was setting up a doll exhibit at Broadway Federal Savings & Loan, a black-owned financial institution. When I caught up with her at the S&L's Midcity branch, she insisted she couldn't break away. "If you need to talk to me right away, maybe you could come here," she suggested. "We're in the middle of setting up for the reception tomorrow night, and some of these dolls are too fragile to leave to the installers."

Realizing this must be the event Uncle Syl and my mother were discussing at Aubrey's, I repeated what she'd said for Thor's benefit, and suggested I could talk to her at the reception. *Do it, now!* he mouthed, shaking his head vigorously.

"We'll be there within the hour," I promised.

Billie and I found her in Broadway S&L's conference room, standing knee-deep in packing materials, unwrapping a delicate cornhusk doll. A dark-skinned woman with broad features softened by a gauzy black scarf loosely covering her head, Habiba Shareef was surrounded by African fertility dolls that looked to be hundreds of years old as well as antique dolls made of clay, bottles, and unglazed porcelain plus the Francines and Chatty Cathys and other black dolls I recognized from my childhood.

"Call it our way of giving something back," she explained after I introduced her to Billie. "After Broadway's main branch burned down in the Uprising, my husband and I decided that in addition to banking here, exhibiting our collection here would be the right thing to do, another way of helping to rebuild our community. But he was shot before we could get it organized. Then we were overwhelmed by his care, and afterward some of the collection were on loan to the William Grant Still doll show. So, here we are." She heaved a mighty sigh. "Better late than never."

Flyers on the table announced the opening of the Malik Shareef Black Doll Collection the next evening and included a quotation. "What action is most excellent?" I read aloud. "To gladden the heart of a human being, to feed the hungry, to help the afflicted, to lighten the sorrow of the sorrowful, and to remove the wrongs of the injured."

"That was my husband's favorite quotation from the prophet Mohammed, peace be unto him," she murmured. "And now that he's gone, it's up to me to carry out his wishes . . ."

Habiba Shareef was attired in a flowing black dress, mudcloth vest, and gauzy head covering, and her brown eyes had the gleam I'd seen in so many other black women who were the widows of great men. Coretta Scott King, Betty Shabazz, Ivy Duncan all took on their husbands' life's work after their deaths, and Mrs. Shareef was clearly casting herself in that role—the dignified yet saddened widow, carrying on despite a tragic loss. And as moved as I was, I had to ask myself—was she for real, or was this an act of penance to assuage her guilt for having her husband murdered?

"I heard about the young man who worked for CZ Toys on the news," she said. "I hoped you'd be getting in touch to give me an update."

I motioned for her to sit down in a chair at the conference table and took the chair opposite her. Billie went around to the other side of the table and started making herself invisible by examining the flyer and checking out the dolls. "We've gotten another lead that we need to discuss with you," I began.

She squared her hips in the chair. "Okay."

As I explained the rumor that had surfaced about her husband's relationship with Alma Zuccari, Habiba Shareef's shoulders slumped, her arms folded across her ample bosom as if warding off a blow. "Why bring this to me?"

"Did you observe anything unusual about Mrs. Zuccari's interest in your husband last year?"

Mrs. Shareef waved a hand in an attempt at casualness, but I didn't miss the pained expression on her face. "Women were always flitting around my husband. He was a very handsome, very charismatic man. But he knew where his home was. He knew who had his back."

"But Mrs. Zuccari *did* spend a lot of time with your husband in the months before the shooting?"

She picked up a carved wooden fertility doll and examined it carefully, lips pursed. "She was very interested in the dolls and in the histories we'd created for them. But why wouldn't she have been? They were beautiful dolls, and beautifully packaged."

"Was she interested in anything else?" I pressed.

Angry tears gathered in Mrs. Shareef's eyes as she placed the doll back on the table. "Who's spreading these lies?"

"It's just that Mrs. Zuccari's interest struck us as unusual, given that she wasn't employed by her husband's company."

"Don't you think I knew that?" she said through clenched teeth. "Alma Zuccari took what Malik believed was a genuine interest in our

dolls, and talked up the deal with her husband. What were we supposed to do—look a gift horse in the mouth?"

"But why would she do that?"

"Maybe you should ask her!" she snapped.

"We will, but we want to know what you think first," Billie said
from her spot across the table, where she was about to pick up a white
baby doll in a red gingham dress.

Mrs. Shareef reached over and snatched up the doll from Billie,
flipping it over to reveal a black doll underneath. "I never talked to her
about it, but Malik said that Mrs. Zuccari believed the line we were developing for CZ Toys would be a great success. That the market for ethnic dolls was bigger than even her husband thought it would be."

"And you believed him?"

"My husband is dead, Detective Justice," she said quietly. "What
difference does it make now whether I believed him or not?"

"It could make a lot of difference if you didn't," Billie replied. "It
could mean maybe you thought there was some truth to the rumor."

Mrs. Shareef pulled herself up to her full height. "And you think *I*
had someone kill my husband over a woman like Alma Zuccari?" Her
voice had grown loud as an angry tear slid down her cheek. "As much
as I loved Malik, and miss him, I would never have done anything to
hurt him."

"What about Alma?" Billie asked.

Mrs. Shareef shook her head. "That poor woman was nothing but
a trophy in Chuck Zuccari's life, nice but completely dependent on her
looks. A woman like that was no threat to what Malik and I had."

"Mr. Zuccari's ex-wife probably said the same thing," I noted, and
watched Habiba Shareef cut her eyes at me.

"Maybe Alma heard about your previous venture with Malik's
brother and his friend," Billie added. "That could have made doing the
deal difficult for CZ Toys."

I expected Habiba Shareef to be surprised at our knowing about
SMA Dollworks, but she dismissed Billie's comment with a wave of
her hand. "The legal department at CZ Toys had worked all that out.
They were going to buy out Malik's brother's and Brother Aycox's equity position for a fair price. Malik insisted on that. To do otherwise

would have violated the Islamic principles of Shari'a, which govern Muslims in all business dealings! We spent a lot of time with Mr. Merrit and CZ Toys' legal staff making sure our transactions were ethical."

"I'm sure you did. Still, some people at the company might have been concerned that your prior business relationship—"

Mrs. Shareef balled her right hand into a fist. "I know who told you this. It was that horrible woman, Renata!"

"Renata Lippincott?" I broke in. "What does she have to do with it?"

"She never wanted to do business with us!" Mrs. Shareef explained, her fist beating softly in her lap. "First, she tried to use our agreement with Rashaan and Brother Aycox to trip us up. Then she tried to say we were making too much of the cultural aspects of the line, that the public wouldn't be interested in a Muslim doll as part of the collection. Then, when we produced research to the contrary, she called me, asking me why Alma was spending so much time with my husband. With that *black man* is what she wanted to say, but she caught herself just in time."

She glanced at Billie as if looking for sympathy, but all she got back was Billie's bland expression.

"I told her Alma was interested in the dolls and the stories behind them, which was a good indication of the strength of the product and the packaging, and she went off, said Alma had no right to meddle in the company's business, that she was a deceitful little witch— although that's not quite what she said—who had to be stopped. That's when I began to wonder whether the ex-wife was just bitter or . . ."

"If Alma Zuccari's interest in your company was legitimate?" I said gently. "Why didn't you tell us this before, ma'am?"

Habiba Shareef sat motionless except for the heaving of her chest. "It seemed so trivial, and after Malik died, I just couldn't let anything . . . tarnish his memory."

"We understand," I murmured, as Billie nodded and made a few notes. "Did you ever confront your husband about Alma Zuccari?"

She nodded sadly. "He denied everything, of course."

I heard the note of reproach in her voice. "Did you do anything else?"

She turned away, too late to hide the tears flowing down her cheeks. "I . . . I was so hurt, so angry, Malik ended up sleeping in the den for three weeks."

"But you eventually made up," I said after a pause. "You forgave him."

"Th-that's just the point." She dabbed at her eyes, and faced me with her chin quivering. "We—I didn't! He was shot before we . . . before . . ."

Billie and I exchanged a look. No wonder Habiba Shareef was so guilty and so intent on preserving just the right memory of her husband and his work.

"The shameful way I behaved toward my husband is something I've got to live with for the rest of my life. So I will not let anyone speak ill of him, or the work we tried to do." Malik's widow sighed heavily and wiped her eyes with a handkerchief. "Can I ask you something, Detective? A friend of mine said whoever killed my husband might not be prosecuted for murder, given his death came as a result of complications of the heart surgery. Is that true?"

"That would be up to the district attorney, ma'am," I replied, wondering where this was headed.

"My husband was in perfect health before he was shot," she insisted tearfully. "I can produce his medical records, if you need them. Just don't let whoever stole my husband from me get away without paying for it, Detective! That's all I ask."

I promised I wouldn't, but as we left the S&L I wondered if Habiba Shareef's jealously hadn't robbed her of her husband as thoroughly as the person who'd shot him.

17

Deceitful Little Bitch

On the ride to Orange County, Billie wondered whether we should obtain a search warrant for Habiba Shareef's financial records. "Those big crocodile tears she was shedding could be hiding a shitload of anger," she contended. "She could have made some big cash withdrawals from her accounts prior to the shooting and paid someone to off her handsome, charismatic husband!"

"I'd rather talk to Renata Lippincott first, see if she corroborates her statement to Mrs. Shareef about Zuccari's wife and Malik. If so, it would certainly bolster our request for the warrant, if we decide to go that way. It *did* sound like something Renata would say, though, especially that 'deceitful little bitch' comment."

"I'm curious about Mrs. Shareef's take on Renata Lippincott. Did Chuck's ex seem like a racist to you?"

"She acted like she didn't want me touching her the day we were at the hospital, but I wasn't sure if it was because I was a cop or I was black. Thor interviewed her after that, but she probably was so busy pulling that 'richer than thou' act on him, I doubt if he got anything substantive out of her."

"Certainly not that she suspected her ex-husband's new wife was sleeping with their joint venture partner," Billie replied. "Maybe she would've responded differently to two black women coming at her. That is, *if* she figured out you're black."

I had a fleeting thought about my mother and certain members of the Curry clan who judged every person they met by the color of their skin—something I swore I'd never do. But I'd danced along the color line before, using other people's ignorance of my race when it benefited a case, and I was not above doing it again. "If she hasn't, then we know who the good cop will be if we see her."

Billie gave me an impish grin. "Sounds like fun to me."

Our first stop was CZ Toys' headquarters, where we met up with Thor, Perkins, and the Feds, who were jointly serving the Zuccari siblings and other company executives with the search warrants. And although Robert Merritt and the company's legal team protested mightily, two hours later our combined teams had fanned out to four different locations to search for documents that would tie CZ Toys, Natalie Johnson, or the Zuccaris to the fraud or the payments to Nilo Engalla.

Billie and I were assigned to search Mario's home in Newport Beach, one of those Orange County cities where houses in the poorer sections of town cost over twice as much as mine in L.A. Mario's place, a newly constructed Mediterranean mini-estate, which sat on a bluff overlooking the ocean, was definitely not in the poorer part of town.

"Not too shabby," Billie noted as she guided the car into the cul-de-sac and got her briefcase out of the trunk. "First home I've ever been in behind the Orange Curtain. I'd better show them my badge, or they'll mistake me for the maid."

Once we were buzzed inside the gates, we walked up the cobblestone driveway to the property, which was landscaped with tropical plants and a burbling fountain. We were intercepted at the door by a young man who identified himself as David Sarkisian, Mario's personal attorney, although the way he was dressed suggested tennis pro or gigolo. Made me wonder if Mario was hiding something behind that good Christian demeanor of his.

Our search warrant was inspected yet again before Sarkisian escorted us across the marble entry to his client's upstairs home office and stood close by while we began to go through the file cabinets. "We really don't need you hovering over us, Mr. Sarkisian," I pointed out as Billie and I put on some gloves.

"I'm here to ensure you confine your search within the strict boundaries of the warrant."

"Don't want us confiscating your client's porno collection?" Billie deadpanned, turning to give me a mischievous wink as Sarkisian sputtered a reply.

A few minutes later, I found Mario's home safe, in the closet of his office. "We'll need the combination for this."

"I don't have it."

"Then call your client and get it, or we'll have to carry it out of here," I told him.

"Let me see if I can reach him," Sarkisian said as he headed for the phone downstairs.

After he was gone, we moved on to Mario's desk. While Billie searched the drawers for the combination to the safe, I looked over the photos on Mario's desk—one that looked like a company party, and a duplicate of the photo I'd seen at the hospital of him, his father, and Alma at that toy convention. Underneath them was a tattered photograph of what must have been Mario as a toddler posing with Chuck and a woman I guessed was Mario's mother. Next to these was a collection of old letters that appeared to have been written by Chuck Zuccari when Mario was at Stanford and a "Thinking of You" greeting card in which Mario had begun to write a note. I was just reading what he'd written when Billie said, "Got something."

"You find the combination to the safe?"

Billie withdrew an envelope. Addressed to Chuck Zuccari, it was postmarked from Jersey City, New Jersey, on January fourteenth of last year, some six months before the shooting. Inside was a Xerox copy of an article from a 1959 issue of *Der Spiegel* entitled "Was Wurde Eigentlich aus dem Schneider der Hitlerjugend?" and a letter handwritten in a spidery hand on off-white parchment. I moved aside the old photograph and letters to spread this one on the desktop so we could both read it.

Until today, I thought the pain your family inflicted on me and mine was behind me. But your evil is far greater than I ever dreamed. If you weren't so arrogant, you would see what you've done is a sin against God. Can't you see who's right in front of you?

Believe me, I will expose you for the liar you are. The enclosed will remind you of the wrongs you have done to me and of the lengths I will go to stop you.

For God's sake, Chuck, please do something before it's too late.

Mrs. William (Belle) Thornton

"Damn!" Billie exclaimed. "I can see why Zuccari hid this."

"The letter seems highly personal, like the writer knows Zuccari," I noted. "But what in the hell is she talking about?"

"A disgruntled former employee, maybe? CZ Toys used to be based in New Jersey, right?"

"Up until Chuck relocated it out here in 'sixty-eight. But I don't know if it was in Jersey City or not." I examined the envelope. "There's no return address, but she signed her name, so she can't be trying to hide her identity too hard."

Billie leaned in a bit closer and reread the note. " 'Pain your family inflicted on me and mine' might refer to Chuck's father's Nazi connection."

"But there was nothing in our original investigation that suggested Claus Zuckerman was more than a hapless dollmaker forced into making uniforms for the Hitlerjugend." I scanned the note again. "And if that's what the writer is referring to, what evil could Chuck be doing that's worse? And what does the writer want him to see?"

"Not what, *who*," Billie corrected, pointing at the document. "Maybe this isn't about the Nazis at all. Maybe this Belle's referring to the deal with the Shareefs."

"But would doing business with a black company qualify as an 'unspeakable sin'?"

"Would if the writer's a white supremacist."

I shook my head. "This doesn't add up." I picked up the letter with gloved hands and held it up to the light to examine the watermark on the paper, then picked up the article and tried to see whether any of the German words leaped out at me. "This article is over thirty years old. And it's definitely about the Hitlerjugend, and I see the Zuckerman name here, but other than that I don't know what it says."

"Can't help you there," Billie said.

"I wonder how Mario got this away from his father."

I heard Sarkisian's footsteps downstairs. "Should we confiscate it?" Billie whispered. "It may not be in the scope of our warrant."

I hastily swept the envelope, greeting card, and other personal effects from the desk inside an evidence bag. "When we get back to the office, let's send it over to Questioned Documents, see what they can make of it. And run this Belle Thornton's name through the system."

"Find anything?" Sarkisian asked from the door.

I whirled to face him. "You got the combination?"

Sarkisian handed me a slip of paper. "Ms. Lippincott will be here shortly."

"I can hardly wait."

Under Sarkisian's watchful eye, we opened the safe, which contained more personal correspondence as well as brokerage, mutual fund, and bank statements. We catalogued and boxed all of the documents, but nothing leaped out at us nearly as much as that letter from Belle Thornton. After another hour, certain we had found as much as we could, we started stacking up the boxes of correspondence and documents in the entryway. Billie had begun to load them into our car when, from the office window, I saw a black Bentley slide behind the gates and stop in the motor court. A black-suited chauffeur hopped out and scurried to open the door for Renata Lippincott, who stalked over to Billie, her heels making angry little stabs in the cobblestones.

By the time I got downstairs I could hear Mrs. Lippincott in the motor court, thundering at Billie. "What in the hell do you think you're doing! David, you have to stop this!"

"I'm afraid their warrant's in order, Renata," Sarkisian replied, hurrying to her side.

"Can't you get Judge Fenwick to block it?" she demanded. "We play tennis together at the club."

"I'm afraid not."

"You're worse than useless!" She waved her arm, striking Sarkisian in the shoulder. "Get out of my way!"

Sarkisian beat a hasty retreat, and Lippincott repeated her demand of Billie, who squared her shoulders and replied: "I'm doing my job, ma'am. Now, if you'll excuse me . . ."

Lippincott saw me approaching and shouted: "Detective Justice! Can you get this . . . this . . ."

Billie took a step closer and produced her badge. "Are you looking for the word *cop*, ma'am?"

Lippincott narrowed her eyes at Billie as if she'd like to strike her, too, then turned to me, working her tight-skinned face into a semblance of a smile. "Can we speak privately?"

I motioned her into her stepson's house, across the marble entryway and down a couple of steps into a cavernous sunken living room. She perched herself on a red leather sectional sofa that faced the ocean view, a monogrammed handbag held in her lap as if it were a shield. From the way she sat and the pained look on her face, I guessed this was the first time she'd been in Mario's house since her split with Chuck.

"Mr. Merritt called about your ridiculous search warrants. But none of your people will give me any more information than that."

"There's nothing for me to say, ma'am. Unless there's something you want to tell me."

"*Me?* Tell you?" She gave me a startled look and started squirming in her little Chanel suit. "Like what?"

I opened my notebook and flipped back to my notes from the meeting Monday at CZ Toys. "For starters, what did your board's audit committee ask the internal auditing department to investigate recently?"

"Nothing!" Lippincott's voice registered the appropriate indignation, but she blinked a few times too many. "I can't believe you're turning our offices and our homes upside down because of something the audit committee is investigating!"

"So they *are* investigating something."

"I didn't say that!" she insisted, clearly flustered. "I don't see what this has to do with—"

"It may have a lot to do with Mr. Shareef's murder. Never mind," I said, pulling out my cell phone. "I'm sure it'll be in the minutes of the audit committee's meetings."

She stretched out a manicured hand, said, "Just a minute!" and withdrew it as quickly. "I don't know why you're asking me! I don't even sit on the audit committee!"

"But as chair of the company's board, I can't imagine the committee keeping its work secret from you."

Lippincott shrugged and gave me an inane stare. I didn't expect her to admit to her own complicity in allowing the company to pay for her Montecito residence, but her lack of cooperation in getting to the bottom of the shootings and murder was pissing me off. "Then tell me this—why wasn't your stepson named CEO of the company?"

Her mouth formed a bright red O. "I don't see what that has to do with—"

"Why don't you humor me, Mrs. Lippincott, and answer the question?"

The housekeeper, a Latina with a long braid down her back and fearful eyes, tiptoed in from the kitchen and asked if we were going to be much longer.

"Oh, I didn't know anyone else was here." Lippincott turned as if relieved for the interruption. "Blanca, get me a Scotch, *por favor?*"

She sat gripping the handles of her handbag and frowning as if trying to think of an answer until the housekeeper returned with her drink. She grabbed the glass and took a long swallow, which seemed to steady her nerves. "The reason why Mario wasn't selected to succeed my husband goes to the very heart of our business strategy. It would be inappropriate to share it with outsiders."

I made a show of closing my notebook. "Don't worry, Mrs. Lippincott, our conversation won't show up in the *Wall Street Journal*. We're just trying to solve the murder of Mr. Shareef and the shooting of three innocent bystanders, among them the father of your daughter."

Embarrassment and something else bloomed on her face. "I'm sorry. It's just that my husb—Chuck was so *vital*. I . . . we . . . the *board* had never considered what the company would do if Chuck was to become incapacitated. Or die."

I looked at the emotions moving across the woman's face. "I understand," I murmured. And I did, because in that instant I realized that after all Chuck Zuccari had done to her, Renata Lippincott probably loved her ex-husband as much as she hated him.

"Chuck had been giving more and more responsibility to Mario." She took another swallow of Scotch and rolled it around as if clearing the distasteful name of her stepson from her mouth. "With the idea that he would eventually become CEO. But the board was developing some reservations, which came to a head last fall."

I wished I could refer to my notes, but I didn't want to interrupt her train of thought. "Were you even on the board last fall?"

She shook her head, lips pressed together carefully. "I'd been gone for almost a year, but I still had several friends who were directors who kept me apprised of the situation and sought my counsel."

I wondered how kosher that was, but let it go. "So these reservations had been brewing for a while."

"Since the previous spring. At the board's annual strategy session, the directors asked Chuck for an update of his succession plan. Nothing cast in stone, mind you, but if Chuck was hit by a car, who would he think could carry on."

"And he named . . . ?"

"My stepson. But last fall, after Chuck was shot, a couple of the directors came to me, quite distressed. Chuck had expressed some concerns to them privately about Mario before the shooting. Nothing formal, you understand, just some concerns."

"About?"

She blinked slowly as if trying to remember, or maybe that was the effect of the Scotch. "Chuck told them some issues had come to his attention that gave him pause . . ."

As her voice trailed off I wondered if Renata Lippincott was trying to figure out how to tell me about the bogus vendor.

She shifted on the sofa, the Scotch clearly taking effect. "But then he was shot, and the board truly didn't know what to do, what with Mario pressing them so hard to name him as successor."

"So you got yourself renamed a director and helped them make a decision."

Lippincott smoothed her skirt and took another long draw on her Scotch. "Yes, I did." Her voice echoed in her glass. She finished her drink and set it on the coffee table. "I think I acted in the best interests of the shareholders."

"You have to forgive me, Ms. Lippincott," I began, covering my annoyance with a smile. "I was a history major undergrad, so I'm a little slow to pick up on this business stuff." I opened my notebook, flipping back and forth through my notes. "How Mario could have headed up the company's operations on two continents, been your CFO for five years, been handpicked by Mr. Zuccari to succeed him, and you *not* endorse him as your ex-husband's successor? Unless you withheld your endorsement for personal reasons."

Renata Lippincott gave me an icy stare. "What are you insinuating?"

Over her shoulder, I saw Billie slip into the foyer and pause near the archway, where she stepped back, out of sight but well within earshot of our conversation. "Your stepson introduced Mr. Zuccari to his current wife, didn't he?" I asked.

The ice in her eyes turned to daggers. "How dare you!"

"Should I take that to be a yes?"

Lippincott's face had turned as red as her stepson's sofa. "I refuse to talk about that deceitful little bitch!"

"I see you don't think much of your ex-husband's new wife."

"Chuck was never that sophisticated about women," she confided. "He married his first wife when they were kids, and he married me soon after she died, so he's really—he really was quite naïve. But the way Alma duped him and bled him dry is criminal!"

"We were led to believe Alma had become quite an asset to him and to the company, especially in assessing the joint venture with the Shareefs."

"The *defunct* joint venture," she corrected, a note of triumph in her voice.

"We were told the venture was very promising."

She leaned in my direction, trying to read my notes. "Who told you that? Alma? Of course *she'd* think so!"

"The Shareefs were very high on it, too."

"They had to be—they were trying to sell us on the idea. But I think the window has closed on that whole ethnic doll thing." She leaned closer, her voice dropping to a whisper. "People don't mind a Diana Ross or a Whitney Houston doll, but an Aisha or Zakiya or Felicidad? Those are *maid's* names, for God's sake!" She sat back and made a face.

"But we understand Mr. Zuccari's wife was excited about the collection," I said, making sure to put the emphasis on the word *wife*. "Maybe she had a different perspective as a younger woman and mother-to-be."

Lippincott bristled, as I'd hoped she would, but her words took me by surprise. "That's not the reason Alma was so enthralled by the Shareefs. She was one of them."

"A Muslim?"

"No, *them!*" She jerked her head in the direction of the front door. "The Afro Americans, Negroes, whatever they call themselves these days!" She leaned toward me and whispered: "Alma Gordone never thought anyone would find out her little secret, but I did!"

As Renata Lippincott congratulated herself on her cunning I was trying to remember whether there was anything in Alma's appearance or behavior that suggested she was passing. I'd noticed her blond hair had dark wavy roots, but I knew some Italians and Jews whose hair was the same way. And while I'd also detected a bit of black slang in her speech pattern, that could have been the case with anyone who grew up near a television in post-segregation America. But passing? Given her age, I would have figured Alma would have been prouder, and more secure, about her racial identity than to resort to a game like that. Passing was something out of a Nella Larsen novel, or *Imitation of Life*—one of those old fifties movies. But, like it or not, I had to admit Lippincott's accusation provided an alternative explanation for Alma's championing the Shareefs' project. How had Malik characterized Alma's interest in their dolls to his brother? *Having a black attack.*

"The way they got married so fast," Lippincott was saying, "and then she started inserting herself in the company's affairs, I knew something wasn't right. What if she was a corporate spy from Mattel or Hasbro? Or she and the Shareefs were in cahoots to steal the company's secrets? Everyone was aware of how much time she spent with him."

"Weren't you being a little extreme?"

"I didn't think so, and neither did Mr. Merritt, head of our company's legal department."

As if a corporate survivor like Robert Merritt was going to disagree with a major stockholder, my little voice said.

"He had Mr. Collins arrange for a private investigator to check into her background for me."

"You have a copy of the investigator's report?"

"Mr. Merritt thought it best that he be the only one to see the actual report," she explained, "just so the company could protect itself in case outsiders tried to get hold of it. Attorney work product privilege, he called it. But he told me the essentials."

She leaned forward, eager to share the dirt that had been dug up. "That story Alma told everyone about both of her parents being dead? All lies! Well, not exactly. I mean, her father's dead, but her mother's in some nursing home in Newark, not far from one of the company's old warehouses!"

I made a note to find out how far Newark was from Jersey City, the postmark on that letter we'd found. "And how did this P.I. discover they were black?"

"The report said the Gordones were pale enough to fool most people—"

Pale like me? I wanted to ask, but I held my tongue.

"The father was a well-to-do obstetrician with a thriving practice in Montclair, which is what deceived the people who sold their home to them in the mid-sixties. But how were they to know? The man was a member of the most exclusive country club in the area!"

Which, I was willing to bet a year's salary, probably didn't accept blacks as members back in the day. Maybe not even now. I made a sympathetic sound. "And here this Dr. Gordone had been examining their wives and delivering their babies."

"Exactly! But when some of the wife's family showed up one Christmas, that's when the truth came to light." She allowed herself a little smile. "Or dark, if you prefer."

"Hm. That must have been quite a blow for Montclair."

"*Upper* Montclair," Lippincott corrected, "which was known at the time as one of the finest neighborhoods in New Jersey." She compressed her lips into an ain't-it-awful expression. "My point is, it was quite the scandal back in the sixties, not the kind of thing a neighborhood soon forgets. The investigator found out that the husband's practice dropped off to nothing, he and the wife divorced, and Alma ended up with her mother, who remarried again before landing in the projects. Served her right, trying to deceive people like that!"

"Why are you telling me all of this, ma'am?"

"Because Alma's just like her mother—trying to claw her way out of the ghetto by deceiving my poor Chuck!"

When I didn't respond, Lippincott leaned forward and demanded: "Well? Don't just sit there."

"What would you like me to do?"

She made a shooing motion with one hand. "Go and arrest her!"

"For what? Pretending to be white?"

"No, for trying to kill my husband! I know Chuck would have divorced her, if he'd had the time. Something like this would have jeopardized every political contact he had!"

Billie emerged from the spot where she'd been eavesdropping, as angry as I'd ever seen her. I raised a hand to stop her, but it was too late. "Whether you know it or not, Ms. Lippincott, interracial marriage is no longer a crime in this country!"

Chuck Zuccari's ex-wife gave Billie a withering look. "I wouldn't expect you to understand."

"So are you saying," I pressed, "that Alma had your ex-husband shot to keep him from divorcing her?"

"I think so, yes," she insisted, nodding her head firmly. "Which is why I think you should investigate."

"We will," I said, flipping my notebook closed. "But what I don't get is . . . why didn't you tell us this before?"

Renata Lippincott's body stiffened and she lifted her head, suddenly above it all. "I would have, but Mr. Merritt advised me to let it go. He said that while the investigator proved Alma was a deceitful little bitch—those weren't his words exactly—lying to trap a man isn't exactly a crime. And if I continued to pursue it, it might stir up problems the company or I personally didn't need."

Like alerting her new boyfriend to his wife's obsession with her ex.

"You said you knew Chuck would have divorced Alma if he'd had time. Does that mean you told him about the investigator's report?"

"*I* wouldn't dream of doing something like that!" Eyes as wide as her face-lift allowed, Renata Lippincott raised a hand to her chest in a sign of feigned innocence.

"But someone else did?"

Her lips twitched. "Mr. Merritt said he would talk to Chuck. I remember he said there were some parts of the story Chuck should hear directly from him."

Or maybe Merritt was trying to spare his boss the embarrassment of hearing the news from his ex. "I just bet he did," I said. But as I watched the fierce gleam in Renata Lippincott's eyes, I wondered if Merritt's motive in talking to his boss privately might be for some other reason entirely.

18

Smiling Faces

After getting the documents processed by Latent Prints back at the PAB, we spent the rest of Friday night discussing what we'd learned in our interviews and reviewing reams of paper from our combined searches. By Saturday morning, guided by Perkins and the guys from the FBI and the U.S. Attorney's Office, we'd assembled an ugly picture of embezzlement at CZ Toys—fifteen million over four years that Wunderlich said topped anything the Feds had seen thus far on the West Coast. But to tie it to the shootings, we needed more, so Thor got MIA to pull a few strings with the commanding officer at SID to get one of their graphologists to join us on Saturday afternoon to review some documents.

"We think we've got enough evidence to tie Natalie Johnson, the company's accounts payable manager, to a scheme involving executives in three of the company's offices worldwide," Thor explained to Terrell Vaughan, a wiry black man from SID's Questioned Documents, who'd been called in to review writing samples from our suspects. "We just need to know if Johnson's signatures approving the payments are authentic."

"You got any other suspects' handwriting you want me to consider?"

I showed Vaughan Mario's handwriting in the greeting card and other items seized from his office and home. "It could have been Zuc-cari's son, Mario. He's the company's CFO and could have been ap-proving the payments, forging Johnson's name."

"Or Felton Carruthers, the company's controller," Perkins said, lay-ing out his handwriting samples next to the documents from Mario's house. "He countersigned most of the approvals. We need to authenti-cate his signatures, too."

Billie placed another packet on the table. "We also need you to com-pare Chuck Zuccari's handwriting in these samples obtained from Mario's house with a note allegedly sent by Chuck to a kid who worked in Accounts Payable, trying to scare him into abandoning his investi-gation into the fraud. We know Chuck Zuccari couldn't have sent it be-cause he was in a coma, but we don't know if it was sent by Mario, or Johnson, or Carruthers."

Arms crossed over his chest, Vaughan leaned over to consider the documents, mouth twisted in concentration, then glanced at his watch. "It's two now. It's going to take me a good eight hours to analyze all these documents. Couldn't this have waited until Monday?"

"Some of these suspects have the means to flee the country at the drop of a hat," I replied. "And without an indictment, we can't just go to a judge and get an order to have their passports lifted. The Feds have got them under surveillance for now, but we need some answers be-fore they get in the wind."

"Look," Wunderlich broke in, "if having these documents exam-ined through the LAPD's lab is going to be too cumbersome, we can send them to our lab for analysis. The embezzlement piece of this case is in our bailiwick, anyway."

Wunderlich was still angling for control of the evidence, and with it the case, but Thor wasn't going for it. "That'll take forever," he ar-gued, "plus if we separate the evidence, it's going to slow us down in making our case on the murder to the DA."

"So far, you don't have a case, Thorfinsen!" Wunderlich reminded him as he and his colleagues gathered up their things. "All we've got so far is the embezzlement, and unless you can come up with something else, we're going to have to take over."

"Give us until the end of the day Monday, Wunderlich, to see what we can pull together." Thor gave Vaughan a meaningful look. "Everybody here understands the importance of hooking up a suspect on the murder, don't we?"

After the others left, Vaughan sighed wearily as he gathered up the documents and signed for them. "I need to look at this stuff in my office," he muttered, "but I've only been authorized enough overtime to work on this until six tonight. What I can't get to today will have to wait until Monday morning."

"You heard what that Fed said, Vaughan. Who do I have to call to get you in here on Sunday morning?"

"I'll get you your results by Monday morning," Vaughan grumbled, "but don't sweat me about Sunday morning—I've got to go to my kid's christening. Some of us do have lives outside of the office, you know."

While getting a hand from us was going to help the Feds make their embezzlement case, I wasn't certain that by the end of the day we'd be any closer to finding our shooter. Yet, I felt in my bones that the documents we'd obtained were the key to breaking open this case. I picked up copies we'd made of the correspondence and other documents seized from Mario's home. "Perkins, you were saying earlier that Mario wrote a lot of checks out of his personal checking account."

"That's been his pattern for the last year," she nodded, leafing through the bank statements. "About fifteen thousand a month, between checks to individuals and those written to cash easily forty, fifty checks a month."

Billie whistled. "That's a lot of checks. He supporting a lover somewhere?"

"Some of that might have been going to whoever he was sending that greeting card to," I noted, sliding the Xerox copy of the "Thinking of You" card I'd found on Mario's desk to Billie. "See, it says: 'I don't want you worrying about money. I've taken care of everything.' The card hadn't been addressed yet, so we don't know who it was intended for."

"I've never seen money sent to a contract killer in a greeting card," Billie noted, giving me an uncertain look.

"As I said, he writes a lot of checks." Perkins leafed through the stack. "There are a bunch to Blanca Ortiz, but those are relatively small."

"That's his housekeeper," I said. "Anything larger?"

"I won't know until I sort all these checks into a list of individuals and businesses and verify their receipt of payment. That could take a week."

"But we've only got until Monday!" I snapped. "Maybe while Perkins is working on the checks, I should dig into Lippincott's accusation about Alma Zuccari. If Chuck found out his wife was passing, that could have given her a motive to have him killed."

"I know you think it's important, Justice, but it just doesn't strike me as a motive for anything."

"This isn't about what you or I would do, Thor. It's about a young black woman who's passing for white being married to a sixty-four-year-old ultraconservative Republican and keeping a secret that could blow the lid off his perfect little world!"

Thor made an impatient gesture. "If it makes you happy, check it out, but don't let it interfere with reviewing the rest of these documents on Natalie Johnson and the other CZ Toys employees. They're our most likely targets."

"Weren't you going up to Oregon to see your granddaughter?" I asked.

He shook his head emphatically. "I couldn't leave you all high and dry."

Don't worry, Thor," Perkins said. "If Vaughan or the Latent Prints guys come up with anything, I'll be here. I need to spend some more time examining Mario Zuccari's and Johnson's financial statements, see if there's a pattern to the withdrawals and deposits."

"And I've got some paperwork to attend to," Billie said, waving him off.

"Go," I agreed, "even if it's just for the day. We've got everything under control. Your granddaughter needs you."

A couple of hours later, Perkins went outside for a cigarette break, and I used the opportunity to walk over to Billie's desk. "While we're killing time," I whispered, "why don't we follow up on Lippincott's accusation about Alma Zuccari."

"Two reasons." Billie closed the blue binder she'd been working on with a thud. "One, the original murder book is full of a bunch of loose ends on the Nazis and the Black Muslims I need to tie off before we turn the file over to the D.A.'s office. And, two, you heard what Thor said—he wants us to concentrate on Johnson and the CZ Toys employees."

The clock on the wall said it was after four. "Thor can't ding us for pursuing it on our own time."

"Damn, Charlotte!" Billie exclaimed, a scowl on her face. "I was hoping to finish this paperwork and get home before sundown. I haven't seen my daughter in the daylight all week. She's gonna think I'm a vampire."

"Sure, go ahead. But while you're playing with Turquoise, do me a favor." I reached for my handbag and unearthed the card Pete Collins had given me at the hospital. "See if Collins can locate Robert Merritt, the head of the legal department at CZ Toys. I want to see if he backs up Renata's story about engaging the private investigator."

"Do you really think this is that important?"

"My maternal grandmother passed all the time in her dressmaking business. There were times she'd publicly deny my darker-skinned uncle if it meant getting some big contract. He used to smile and laugh about it, but it had to hurt."

"But enough to make somebody want to kill?"

"I don't know. But you know like I do, color prejudice is one of America's dirtiest little secrets. The only question is—how far would Alma Zuccari go to keep hers?"

Billie reluctantly took the card and tucked it into her jacket pocket. "But what are you going to do?"

"See a woman about a doll."

You would have thought it was a film premiere the way the cars were inching along Venice Boulevard toward Broadway Federal S&L. Inside were the usual hodgepodge of notable black Angelenos— the bankers and doctors, divas and dilettantes and various poseurs in between—interspersed with an equally diverse group of the city's African American Muslim population, if the subdued garb and covered heads were any indication. From high yellow to espresso black, in kuftis and cashmere, these two very different sides of black L.A. had come together, not to see Spike or Clint's latest film but the unveiling of the Malik Shareef Black Doll Collection.

I thought I was going to have to drag Aubrey kicking and screaming to the event. He wouldn't stop complaining until I told him I thought my family would be there as well. "Come on honey, it'll be fun," I wheedled when I'd called him about it from work.

"Why are you just now telling me?"

"You'd gone inside the other night when Mother mentioned it," I replied as if my mother and I had planned this excursion all along. "You're the one who's been telling me I should show up for more family events."

But Aubrey wasn't buying it. "Don't bullshit me, Char! This is not a family event. This is about the Smiley Face shootings and you know it."

"I just need to ask Malik Shareef's widow one question, then we can leave. Besides, I know how you enjoy talking to my father."

A pause, then: "If your dad's going to be there, I guess I can run through there with you. But you owe me a decent dinner afterward!"

"Campanile?"

"And dessert afterward, and I'm not talking profiteroles!"

But first Aubrey had to get through the dozens of dolls on display throughout the small branch. "Good thing they're serving drinks," he said, a comment I heard echoed by more than one man as their wives and girlfriends moved among the display cases, oohing and aahing over the rare dolls and artifacts while the men stood in protective little clusters, arguing over the NBA standings or the latest scandal in the current mayoral race.

Aubrey said, "I see some of my fellow Omegas got shanghaied tonight, too," as he walked toward the bar and a short dark-skinned brother I didn't know. On the other side of the room, I spotted Habiba Shareef talking to the bank's young CEO. I was about to head that way when I felt a tap on my shoulder.

"Hey, girl," Louise said, giving me a hug. "Your mother didn't tell me you were coming, too."

"I wanted to surprise her." Over Louise's shoulder, I saw Joymarie and Uncle Syl dragging my father to look at the dolls while Perris strode toward the bar and gave Aubrey and the dark-skinned guy the Omega Psi Phi fraternity handshake. Other than looking more tired than usual, the Dark Prince was doing his thing, smiling and glad-handing, laughing with his frat brothers as they saluted each other with the old Omega phrase—*Q Psi Phi 'til the day I die.* But every once in a while I saw my brother's eyes rake over the crowd. Was it just another leftover habit from his days on patrol, or was Perris looking for his frat brother Paul Taft, the Q who wasn't there? "I see my big brother is up to his usual tricks."

"He'd better be getting a Coca-Cola," Louise replied, craning her neck to see what Perris was doing. "We had a long talk after Film Night, Char. He's promised he's going to stop drinking. He even went to a meeting this afternoon."

"AA's a start." Across the room, Perris caught my eye and gave me a wary nod. "Did he tell you I called the other day?"

"No! Did you two talk?"

"Not yet, but I left a message, which he hasn't returned."

Louise put a hand on my arm and gave it a reassuring squeeze. "Well, I know he wants to talk to you. He said he needed to get some things straightened out."

"Yes, he does," I murmured, wondering if Uncle Henry had warned him I was on the warpath about Keith's files.

"I told him if he didn't do it soon, I was going to make him sleep in the garage!"

I hugged Louise again, whispered, "Thanks, sis," and continued on toward Mrs. Shareef, where I hung back a few feet until she was finished with her conversation. "What is it now, Detective?" she whispered, leading me out of the flow of well-wishers and the press.

"Just need to get your reaction to some new information."

Her eyes on the crowd, Mrs. Shareef went over to give a kiss on both cheeks to a Muslim female, then shook hands with a lawyer here, a state assemblywoman there. "I'm not going to have you drag my husband's memory through the mud in front of all these people!" she hissed out of the corner of her mouth.

"This is not about Malik. It's about Alma Zuccari."

Habiba Shareef's expression hardened as she turned on me. "Haven't I heard enough about that woman?"

I told her what we'd learned about Alma and her family, which caused Mrs. Shareef's brow to unfurl and her face to go slack with relief. "So *that's* what it was! Malik always said she was a troubled spirit, but I don't think even he would have guessed she was passing! And now that you say it, her behavior makes sense. Did I tell you she even asked us to add an ultra-fair-skinned doll to the collection? Too bad she just couldn't come out and tell us. All that exposure to our dolls didn't teach her a thing about loving herself."

"Maybe it did," I replied, wondering for the first time if Alma's obsession with the Shareefs' dolls could have drawn the wrath of her husband.

I heard a throat clear behind us. "Char, can you introduce us?" Louise had slipped up behind me, my brother in tow, beaming at Mrs. Shareef as if she were Coretta Scott King and Ethel Kennedy rolled into one. "My husband and I are great fans of your and your husband's book. Are any of the dolls your husband used in his research here in the exhibit?"

Habiba Shareef walked Louise over to the topsy-turvy doll and began explaining how it was used in focus groups to determine children's racial preferences. Perris lingered behind, gazing off in another direction, his body turned slightly away from me, as if positioning himself for a quick escape. "Uncle Henry called. He's pretty pissed off at you for forging his signature."

"I'm just trying to reconstruct a file that seems to have gone missing. You have any idea what I'm talking about?"

"Look, Char, I—"

"Let's cut to the chase, Perris. What do you want?"

"I got your message about Paul Taft," he mumbled.

"You didn't call me back."

"I had walked over to invite you to breakfast in the morning," he replied. "I was hoping we could talk face-to-face, clear up a few things."

I positioned myself so I was in his line of sight. "We're face-to-face right now."

He turned the other way. "This isn't the place, Char—"

I stood in his way again. "We can take it outside."

Perris looked at me sharply, as if I'd challenged him to a fight. "Fine," he sighed at last. "Might as well get this over with."

We stepped into an evening that had cooled off considerably, dark clouds backlit by moonlight as they skittered across the sky. "You know Paul Williams designed this building," Perris began, leaning against a column and jiggling the ice in his cup. "The bank's CEO is his grandson."

"Spare me the black L.A. history lesson." I grabbed his cup, sniffed its contents. "What was in here, a screwdriver?"

"Orange juice. I've stopped drinking."

"Congratulations." I handed it back. "How long has it been?"

He looked away. "Three days. Since I got your message."

"I called *Uncle Henry* on Wednesday, Perris. I didn't call you until yesterday."

He turned up his cup, trying to play it off. "One day, three days. What does it matter?"

"Look, I didn't come out in the cold to talk black history or architecture or your journey to sobriety, for that matter. I want to know why you took Keith's files and what's going on with you and Paul Taft."

At the mention of Taft's name, Perris started looking around as if the FBI agent were going to jump out from between the parked cars. "Why don't we sit in my car and talk?" he suggested, hustling me over to his Beemer, which was parked a few yards away, facing the bank. He looked around again before unlocking my door and opening it for me.

"So, what's the deal?" I said, once we were inside. "Why are you so nervous?"

Perris got in the driver's seat and sat for a few minutes, breathing deeply. "I prayed for years that I'd never have to do this," he muttered as he started the car and turned on the heater.

"Do what? Stop being such a drama king, Perris, and just spit it out!"

Just then, my cell phone rang. It was Billie. "I just finished talking to Robert Merritt," she said excitedly. "You're gonna trip when you hear what he had to say!"

"I'm in the middle of something right now. Can I call you back in five, ten minutes?"

"Sure. I've gotta make a few phone calls anyway. But be sure and call me back."

I broke the connection and returned my attention to Perris, who had switched the radio to an oldies station and was idly humming along with a group the DJ identified as The Undisputed Truth. "So?"

He stopped humming and took another breath. "Okay. Remember how I used to talk with Keith about gangs, back when you first started bringing him around?"

The question caught me off guard. "Sure. You said Keith's knowledge could help your work on the streets."

"The spring before he was—" He stopped himself and started again, head down this time. "That spring, Keith had started researching the Black Freedom Militia."

I waved a hand in front of his face. "Earth to Perris! I was working with him, remember?"

"You were working on the *data* end of the study," he reminded me. "Keith wanted to go into the field, do some primary research, something I had urged him not to do."

Despite the heater, Perris's words made the air in the car turn cold. The Undisputed Truth was singing something about truth being in the eyes, but Perris refused to look in mine. "Keith never told me that."

But Perris wasn't listening to me or the radio. His attention was drawn to the activity inside the bank. "The department had started its own investigation of the BFM. Keith nosing around had the potential to get in the way. Plus I didn't want him blowing my cover, in case we ran into each other at one of their meetings."

"You worked undercover?" So Taft hadn't been lying about *that*.

"In the beginning, I didn't tell you because of the nature of the assignment," he replied, his voice flat. "And later, when I thought I should, Keith made me promise not to. He was afraid you'd try and stop him."

"Stop *him*?" I grabbed his arm. "From doing what?"

"Just let me get this out, okay?" he said, his voice growing thick as he carefully disengaged my grip. "I was already inside the organization, had gotten pretty close to Cinque Lewis and his girlfriend—"

"Sojourner Truth."

He nodded. "My assignment was to destabilize the BFM from within, which I was doing by feeding Truth information about Lewis's infidelity.

"Keith showed up at an orientation meeting right after I had talked to her, asking his standard set of research questions. But she was so angry about what I'd been telling her, she started spilling her guts to Keith about the inner circle of Lewis's advisors and the drugs they were dealing."

I'd heard part of this story before when I'd interviewed Sojourner Truth in connection with Lewis's murder, and even before that when Cinque Lewis began to threaten Keith and our family if he published his findings. But the spin Perris was putting on the story gave it a different, more ominous feeling.

"Keith came to me," Perris was saying, "concerned for the children in the BFM's after-school programs, and asked me what should he do. I told him he had to get the hell away from the BFM, that they were too volatile, but he said he wanted to stay and help us get as much information on the organization as possible. To help those kids, you know?"

Perris's words sent a deeper chill down my spine and set off a war in my mind. One part of me couldn't believe Keith could be so foolish, while the other part knew it was exactly what my headstrong, idealistic husband would do. But in addition to the argument raging inside my head, there was one voice I could not ignore, which was screaming: *He put you and your baby in jeopardy!*

I covered my ears to drown out the noise in my head. "You're lying to me, Perris! You talked Keith into this. I know how you are!"

My brother shook his head rhythmically, eyes shut tight. "I wish it was different, Char, but Keith insisted on helping us. He said he wanted to put all that data he'd been collecting to use in the real world."

That, too, sounded like something Keith would say. As the tears slid down my face and my throat closed up, I could see my father inside the bank, saying something to Aubrey and his frat brother that made them laugh. I opened my handbag and felt around for my inhaler, my Altoids tin, anything to stop the feeling that I was going to choke to death inside this car. I found instead my yellow marble from Dr. P's office. "You did this to Keith. You caused his and Erica's deaths as surely as if you pulled the trigger yourself!"

"Oh, God, Char, please don't say that! When Lewis and his gang came after Keith, we all tried to protect your family."

"We who? You and Burt Rivers?"

"Uncle Henry, too."

"You're saying my godfather knew Keith was working with you?"

"He was our captain and C.O. of Southwest," Perris reminded me. "He authorized the operation in conjunction with PDID. How do you think your family got around-the-clock protection so quickly?"

I stared at the smiling faces of Aubrey and his frat brothers inside the bank in disbelief.

Smiling faces tell lies, The Undisputed Truth sang to me. *And I've got proof.*

What was the proof? I'd read bits and pieces of the PDID files on the BFM years before. They were largely the report of a police informant placed inside the organization. But I hadn't put it together then, nor when I met Sojourner Truth and her adopted son, Cinque Lewis's brother Peyton, years later and she'd told me about a brother named Q-Dog pulling her coat about her man sleeping with another woman in the BFM. No wonder Perris took Keith's files, and Uncle Henry was so intent on my cutting Perris some slack, and Burt was advising me on what Keith would want me to do. They'd all been in it together— Burt Rivers, Henry Youngblood, and, at the center of it all, my brother, the Dark Prince, Mr. Q-Psi-Phi 'til the day I die.

But now I felt like the one who was dying, and Perris was to blame. "You were the informant in those files! You were Q-Dog!"

He nodded slowly, his face contorted with pain. "Since we Omegas called each other Q-dogs, I figured Quincy Dash wouldn't be a hard name to remember."

I slapped him, all my strength behind the blow. "So that's why everyone's been covering for your sorry ass!" I slapped him again. "All these years!" And again. "You sorry motherfucker!"

"I was only doing my job, Char!" Fending me off, Perris grabbed my sleeve, but I yanked my arm away, sending the yellow marble I'd been clutching flying. As I felt around the floor of the car my arm brushed against my holstered gun.

It would take so little effort to keep reaching back, to pull out that gun and blow him away.

To watch his brains splatter all over the driver's seat of his shiny Beemer, the way Keith's were splattered in my driveway.

So easy.

As if he'd read my mind, Perris let go of my arm. "I wouldn't blame you if you wanted to kill me, Char." He stared at the happy people inside the bank, tears streaming down his face. "I wanted to kill myself, many times, after seeing what their deaths did to you. It's why I had to leave the department. I just couldn't take it anymore."

I picked up the marble and held onto it for dear life. The voices inside my head were screaming so loud I couldn't stand it. "Just tell me what happened."

He pressed his palm over one eye as if to stop the flow of tears. "The day they—that day, I was on my way over to your house to work my shift, when Lewis waylaid me at the cover apartment the department had set me up with. Someone had tipped him off that I was a cop. He shot me as I was getting into my car. Otherwise, I would have been there at your house that day. I could have stopped him, Char. I would have gladly taken those bullets to stop Lewis!"

My brother's tearful confession reminded me of how, after Keith and Erica's murders, he would come to my house, drunk and crying. And I'd thought it was because of sympathy for me or reliving what had happened to him the day they died.

Now I knew. It was both, and more. "Who else knows about this besides Uncle Henry and Burt?"

Perris gulped as he scanned the crowd in the brightly lit bank. "I told Mom right after it happened."

No surprise there, my little voice reminded me. *Those two are thick as thieves.*

"She told me to try and let it go, go on with my life and not burden you with things that would only hurt you even worse than Keith and Erica's deaths."

That sounded like my mother—doing her part to keep up appearances, even if it meant watching her daughter suffer not knowing the truth, or her son, who knew the truth all too well. And it also explained why she was so outraged when I joined the department shortly after Keith's death, why she and Perris had been sniping at me about quitting from Day One.

I smiled bitterly. "So my dear darling mother has been lying to me for almost thirteen years."

One lie calls for another and another, I could hear my grandmama Cile say.

"Not lying, Char. Just selectively editing the truth down to what you could handle."

"That should have been my choice to make, not hers, or yours!"

"We couldn't do it, not as fragile as you were!"

"I haven't been fragile for the entire thirteen years, Perris! Did you tell Daddy, too?"

"I haven't, but Mom or Uncle Henry might have."

Even if my mother didn't have the nerve to do it, Uncle Henry would have certainly confided in his best friend. Which meant Grandmama Cile probably knew, too. Was I the only one in our family who'd been left in the dark?

The possibility made me replay conversations with my family about Keith or about my being on the department—scores of them over the years, over countless barbecues and card games and Justice Family Film Nights. Was Matt Justice's love and concern for me genuine, or was it all to cover the Dark Prince's trail? How long had he and my mother been smiling in my face, and stabbing me in the back with their lies and half-truths? Now something my grandmother said about Perris and my mother taking those files, just last week at a card game with my father and Uncle Syl, came back to me, its meaning suddenly crystal clear.

"Why they want to dig up the past?" she'd said. *"You go diggin' in the past, all you gon' get is dirty."*

I fished some more antacids from the Altoids tin to fight back the waves of rage and nausea threatening to drown me. "Are you okay, Char?" Perris asked.

As if he cared. "How does Taft fit into all of this?"

"The FBI was investigating the BFM the same time as the LAPD. Taft was the Bureau's plant inside the organization. When he found out I was working undercover, too, he tried to get me removed from the case. Then, after I got shot and Lewis disappeared, he transferred to Birmingham."

"And you never spoke to him again?"

He shrugged. "Not until he started calling me recently, trying to locate Sojourner Truth and Peyton."

"For what?"

"He wouldn't say, but he threatened to tell you the whole story if I didn't help him."

"Which is why you took Keith's files, to keep me from figuring it out on my own."

He nodded. "Up until Taft showed up, I had just tried to put the whole mess out of my mind. But it was hard. I was so bitter about how nobody backed me up the day I got shot."

And had used that bitterness, in his law practice, to become one of the biggest thorns in L.A. law enforcement's side. But he'd paid a heavy price, too. In the reflected light of the reception, I could see the scar over my brother's eye, the one from the car accident he'd had while driving under the influence, one of the countless ways he'd tried to "put the whole mess out of his mind."

Perris saw me staring and fingered the scar on his cheek. "I deserved this and every other bad thing that has happened in my life, for letting Keith take such a foolish risk, for not coming clean to you. If I had, maybe together we could have made him stop."

"Don't you dare!" If I had to sit here another minute I was going to throw up. I grabbed my handbag, got out of the car, and walked angrily toward the bank. "Don't you dare put this on me, Perris! You're the one who let Keith get himself killed!"

"I'm sorry, Char," he called after me. "I wasn't trying to say—"

"Stay the hell away from me, Perris!"

nside, Aubrey was talking to Uncle Syl and my mother, who had her back to the door. If I could have stabbed her between the shoulder blades at that moment, I would have. "Let's get the fuck out of here," I muttered to Aubrey.

"Language, young lady!" my mother warned, glancing around to see who had heard me.

Uncle Syl did, and frowned at the expression on my face. "Why are you hatting up so soon, Baby Girl?"

"I've heard enough bullshit for one night!" I snapped, glad to see my mother cringe.

Aubrey had moved to my side and put a supportive hand on my back. "Char's had a long week. So, if you'll excuse us, I've promised her a fabulous dinner at Campanile."

"I'm not in the mood for all that pomp and circumstance!"

"Me, either," he whispered in my ear as he steered me toward the door. "Let's just get you out of here."

Aubrey called ahead and ordered takeout from his favorite Italian restaurant. On the way there, I told him about Perris, surprising my-self that I didn't cry once in the retelling.

Although sympathetic, Aubrey was not surprised at all. "All that trash Perris and your mom were talking about how you'd handle clos-ing up your house, and the way they were sneaking around the day they found those files let me know something wasn't right."

"Well, I wish you had said something!"

"I *told* you what they were doing!" he snapped back. "How was I supposed to know what kind of games they were playing or what they'd done?"

I massaged my forehead, trying to will away the headache that had my head throbbing. "You're right. I'm sorry—I just can't believe my family would do something like this to me."

Aubrey stopped the car in front of the restaurant. "The trip of it is, I don't think they meant to harm you, Char. In their minds, they prob-ably thought they were protecting you."

"That's the same line of BS my brother was trying to sell me! You shouldn't need protection from the truth."

Aubrey raised his hands. "Hey, don't shoot the messenger! I'm just trying to show you the other side."

"I'm tired of seeing the other side. I need someone to see *my* side!"

"That's what I was trying to do!" Aubrey snapped, slamming the car door and stalking inside to get our food.

After eleven, after we'd had dinner and way too much red wine, Aubrey snaked an arm around me in bed and drew my hips close. "I know you're hurting, Char," he whispered, "but you've got to try and let it go. Don't spend another thirteen years grieving over something you couldn't have controlled in the first place."

I nodded, but I didn't believe a word of what he was saying. I knew Keith would have listened to me, would have stopped messing around with Lewis and the BFM, if I had asked him to. Wouldn't he?

Aubrey hugged me close and kissed the back of my neck. I moved his hand higher, demonstrating how I wanted him to knead my breast, almost as if he could reach through my bones and massage my cold, dead heart back to life. After a few moments, I felt him harden behind me and pull his hand away. "This isn't right, Char," he muttered. "You don't need me pushing up on you right now."

"Baby." I turned over and reached down, felt Aubrey shudder beneath my probing hand. "That's exactly what I need."

What I did that night was wrong; I know it was. I used Aubrey's body to work out my pain, accepted and returned his thrusts as if they were driving something evil out of my soul. Was I trying to dispel the pain, or the anger behind the memory of all those nights of lovemaking with Keith? I didn't know, and at that moment I didn't care. All I wanted that night was to know that somebody loved me, and as I touched and was touched, bit and was bitten, rode and was ridden into a babbling, tearful release, I knew without a doubt that Keith was dead and gone out of my life forever, along with Perris and my whole family, people who'd betrayed my love and trust to suit their own ends. It was only later, after we'd exhausted ourselves and Aubrey had rolled over and gone to sleep and I'd slipped out of bed to return Billie's call, that it occurred to me that maybe I'd just driven my lover out of my life as well.

19

The Passing Game

lthough I was in my robe and slippers, I felt chilled by Billie's words. I whispered: "You think the woman who wrote the threatening letter to Zuccari is Alma's *mother*?"

Billie had gotten a verbal summary from Robert Merritt of the P.I.'s report and had made the connection between Alma's mother and the writer of the letter to Chuck Zuccari. "Merritt never saw the letter, so he didn't recognize the name Belle Thornton. But when he told me Alma's mother's name was Isabelle Thornton, I figured it had to be the same person."

"How'd he find her?"

"Alma provided next of kin information when she was hired by the modeling agency that sent her to that toy convention. How many Isabelle or Belle Thorntons do you think there are in Newark, New Jersey?"

I was about to argue the point, then remembered Alma and Chuck Zuccari's daughter's name was Cara-Isabella and bit my tongue.

"The P.I. did some digging on Thornton and found out she'd been married previously to an OB/GYN, Dr. Earl Gordone. That's when he flew out to New Jersey and got that information he passed on to Renata Lippincott about the Gordones passing for white."

"But how did he connect her to Chuck Zuccari?"

"The P.I. pulled her marriage license and traced her through her maiden name. He finally found someone who remembered that Isabelle Kendry had moved to Newark after high school and taken a job as a payroll clerk at CZ Toys, where she met and married the boss's son."

According to the wedding announcement in the local paper, Chuck was twenty-five and destined for great things when he fell head over heels for the eighteen-year-old brown-haired, blue-eyed Isabelle Kendry. "But then, a few years later, when Mario was about two, Isabelle Zuccari dropped off the scene, resurfacing a year later as Belle Gordone of Upper Montclair, New Jersey, wife of Dr. Earl Gordone and mother of a baby girl, Alma."

"The Zuccaris must have found out she was black and paid her to disappear," I said.

"That's what the P.I. pieced together after interviewing Belle last year. Bottom line is, with her out of the way, the Zuccaris could pretend to Mario and everyone else that his mother had died. Only now that lie has come back to bite them all in the butt."

My grandmother's voice came to me again, reminding me: *One lie calls for another and another.* I could only imagine the pain Isabelle Zuccari had felt, separated from her child because of her lies. Or the half-hearted love Mario must have gotten from his family, who knew the truth and withheld it from him. Or Chuck, who must have been riddled with guilt every time he lied to Mario about his mother being dead. I could see how Mario became such a straitlaced, dutiful son. Probably desperate to win his father's approval, he'd devoted his life to the family business and adopted his father's politics, his religious beliefs, and God only knew what else.

"So you were right about that letter being personal," Billie was saying. "Alma's mother was writing about how the Zuccaris took her son from her, not their Nazi connection. She probably just put the article in there to remind Chuck she had some dirt on his family, too."

The enclosed will remind you of the wrongs you have done to me, Isabelle had reproached her former husband, *and of the lengths I will go to stop you.*

Now the truth lay heavy in our hands, but I was completely baffled about what to do with it. How in the hell were we going to tell Alma and Mario that Chuck was once married to Alma's mother, making them not just in-laws but half sister and brother? Then a thought struck me. "Mrs. Lippincott said Merritt was supposed to talk to Zuccari about the P.I.'s report. Did he?"

"Sort of. Merritt sent Zuccari a copy of the report and the invoice with a memo telling him how the P.I. was engaged at the insistence of his ex and asking how he wanted Merritt to handle payment. Zuccari wrote back and said to pay the invoice in full, along with a hefty bonus, in exchange for the original case files and notes."

"And that was it? Zuccari never discussed it with Merritt directly?"

"Would you? But Merritt said he kept a copy of the P.I.'s report in a safe at the office, just to cover the company against some future claim by Thornton."

Merritt had promised to go into his office in the morning and fax a copy of the report to us so we could go over it ourselves. Which we would, with a fine-toothed comb. Yet the prospect of what lay ahead sent a chill straight through me, making my little office in Aubrey's house seem even colder than it was. I checked the time. Almost midnight. "You know, it's going to be creepy having to tell Alma and Mario about this."

Billie agreed, but advised we wait until morning. "Zuccari's taken a turn for the worse," she said. "When I checked in with the Feds surveilling Mario and Gabriella, they told me they both drove down to the hospital about nine and just got back home. And the nurse I called on Chuck's unit said Alma was still there. It doesn't sound good."

Given the hour and the circumstances, I agreed that we'd let it rest until morning, allowing us to be better prepared for the difficult interviews that lay ahead. "But what the hell are we going to tell Alma and Mario, Charlotte?" Billie asked.

"The truth."

Alma Zuccari agreed to come in at eleven, after she had visited her husband at the hospital. But Mario Zuccari, speaking through his attorney, Sarkisian, asked if he could meet with us first thing Monday morning, ostensibly to allow him time to participate in an Easter pageant rehearsal at his church.

"Pageant my ass!" Thor scoffed over the phone as Perkins, Billie, and I sat in MIA's office, giving him an update. "The only pageant Mario Zuccari's involved in is the one with him and his attorneys, trying to get their ducks in a row."

"He *could* be in church," Billie added, "praying he can keep the embezzlement from hitting the news until after his family can dump their stock!"

"Hopefully, they're not that stupid," Perkins said. " 'Cause if they are, the Feds could hook them for insider trading on top of the embezzlement."

"Want us to go down there and bring him in?" I asked.

"No, let him do something stupid," Thor replied. "It could give us some leverage, especially since we don't have anything conclusive to tie him to the embezzlement or the shootings."

"But we've got one hell of a smoking gun," Billie put in. "That letter from Mario's mother to his father we found hidden in his desk. If he realized who she was and that his father had kept them apart all these years—"

"He could have contracted to have his father killed himself," Thor interrupted, "and then paid off Engalla to make it look like he was responsible."

"We'll know if that's the case soon enough," I said. "Latent Prints left a message that they'll have complete results on the prints they lifted off the letter to Engalla by Monday. If you want us to hold off on Alma Zuccari until then, we can."

"I'd rather not. I don't want to run the risk of Merritt giving Alma a heads-up before we can interview her. In fact, I'm a little concerned we may have blown the element of surprise by not interviewing her last night."

"I didn't think the time was right," I said, explaining what we knew about Chuck Zuccari's condition. "But we should have checked it with you. After all, you *are* the supervising detective on the case."

"No, that was a good call," he conceded. "You know what you're doing as much as I do."

It was one of the few compliments I'd received from the veteran detective since he'd come onto this case, and I didn't know quite what to do with it.

As I mumbled thanks, Thor said: "I should have listened to you about that passing thing, Justice. I just never thought it was that big a deal."

"It was to Alma Zuccari and her mother."

"And from what the P.I. found out," Billie added, "it was a whole lot more than that to Chuck."

Thor grunted. "That whole family is choking to death on its secrets. Question is, how far were they willing to go to keep them."

At one, Alma Zuccari was wheeled into the interview room by a fiftyish, toupee-wearing suit I'd not met before. Her face pale and drawn, she looked worse than she did the day I saw her at the hospital, reminding me again of the havoc that crime can wreak on families. "This is Jerry Gales. Mr. Gales is a political associate and friend of my husband's," she explained, after I introduced Billie.

Gales snapped a card in my direction. "And the family's personal attorney."

"I'm sorry I'm late," she went on, the agitation clear in her voice. "My husband's developed an infection that's causing his kidneys and other organs to fail. They've had to put him on a ventilator, and the first EEG was flat. I'm afraid he may be . . . ."

I glanced quickly at Billie as we chimed "I'm so sorry" in unison.

But Alma didn't want our sympathy. "All I care about is that you arrest whoever shot my husband before he . . . before I have to . . ." She shifted uncomfortably in her chair. "It might help me to let him go, to know the guilty party will be punished."

"We'll do our best, ma'am," I promised, and shot another look at Billie, wondering how she was interpreting Alma's response.

After an awkward silence, Gales said: "Mrs. Zuccari tells me she never saw the shooter that night and doesn't remember much of what happened before or after she was shot. So, if you've called her up here to identify that boy suspected of embezzling funds from the company, I'm afraid you're going to be disappointed."

I carefully placed the attorney's card in front of me on the table. "Thank you, sir, we've already got your client's statement on where she was at the time of the shooting."

"So you agree she can't possibly identify Nilo Engalla." Gales sat back in his chair, proud of the point he thought he was scoring.

"Yes, sir, we do. But Mr. Engalla is not a suspect at this time."

"Then why are we here?"

I addressed Alma Zuccari directly. "I was wondering, before we begin, if we might speak with you privately, ma'am, completely off the record?"

Gales again placed his hand over Alma's. "Don't you believe them, my dear. Nothing is off the record with the police!"

"We're not trying to entrap your client, merely protect her privacy."

Alma gave me a puzzled look. "Protect my privacy from *whom*? Mr. Gales is our attorney!"

I fingered the card in front of me. "Yes, ma'am," I said, "and a family friend and political associate of your husband's. You explained that."

Alma watched me intently, blinking as she slowly withdrew her hand from Gales's protective grasp. "Jerry, could you get me some water? I promise I won't confess to anything while you're gone."

"There's a watercooler in our break room, sir," Billie offered. "If you step outside and turn to your right, Detective Perkins can direct you."

"Ten minutes, Jerry," Alma promised as she turned and mustered an encouraging smile for her skeptical attorney. "Then you can protect Chuck and me to your heart's content."

She waited until she could no longer hear Gales's footstep in the hall. "What's this all about?"

"We wanted to talk to you about Isabelle Thornton," Billie told her.

Alma started as if Billie had slapped her. "My mother?" she whispered. "How did you find her?"

"We didn't," Billie replied as she explained about the P.I. Renata Lippincott had had CZ Toys hire.

Alma shook her head, her eyes welling with tears. "I kept telling her someone would eventually find out. How is she?"

"I'm sorry to say she's had a stroke, ma'am," Billie said gently.

Alma drew in her breath, the color draining from her already pale face. "Is she all right?"

"When the P.I. filed his report, she was in a nursing home, but that was over a year ago. Is there a reason you two haven't communicated?"

Alma nodded fiercely as she fumbled in her pocket for a tissue. "That's how she wanted it. She wanted me to get as far away from the past as possible."

"And your racial identity?" Billie asked.

Alma gave Billie a crooked smile. "I told Mother it was ridiculous, playing that stupid passing game in this day and age, but she couldn't stop. Kept shuttling us around these small towns in Connecticut and New Jersey, lying to get us into better neighborhoods, and me into better schools."

"And for her, better meant white," Billie said, her clipped tone betraying her disapproval.

Alma nodded, a guilty look on her face. "I hated every minute of it, especially when I'd get beaten up when the white kids at a school found out I was black. But my mother would just pick us up and move again. It was like, after the mistake she made with my father, she had to get it right."

"You're referring to what happened to Dr. Gordone's practice in Upper Montclair?" I asked.

"I'm sorry, I'm not being clear." Alma sighed, wiped her eyes, and folded her hands in her lap. "Dr. Gordone was the only father I've ever known, but he wasn't my birth father—something Mother didn't tell me until after he died. No, the mistake she was referring to was with my *real* father."

Beside me, Billie ducked her head and started writing in her notepad. I glanced down and read: OH, SHIT!

"My mother and father married when my mother was very young," Alma was saying. "But when his family discovered she was black, they had the marriage annulled, and they never saw each other again."

It was bad enough, trying to figure out how to tell Alma about her mother's marriage to Chuck Zuccari, but what she'd just told us left me sick at heart and not knowing quite how to proceed. Chuck Zuccari had married his daughter and fathered her baby!

I glanced at Billie, who was tapping her pen on her notepad, the same awful realization written all over her face. "Did you ever meet your father, ma'am?" I asked carefully. "Or find out who he was?"

"Mother wouldn't tell me his name, and naturally my birth certificate said my father was Earl Gordone. She and Dr. Gordone had gotten married right after her marriage to my father was annulled, so I don't know if even he knew the truth." She looked up at us, tears again in her eyes. "But I know my mother never got over what my father and his people did to her. And what happened to us in Montclair only made her worse. By the time I was in my teens, she'd married and divorced again—"

"This would be Mr. Thornton?" I asked, my mind still reeling.

"William Thornton, that's right." She nodded, a frown crossing her face. "Right skin tone, but he was a gambler, and violent, too. We ended up broke and on the wrong side of the tracks in Newark, this time with the black kids beating me up because they thought I was white. But then I went away to college, where nobody knew me, and things were better. My mother made me promise to keep my mouth shut and let people make their own assumptions about who and what I was."

Alma looked from me to Billie, her face flushed with embarrassment. "You must think I'm a pitiful excuse for a black person," she said as she blew her nose, "but I never tried actively to pass. I just fell into it. And when my mother found out, she was so thrilled that I'd been able to accomplish something she hadn't. After I graduated, she convinced me it was better not to come home, lest someone found out. I used to write, but she never wrote back. Then she moved again and I lost track of her completely. I haven't seen or heard from her in almost three years now."

During which time Alma had settled into her new life—the one her mother had struggled so hard for her to have—and stumbled straight into hell. But as much as her story sickened me, I hadn't lived Alma's life, or her mother's, so how could I judge. "But you should know," I said, "that in addition to Ms. Lippincott, Mr. Merritt discussed the P.I.'s report directly with your husband."

"Chuck knew?" she whispered, her lips barely moving. "For how long?"

"Why do you ask how long your husband knew?" I asked, noting the stricken look on her face.

Alma beat a fist into her lap. "I *knew* it was something!"

"Why do you say that?" Billie asked.

"I kept asking him what was wrong, but Chuck said it was nothing."

"But you weren't convinced," I prompted, glancing at Billie.

She shook her head. "When Chuck found out I was pregnant, he was thrilled at first. Then in the late spring, around the end of my first trimester, everything changed. He became distant, even hostile at times, questioning whether the baby was his and then badgering me to abort it."

I felt my pulse quicken. "Do you know any other reason he could have had a change of heart about your baby?"

"I never cheated on my husband, so don't even go there!" she whispered fiercely. "I just thought he was just having an old man's doubts. Not that my husband was old, mind you, but . . . he just changed so *completely*, I figured it was those kind of doubts, or him being turned off to me being pregnant . . . I mean, he even stopped sleeping with me."

Embarrassed, she fell silent. Billie and I exchanged pained looks, then Billie took a breath and said: "And you never thought the changes in your . . . husband's affections had anything to do with the secret you were keeping about your race?"

"Or anything else?" I added.

"Never!" She shook her head, bewildered. "What are you driving at?"

"Ma'am, I need you to prepare yourself." I took in a deep breath, and looked her in the eyes. "What I need to tell you is going to be hard to hear."

"For God's sake, tell me!"

And so I did, as gently as I could, everything about the lies her mother and father had kept to themselves and told each other and how the secret of her birth that her mother had kept all these years had surfaced to poison them all.

Alma's face went slack, and her eyes dull. "You're wrong!" she murmured. "Surely there's been some mistake."

"I wish there were, but given what you've just told us and the P.I.'s report, we're pretty sure of it. Chuck Zuccari is your father."

Alma sat, her eyes filled with unbelieving tears. And then, from somewhere deep in her soul, she moaned, a sound of betrayal that dissolved the space between us. I could feel myself slipping inside her skin, feel the corrosiveness of old secrets eating away at her life, as they had at mine, eat away at flesh and bone, blood and marrow.

But the moment passed and I was back in my own skin, watching Alma gulp and gasp for air, hyperventilating to the point where she began to slump in her wheelchair. I hurried to her side and held her steady while Billie exited the interview room, blowing past Jerry Gales, who was waiting outside.

"What happened?" Gales demanded as he stepped into the room. "What did you say to her?"

"She's had a bit of a shock is all, sir," I assured him. "She'll be all right."

Billie returned with a cup of ice. After a few minutes of ice applied to Alma's neck and gentle reassurance, we were able to bring her back. But as her eyes opened I could tell this was not the place she wanted to be, nor Gales, Billie, and I the people she wanted to see. "I need to talk to my mother," she whispered.

"At the appropriate time, we can give you the number we have for her," I assured her.

She motioned me closer and whispered, her lips barely moving: "Please don't tell Jerry about . . . I'd hate for something like this to tarnish Chuck's legacy."

After the hell Chuck Zuccari's lies had put her and her mother through, I was stunned at Alma's willingness to protect the man. "We'll do our best, ma'am."

Gales moved behind her chair. "Perhaps I should be getting Mrs. Zuccari back home, Detective," he said, oblivious to how she cringed at the title.

"Of course, sir, but I just have a couple more questions for your client."

"Haven't you badgered this poor woman enough?" Gales said.

Alma held up a hand. "No, Jerry, let them do their job. We've got to get to the bottom of who shot my . . . Chuck and killed poor Malik."

Unless she was the greatest actress on earth, Alma's willingness to go on just convinced me she had nothing to do with the shooting. I motioned Gales to a seat and gave Alma a few more moments to compose herself. "Did your—did Chuck mention a project he was working on with Mr. Engalla shortly before the shooting? Or mention any concerns he had about Mario, or an employee named Natalie Johnson?"

"The only thing Chuck talked about during that time was the joint venture with Malik and Habiba Shareef." Again her blue eyes welled up with tears. Had it occurred to her that Chuck might have pushed her toward the Shareefs and their venture because he knew who she was?

Oblivious to what was transpiring, Gales patted Alma's hand reassuringly. "We understand the LAPD and FBI seized records from the company and Mr. Zuccari's children. Are we to assume Mario and this Johnson woman are suspects in the shooting?"

Disregarding his question, I spoke directly to Alma. "It would help us tremendously if you could provide us access to Mr. Zuccari's personal financial records. We need to be sure someone wasn't trying to blackmail him."

"Why would someone want to blackmail Chuck?" Gales said, antennae up.

Ignoring the question, Billie asked Alma whether Chuck had told her about the threatening letter. "He mentioned it," she replied, "but he never showed it to me. Now I can understand why."

Gales looked from Alma to Billie to me, a baffled look on his face. "Am I missing something here?" he asked.

"So was my—" Here, Alma hesitated, unsure of what to say. "Is that who you think might have blackmailed Chuck?"

"It's something we have to look at."

"I see." The possibility seemed to shake Chuck and Isabelle's daughter to her core. "You have my permission to review anything you like."

"Alma," Gales broke in. "Are you sure you want to open Chuck's personal affairs to the police and the Feds without a subpoena?"

"We can certainly obtain one," I assured the attorney. "But we'd be wasting valuable time that I frankly don't think we have, given Mr. Zuccari's condition."

Alma turned to her attorney. "She's right, Jerry. I want to be able to go back to that hospital and tell my—tell Chuck they've arrested the person who shot him and my baby." Focusing her attention on me, she said: "If you can provide Mr. Gales with a list of items you need, we can have everything sent up to you tonight."

"It would be faster to have one of our people go with you and pick them up."

While Billie walked Gales out to Detective Perkins to get a complete list, Alma sat in her wheelchair, her face suffused with pain as her emotions caught up with her. "D-does this mean Mario is my brother?"

"Most likely, yes."

She nodded as if confirming something to herself. "You know, from the day I met him at that convention, I felt like I'd known Mario all my life. He was like a kindred spirit . . . so intent on succeeding, and yet so sad. It's like there was a piece of him missing. Just like in me." She frowned suddenly and asked: "Is it possible—could Mario have known about all this?"

"Why do you ask?"

"Last night, when Chuck took a turn for the worse, I called Mario and Gabriella. After all, they *are* his children." Her voice faltered, perhaps sensing the irony of her words, but she struggled on. "When Mario got to the hospital, he said something about chickens coming home to roost that I thought was sort of odd, but I thought he was still upset about not being named as president. Now I'm not so sure what he meant."

"I appreciate you telling me this, ma'am," I said as I gathered up my notebook. "And we'll certainly follow up on it. But in the meantime, it's essential that you not say anything about this to Mario or anyone else."

She smiled bitterly. "Who could I tell something like this?"

She seemed to have aged another ten years since coming through the door. "If there's nothing else, Detective Justice, I need to head back to find those documents, and go back to the hospital." She slowly moved her wheelchair to the door.

"There is one more thing." At Alma's mention of the hospital, a memory flickered into my consciousness that sent me back to my notebook. "Detective Thorfinsen asked you something at the hospital on Monday about the night of the shooting that I just need to double-check."

I found my notation, hastily scribbled when I'd walked in on her conversation with Thor. " 'The last thing I remember,' you said, 'was Chuck turning around and pushing me away from him as we were waiting for the valet to bring our car.' You said you couldn't remember whether he pushed you toward the building or the street."

Her gaze focused on the far wall, Alma seemed lost in thought. Then she shuddered, her attention back on me. "I remember now. It was toward the building."

"You're certain?"

"Of course I'm certain!" she said, that same agitated note in her voice that I heard when she spoke to Thor. She reached into her hand-bag. "He was trying to shield me from that car!"

I watched as she started rearranging items in her bag, aware that she seemed unable to look me in the eye. Billie had just reentered the room when I said: "Frankly, ma'am, I'm confused."

"Confused about what?" Annoyed, Alma looked up from what she was doing and shifted her shoulders against the back of the chair. "I told you what happened!"

"But how can you be so sure in which direction he pushed you today when you've never been able to remember anything else about the moments leading up to the shooting or much of what happened afterward?"

Alma's hands started fluttering in her lap. "I guess the shock of all this jogged my memory." She sighed again and clenched her hands over her bag. "Up until ten minutes ago, that was the worst day of my life, Detective. Can you blame me for not being able to remember until now?"

I saw the defiance and pain on her face and flipped my notebook closed. "Thank you for your time." I walked over and took her hand. "Please call us if anything else occurs to you in the coming days. And we are truly sorry about everything."

She nodded, swallowing hard. "So am I, Detective."

Billie and I watched her move slowly down the hall. She was joined by Gales and Perkins, who Billie told me was going to follow them to Chuck and Alma's house to get those records. "What was with the question about which way her husband pushed her?" she asked.

"When she was talking to Thor about it on Monday, something just struck me as odd. And just now it hit me—we've been wondering if Alma might have had her husband shot to keep him from finding out she was black, or Chuck contracted to have her killed when he heard the news from Merritt. But what if it was more than that?"

I read to Billie from my notes. " 'That's about when my memory of that night runs out,' " she said. "Then she asked Thor if it mattered."

Billie frowned. "I'm not following you."

"See, I think she may have had her suspicions about Zuccari even then, but us telling her about his true identity just pushed her over the edge." I trailed Billie to her desk. "Think about it. We tell Alma Zuccari that her husband—this paragon of perfection—not only found out she was passing for white but is most likely her father, and all of a sudden she remembers on the night of the shooting that he pushed her out of the line of fire. Maybe our conversation has made her wonder if he contracted to have her killed, and pushing her was part of the plan, but she doesn't want to admit it."

"How on earth can we prove that?"

I brought my hand down on the original murder book from last summer. "Check the crime scene photos and witness interviews. Then talk to the uniforms on the scene, see if they remember the exact location of Alma's body in relation to Zuccari's."

"How about Habiba Shareef? Maybe she saw something."

"Good idea."

While Billie got busy I called Thor to brief him on our interview with Alma, catching him just as he was about to leave his daughter's house for the airport. "Good God!" he exclaimed. "Are you sure about Zuccari being Alma's father?"

"As sure as I can be without a paternity test talking to Belle Thornton myself. The latter of which I intend to do as soon as we're off the phone."

"Good. I drew a diagram of the crime scene as Alma described it at the hospital, if that'll help Billie."

"I'll have her compare it with the one I drew last summer. Meanwhile, I'm also going to talk to the D.A. on call, see if we should try for a court to stop Alma from pulling Zuccari off of that ventilator."

"Is he that far gone?"

"That's what it sounds like. And if Alma Zuccari's as angry at what Chuck's done to her and her mother as she ought to be, the last thing we want is her making a decision about whether he should live or die."

20

Nothing But the Son

By the time Mario appeared in our offices on Monday morning, flanked by the attorneys Merritt and Sarkisian, our team had been at it nonstop for almost twenty-four hours, making phone calls to Belle Thornton's nursing home in New Jersey finalizing the review of Mario's financial records, going over Chuck Zuccari's, getting reports in from SID's Latent Prints and Questioned Documents technicians, and conferring on strategy and jurisdictional issues with the Feds. While Billie was tracking down the officers at the scene that night, Thor, Perkins, and I met with Mario in MIA's office, where we'd arrayed ourselves and all the paperwork at one end of the conference table. Wunderlich and an FBI agent we'd met on Friday occupied the other end, forcing Mario and his attorneys to sit in the middle.

Before we could begin, Sarkisian said: "My client would like to make a statement."

"Okay." Thor raised an eyebrow at our team while Wunderlich and the FBI agent sat up a little straighter in their chairs.

Mario pulled a typed sheet out of his jacket pocket and began to read. "As long ago as last September, I began to suspect that my father, Carlo Zuccari, had entered into a conspiracy to murder Mr. Malik Shareef, a business associate."

Looks were exchanged around the room, but no one said a word.

Mario licked his lips and continued. "The reasons for his actions, I believed, stem from his belief that his wife, Alma, was having an affair with Mr. Shareef. I have since confirmed that Pete Collins, the company's security director, introduced my father to Jeff Leykis and Luis Ybarra, convicted felons known to Mr. Collins, whom my father paid to kill Mr. Shareef."

Last night Perkins had found canceled checks that Chuck had written to Leykis and Ybarra for twenty-five thousand each shortly before the shooting as well as several small checks Mario had written to them totalling the same amount, so Mario coming forward with his statement now was too little too late. He was about to continue when I interrupted him. "You can save the prepared statement for the press, Mr. Zuccari. How did you come by this information?"

"Ah . . ." Mario looked hesitantly to Merritt, who nodded encouragement. "Pete came to me last October, saying that Leykis and Ybarra were demanding an additional payment for an undisclosed assignment they'd undertaken for my father. It didn't take much to figure out what their assignment was and that what they were trying to do, in essence, was extort money from the company in exchange for their silence."

Thor smiled grimly. "And you're in the habit of opening your checkbook for every lowlife who comes knocking on your door demanding money?" As Mario blanched, Thor added: "We've seen the checks you wrote to them."

"There'd been rumors about Alma's interest in Mr. Shareef," Mario replied. "So I thought it best to pay them to go away. When they didn't, I figured maybe we should hire them to watch over my father and Alma, inasmuch as I didn't want to run the risk of retaliation from Mrs. Shareef for my father's indiscretion."

"*Indiscretion?*" Thor exclaimed, his smile growing to one of complete disbelief. "This little twerp did not call conspiracy to commit murder an indiscretion!"

At the same time, Wunderlich was saying: "That's it. I've heard enough of this crap." He gestured to his FBI colleague, who removed the handcuffs on his belt and approached the middle of the table. "Mario Zuccari, you're under arrest for embezzlement."

"What the—?" Merritt exclaimed as the agent pushed him aside, cuffed the protesting Mario, and moved him to their end of the table, where he sat squirming.

"Just a minute!" Sarkisian objected. "My client came here with every intention of cooperating in solving the murder of Mr. Shareef. Why are you accusing him of embezzlement?"

"Sit down and shut up, Mr. Sarkisian," Thor ordered, while Mario was being read his rights. "I don't know what kind of game your client is playing, but it's over now." He turned to Perkins. "Go on, Jackie. Tell them what we've got."

"Natalie Johnson and Felton Carruthers have been conspiring for four years with one of your managers in the Phillipines to embezzle funds from the company, at a rate of one to four hundred thousand per month." She flipped open a file and leafed through some papers. "Jose Agnafilo, a vice president in the company's Philippine operations in Laguna, approved the phony invoices for payment to Sonrisa Safety and Security and then Johnson would countersign them, except for two or three which were countersigned by Carruthers when the amounts exceeded her authorization limit. We suspect Agnafilo then funneled the money back to accounts Johnson and Carruthers had set up here and in the Philippines, judging by the bank statements we seized from their homes."

"Funny, your statement failed to mention any of this," Wunderlich said to Mario, toying with him like a cat with a ball of yarn.

"We thought the LAPD was more interested in the murder than the embezzlement," Merritt explained.

Thor snorted. "That's the lamest excuse I've heard in a long time. We're interested in whatever Mr. Zuccari has to tell us that's relevant to our investigation!"

"In exchange for?" Merritt asked.

"Mr. Zuccari's in no real position to bargain," Wunderlich replied, "given that he's known about the embezzlement for a year and has done nothing to stop it."

Mario's jaw tightened as he glanced nervously at Merritt, who cleared his throat. "We've suspected Natalie and Felton for some time," the attorney said. "At the board's direction, Mario was investigating it quietly, through the company's internal auditing department."

"We were hoping we could get Johnson and Carruthers to make restitution," Mario added, "and save the company and its stockholders a public scandal that could destroy shareholder value."

"Seems your client wants to do everything quietly," Thor said sarcastically, "even be an accessory after the fact to embezzlement and murder, as long as the company's precious stock price isn't compromised!"

"Wh-what are you talking about?" Mario's voice came out in a squeak. "I had nothing to do with any of this!"

"Then how do you account for your forging Felton Carruthers's signature on these authorizations to pay Sonrisa?" Perkins said, her hand resting on the report we'd received from Questioned Documents. "You signed them back in March of last year, a month *after* the audit manager from Shuttleworth and Bezney came to you with his suspicions."

"That's—that's not my signature!" he sputtered. "Felton must have done that on his own."

"Just like it's not your signature authorizing hiring Mr. Leykis and Mr. Ybarra?" Thor asked.

"I explained why we hired them!"

"Ah, yes, the extortion," Thor said, and shook his head. "Sorry, son, but we're not buying it. I think you're telling us about Leykis and Ybarra now because you knew we'd find the canceled checks you and the company wrote to them and wonder why they were being paid so handsomely. What happened—were these guys thugs you hired to shoot your father and then couldn't get rid of after they botched the job?"

"I would never pay someone to shoot my father," Mario said through gritted teeth.

"Why not?" I asked. "After all, he turned against you as his successor."

"That's not it!"

"Then why not?" Thor repeated, taunting him now. "Because you're such an upstanding citizen?"

"No!" Mario shouted. "Because, for all the sins my father's committed, God's got a greater punishment in mind for him than I could ever imagine!"

I picked up a file, walked over to Mario, and sat in the chair next to him. "I know you haven't been exactly chomping at the bit to help our investigation these past few days, Mario, but I'm surprised at this outright hostility toward your father. You've always impressed me as a loyal and dutiful son. Why the sudden change of heart?"

"The truth needed to come out." He turned away from me a bit, head down as he mumbled. "He's been lying for too many years."

I leaned forward and caught Thor's eye, saw him nod encouragement. "Lying about what, Mr. Zuccari?" I watched as Mario sat awkwardly in his chair, hands cuffed behind his back, his jaw working furiously. I leaned over and whispered: "Frankly, Mr. Zuccari, this bull you've been spreading around about your father contracting to have Malik Shareef murdered is a little hard to accept, especially given the fact that *you* were the one who was paying hush money to Leykis and Ybarra."

"Don't forget the money he paid Nilo Engalla to stop investigating the embezzlement," Perlans added.

"I did no such thing!" Mario asserted, but his eyes told me otherwise.

"I'm sorry, but my client doesn't have to listen to this," Sarkisian said, rising from his chair.

"Yes, David, he does!" Merritt interrupted. "We've got to get to the bottom of this if we have any hope of putting a face on this thing, what with the embezzlement, the conspiracy, and now Chuck's condition taking this unexpected turn."

"But you've already got Gabriella in place, running the company!" Sarkisian protested.

"Gabby's just a placeholder to appease her mother and get us through this transition," Merritt scoffed. "Everyone knows that Mario's the brains in this company. So if he's going down, I need to know so we can develop a strategy with the analysts."

He turned to Mario. "You know we've called a press conference for two, which is the timing the PR consultant advised to mitigate damage to the share price before the closing bell. Mario, please, for your sake and the sake of the company, help us get this thing resolved."

After a long silence Mario shrugged a reluctant agreement. From the folder we'd received from Latent Prints that morning, I laid out the photos and reports for the attorneys to see. "Our Latent Print technician matched Mario's thumbprint on the envelope used to send the money to Nilo Engalla."

"But they never took my fingerprints!" Mario protested to Sarkisian.

"Didn't need to," I said. "We had these." I spread out the photographed fingerprints from the old letters Chuck had sent to Mario while he was in college as well as those taken from Mario's bank statements and the letter from Belle Thornton to Chuck. "Your prints are on all three."

Thor added: "All we have to do now is get a print from you to confirm our suspicions."

"And there's more." I picked up the copies and walked back to my chair. "I think this letter that we found taped under a drawer in your desk is the real reason you've had a change of heart toward your father. Your thumbprint was on it, too." I slid the plastic-encased letter from Belle to Zuccari across the table for Merritt to read. "Does this sound familiar, Mr. Merritt?"

Merritt leaned over to examine the letter. "I never saw the original, but it reads like the letter Chuck got from that nutcase last year."

"She's not a nutcase!" Mario protested.

"You know this woman?"

"The nutcase is Mario's mother," I said softly, sliding the photo of Mario, Belle, and Chuck across the table for Merritt to see. "He's been visiting her and paying for her care for the last seven months, according to her nursing home. How long have you known she was alive, Mario?"

Mario fingered the photo, and swallowed hard to hold back the tears. "Since February. She called the office, told me about the private investigator tracking her down, and asked if we could meet. So I went to New Jersey, and she was able to explain a lot of what happened when I was little, before that second stroke paralyzed her."

Merritt fell back in his chair. "Are you sure this isn't some kind of hoax?" he asked faintly. "I was under the impression your mother died a long time ago."

"So were a lot of people." I proceeded to give the attorneys a run-down on the strange family history which the two men listened to quietly while Mario fumed. But when I got to Alma's connection to the Zuccari's first wife and son, Mario's shoulders slumped and he moaned as if he'd been sucker punched. Obviously, Belle hadn't shared this part of the story with her son.

When I was finished, Merritt groaned and lowered his head into his hands while Sarkisian just stared at his client in disbelief. "This is a disaster!" he muttered. "When news of this leaks out, the stock is going to drop like a rock!"

But Mario just stared, his gaze fixed on some distant shore none of us could see. I approached him again cautiously, aware that the interview could go sideways any minute. "Mario," I began softly. "I don't blame you for forging those payment authorizations to Sonrisa. You'd discovered how your family had sent your mother away. The money Johnson and Carruthers were kicking back to you was a small price for how your family ruined your life."

Mario just stared, his head barely nodding.

"I wouldn't be surprised if you used the money to pay for your mother's nursing home care."

"My mother said them taking me away from her like that was as good as killing her," he whispered. "She said her life was never the same after that."

"Not another word!" Sarkisian shouted.

Merritt cleared his throat. "David's telling you right, Mario."

"I don't care anymore," Mario insisted, pushing away his statement. "Dad never told me he suspected Alma of infidelity. I heard that from Gabriella. I said that because I couldn't think of any other reason Dad would have hired those two to do something so horrible. But now I get it—Dad wanted Alma and the baby dead. The sin he had committed was too much to bear."

"You're saying your father *did* hire them?"

He nodded. "They had a note in Dad's handwriting, detailing his and Alma's movements for the entire week, and highlighting the dinner arrangements at Ristorante Rex that night and what time they'd be leaving the restaurant. They waited a half block away from the restaurant until ten, the time Dad promised to have everyone outside."

"Where's this note now?"

"Leykis and Ybarra kept it for insurance purposes, they said."

"Where would Leykis and Ybarra be now?"

"Where they always are on Mondays," Mario replied. "At the hospital with my father and Alma."

H ow'd it go?" Billie asked as we emerged from MIA's office.

"Got him dead to rights on the embezzlement," I replied, "but he wouldn't cop to the conspiracy to murder charge. Swears his father was the one who contracted with Leykis and Ybarra. Claims there's a letter in his father's handwriting that spells it all out."

"Who was the intended victim?" Billie asked.

"Mario thinks Alma. Why?"

"My interviews with the responding officers and the diagrams of the crime scene back up that theory. She and Zuccari were only a few feet apart when they fell. So, if Chuck Zuccari really *did* try to push her away when he saw the car coming, he didn't do such a good job."

21

After the Dust Has Settled

By noon, **Mario** and his attorney were on their way to booking on the embezzlement, the FBI was working with Merritt on the logistics of hooking up Natalie Johnson and Felton Carruthers at the company's headquarters, and Wunderlich and Perkins were wrapping up the transfer of files to the Feds' custody. While Thor was updating our lieutenant, Billie had gotten home addresses for Leykis and Ybarra from CZ Toys' human resources department, and the two of us had prepared and obtained a judge's signature on a warrant to search the apartment they shared in Cerritos as well as the office they maintained at the hospital.

We'd hit their apartment first and spent two fruitless hours tossing it. Now it was three, and Billie and I were heading farther south, dropping behind that Orange Curtain as we led the way for the black-and-white containing Thor and a couple of uniforms from Central Bureau. As I guided the car down the same stretch of I-5 I'd covered with Thor just a week ago, I couldn't help thinking what a difference a week had made—in this case and in my life. But although I'd uncovered the reasons behind my brother's behavior, I still hadn't cracked the mystery of Paul Taft, just as there was something about Chuck Zuccari's behavior and motives that still puzzled me. "I know we've been over this before," I said to Billie, "but do you really think Chuck Zuccari contracted with those roughnecks to kill Alma and her baby?"

"Before your interview and my reassessment of the crime scene, my money was on Mario," Billie conceded. "And even though he's got a motive, too, the more I think about Chuck Zuccari, the more I'm liking him for the shootings."

"Just because Mario says so?"

She shook her head vigorously. "If the truth about Zuccari's marriage to Alma ever got out, it would have ruined him socially and politically as well as done some serious damage to his company. And given what I've heard about him being so sensitive to appearances, he could have resorted to murder to save face."

"Zuccari just doesn't seem the type to take such overt action."

"I disagree. From everything I've heard and read in the files, Zuccari's been a shrewd businessman for almost thirty years. All the deals he's done, and the risks he's taken to make his company a success—I don't see him letting it go down the tubes because of something in his past."

"But the man's a weasel when it comes to his personal life! He let his family run his first wife away on a humbug, then lied to his son about what really happened."

"What would you have done under the circumstances?" Billie asked.

"Told the truth, for starters!" I snapped.

"Chill, Charlotte!" Billie said, glancing at me sideways as I maneuvered through traffic. "There's no need to run us off the road because Zuccari lied to his kid!"

Or because your parents lied to you, my little voice chided. "Sorry. But I could sooner imagine Chuck Zuccari making up some excuse and divorcing Alma than contracting to have her killed. And, if he did, why have it done in the front of the Oviatt Building, with all those witnesses? A dozen places would have been easier logistically than downtown L.A."

"Yet, in a perverse sort of way, I understand it," Billie said. "Remember that guy in Boston who killed his wife and claimed it was some ubiquitous black man? He had the Boston PD scooping up every black man in a jogging suit for miles around. At least Zuccari didn't play the race card!"

"We did it for him," I replied. "We were so preoccupied running after gangbangers and Black Muslims, the suspect right under our noses almost got away. Even from his hospital bed, Chuck Zuccari's been playing us for chumps all along."

Billie snorted. "Player got played, far as I'm concerned. He's the one who's near death, not Alma or his kid."

"Yeah, but look at the damage he's done to them, physically and emotionally. Neither of them will ever be right after this."

I pulled into the parking structure, showed the attendant my ID, and told him to let Ms. Gipson in Administration know we were there. Before we left, Thor had notified the hospital's chief nursing officer and the Orange County Sheriff's Department of our intention to inter-view and possibly arrest Chuck Zuccari's security guards so they could provide adequate backup. Gipson had asked that we call as soon as we arrived so someone could meet us at the entrance.

"Justice, you and I will interview Leykis and Ybarra in the adminis-tration suite while Billie and the guys here search their office," Thor explained after we joined him and the uniforms around the black-and-white. "One way or another, we're hooking them up, for either the ex-tortion or the murder for hire."

"Won't they get suspicious if they get a call to report to Administra-tion?" I asked. "It would be better to surprise them."

"The hospital's administrator and the OCSD determined they didn't want to risk jeopardizing anyone's safety if things go sideways, so this was the best alternative."

"Seems like a lot of trouble for a man who's brain dead," Billie said.

"Even so, they've got to think about patient safety first, Zuccari's or anybody else who's on that floor." Thor checked his watch. "Alma was due in Administration by three. Gipson said she'd call the unit and get her to come down on the pretext they needed to meet with her to re-view some paperwork related to disconnecting her husband's ventila-tor. Then she was to call Leykis and Ybarra down, have the deputies intercept them and hold them for us."

A redheaded male in a brown uniform hurried toward us, said, "Heard you arrived," and introduced himself as Lieutenant Cordell Doyle, chief of police for the sheriff's Mission Viejo division. "There's been a change of plans. We've set up a SWAT command post right off the lobby."

"SWAT?" Thor frowned. "What happened?"

"We've got a situation," he said, leading the way in a trot.

As we moved quickly to the entrance and through the lobby it was obvious from the number of cars and deputies milling about that the initial plan had backfired. "Our deputies had taken positions at the main elevator lobby on one," Doyle explained. "Zuccari's wife came down as planned, no problem. But Leykis and Ybarra took the stairs, saw two of our deputies, turned tail, and ran back upstairs. At the top of the stairs, they drew their weapons and fired on Deputy Locke, who returned fire, wounding one of the assailants."

Locke and his partner had ended up in the ER, Leykis and Ybarra in Two South. "They've taken Zuccari's nurse as their hostage," Doyle explained.

"What about the one who's wounded?" I asked.

"Luis Ybarra," Gipson supplied. "Nurse O'Farrell's tried to patch him up, but she said it's serious."

"So you've opened negotiations?" Thor asked.

"With Leykis, about ten minutes ago," Doyle confirmed.

"Any demands?"

"Just that we get someone in there to patch up his buddy."

"Will you?" I asked.

"Not if it means jeopardizing anyone else," Doyle snapped.

In the makeshift command post they'd set up in Admitting, one of the interior conference rooms had been given over to OCSD communications equipment and hospital floor plans. Another white male whom Doyle identified as Lieutenant Ingram, the SWAT commander, was talking via walkie-talkie to his colleagues while a brown-uniformed female and her male counterpart were poring over the floor plans with a clearly tense Avis Gipson and an engineering type. Off in one corner, Alma Zuccari sat in her wheelchair, the activity around her barely registering in her lost eyes.

While Billie went to comfort her I asked Doyle whether we knew Leykis and Ybarra's exact position. The female deputy, a brown-skinned Asian with FERGUSON on her nametag, replied: "They won't tell us, but we've been able to observe a trail of blood down the main corridor of the unit, leading off to the right."

"So they're probably in Mr. Zuccari's room," Gipson added.

"Is there another way onto Two South other than the main entrance?" I asked.

"There's a service entrance that opens up onto the main corridor," the engineer said, indicating a door to the left of the unit's entrance on the plans.

I felt the glimmer of an idea and said, "If you cut power just to that Two South Unit"—and saw the engineer's hesitant nod—"what happens to Mr. Zuccari's ventilator?"

"Nothing. The backup generator will kick in."

"How long does that take?"

"Just a few seconds," he replied.

"In those few seconds, will the loss of power set off the alarms on his ventilator?"

Gipson nodded. "It should, but—"

I glanced at Billie and Deputy Ferguson, the glimmer coalescing into a plan. "What sizes do you ladies wear?"

By two, the three of us were dressed in blue scrubs, white lab coats, and IDs cobbled together by Human Resources. We waited on the second floor, a dozen yards from the entrance to Two South and a red crash cart at the ready, while Doyle stood at the elevator lobby, walkie-talkie in hand, waiting for a signal from the command post.

Earlier, when we were working out our plan and contingencies downstairs, I had argued that it was important that the team sent in there be female. "A couple of ex-cons like them will smell cop all over your guys or ours. At least we stand a chance."

And since I was the only female officer who'd been on the unit before, I'd insisted that I be part of the team sent in. So they'd found Ferguson, Billie, and me some surgical scrubs and masks, with a flowered surgical cap for me as an extra disguise. Ferguson and Billie had gotten a lesson in the maintenance of ventilators from the engineer, and Gipson had given me last-minute instructions on how a physician would approach and treat Ybarra's injury. As I listened I had a fleeting thought that I should call Aubrey, but since I hadn't seen or talked to him since going to the office Sunday morning, I couldn't figure out what I would say.

Maybe you should start with I'm sorry.

Mistaking the look on my face, Thor had taken me aside. "Are you sure you're up for this?" he'd whispered, the concern on his own face plain.

"You worried they'll recognize me, or that I'm not ready to handle this kind of situation?"

"I'm worried about you putting yourself in unnecessary danger," he replied.

"I appreciate your concern, Thor, but I'll be fine." I moved to the crash cart and double-checked the location of the items I'd need. "I'll be the last one in, anyway. They'll be so focused on the cart, they won't even see me."

Let's hope so, my little voice had fretted.

Now that I was waiting outside the entrance to Two South, that little voice had progressed from fretting to praying. The psalm my grandmother gave me. Snippets of meditations. Whatever I could think of. I felt in my pocket, remembered I'd left the yellow marble from Dr. P's office in my blazer. Remembered I had an appointment with him this morning that I'd forgotten to keep. I hoped I'd be able to tell him why tomorrow.

Billie leaned over and whispered: "You okay?"

"Just wanting to get this over with."

Doyle's walkie-talkie crackled to life, and he gave us the nod. The lights flickered, then went off, the air circulation system shuddering to a stop. The ensuing silence was soon filled by the faint squeals of monitor alarms alerting staff to the loss of power to equipment all over the floor.

A voice came over the hospital's loudspeaker, reading the message we'd scripted with Engineering: "We are experiencing a temporary loss of power on the second and third floors. Nurses, please reset the alarms on patient equipment and await arrival of biomedical engineers to recalibrate your equipment."

"You think this will work?" Billie whispered as the voice repeated the message.

"I hope so, for everyone's sake," Ferguson said.

About five minutes later, Doyle's walkie-talkie crackled again. Doyle listened, then trotted down the hall to where we were positioned. "Gipson just got off the phone with Leykis. He said only the surgeon and one biomed tech can come onto the unit."

"What do we do now?" Billie asked me.

"Go to Plan B."

Ferguson asked if I was ready. "As I'll ever be."

I fell in step behind her, pushing the crash cart, grateful her height would block their field of vision until I could get into the room. I put my weight behind the crash cart and I felt it pick up speed until I had to trot to catch up. We started the diversionary chatter we'd rehearsed earlier with Gipson, about the new signage that had just been installed and our take on the cute new radiologist who'd just been hired.

When we hit the door to Zuccari's room, we found Jeff Leykis, standing like a monolith by the window, legs apart, gun trained on whoever came through that door. Michaela O'Farrell was dividing her attention between Chuck Zuccari and Luis Ybarra, who was lying in the fetal position on the other bed in the room, his breathing almost as mechanical as the all-but-dead man's on that ventilator. Ybarra's left shoulder oozed blood, which the nurse was trying to staunch with a towel.

Ferguson positioned the cart between the two beds and went to the head of Zuccari's bed, next to the ventilator, and started fingering the dials and studying the readout.

"Thank God you're here . . . Doctor Scott?" O'Farrell said, giving my name badge a quizzical look.

"Put this on." I handed her the mask, squeezing her hand as I did so. "Don't want to risk contaminating the patient's wound."

Ferguson offered a mask to Leykis. "Put it on the foot of the bed there," he ordered, gesturing with the gun. She sneaked a look at me. So much for her getting close enough to take the gun from him the way we'd planned.

Nurse O'Farrell had moved to the crash cart, positioning herself so Leykis couldn't see what I was doing. "They wouldn't let me leave the room, and I'd run out of four-by-fours," she explained, opening several packages and passing them across the bed to me, then rummaging around in the drawers of the cart until she found a larger package. "I'll just open the pressure bandage for you."

Ybarra moaned as I applied pressure to the wound with the four-by-fours. "That shit hurts!"

"It's going to hurt more when I apply this." I pressed the bandage over the gauze, saw it wasn't going to do the job, and asked O'Farrell for more four-by-fours.

Ybarra's eyes fluttered, and he muttered something unintelligible. "What's he saying?" Leykis demanded.

"He's going into shock," I said, remembering my briefing with Gipson. "We're going to lose him unless I can get him into surgery."

"No way," Ybarra mumbled. "Do it here!"

I saw Ferguson frown behind her mask. "These aren't sterile conditions!" I protested.

Leykis pointed his gun at O'Farrell. "Figure it out, or I'll blow her head off!" He glanced over at Ferguson. "Aren't you finished yet?"

"I need to ask the doctor a question," she said mildly.

"So ask it and get the fuck out of here!"

"Not now!" I snapped at Ferguson and moved to the cart.

"Where are you going?" Leykis demanded, turning the gun on me.

I stopped and said, "To get the Versed," hoping I remembered the name correctly.

"What's that?" Leykis asked suspiciously as O'Farrell tied off Ybarra's arm.

"Something to tranquilize the patient. Unless you want him to bite down on one of those bullets in your gun while I operate on his shoulder."

Leykis jerked his head toward O'Farrell. "Let her get it."

I nodded to the nurse, watched as she got the syringe from the second drawer, wondered if she felt the gun I'd hidden in the back. "I'll give it to him," she volunteered.

"Let the doctor do it," Leykis said.

"Doctors couldn't find a vein to save their souls," O'Farrell said with a nervous twitter as she inserted the needle into Ybarra's vein.

"That's why God created nurses," I added.

"Take off that mask!" Leykis ordered. "I can't understand what you're saying."

At Zuccari's bed, I could see Ferguson pause, her eyes wide. "You heard what Dr. Scott said," O'Farrell spoke up, dropping the syringe in a wastebasket. "She can't, unless you want to infect the wound and lose your friend. And you should put on your mask, too."

Leykis refused. "I'll be fine over here."

I glanced down at Ybarra, who was already on his way out. I took a deep breath and said: "Let's get started."

We'd been there two minutes over the five we'd estimated. I saw Deputy Ferguson glancing at the clock on the wall and knew she was aware of the time, too. "Before you begin, Doctor, can you take a look at the levels on this ventilator?" she asked. "I'm not sure they're correct."

"I need to read the patient's chart, to see what the order was."

"To hell with Zuccari!" Leykis snapped. "You need to take care of Luis."

"This'll only take a second." I grabbed the chart from the foot of Zuccari's bed and moved past Leykis to where Ferguson stood, my back to the gunman. "Nurse, start prepping the patient. There are some drapes in the bottom drawer of the cart."

Nurse O'Farrell crouched on her haunches. "I don't see them."

"I know they're down there." I moved back to the cart. "Let me show you."

I opened some drawers, found the one with the second gun at the bottom. "Here they are," I said, pushing O'Farrell down as I crouched and turned.

And prayed Ferguson had given the signal like we'd agreed.

"What the—" Leykis exclaimed.

It was the last thing he said before all hell broke loose.

With as much death as I'd seen over the last few years, I thought I might feel fear or revulsion to see one more dead body. But I must confess I felt nothing but relief to learn, after the dust had settled, that my, Ferguson's, and the SWAT team's bullets had hit Leykis six times—three in the chest, two in the stomach, and one in the head. Of course, I'm assuming that last bit, because there wasn't much of his head left after the shooting was over.

Things happened fast after that. Ferguson went out to signal the all clear, which allowed the team of doctors and nurses from ER to enter Zuccari's room to ensure his ventilator was still working. Ybarra, fully unconscious from the drug, was taken out on a gurney and to another room, where he would be monitored under guard until he came to. "You did that very well," I heard Ferguson compliment the nurse as she escorted her from the room. "I'll have to remember to request some of that Versed if I ever have surgery."

An hour later, the crime scene had been isolated, and I had just been turned loose by one of the OCSD detectives sent out to investigate the shooting. I found Billie waiting for me outside in the hall. "Where's Thor?"

"Down in the command center, talking on the phone to Lieutenant Stobaugh. I told him I'd wait for you." She squeezed my arm. "How're you doing?"

"Better than I would have thought."

One of the other OCSD detectives popped his head out the door, holding a couple of bloodstained pages in his hand. "Found this in Leykis's wallet. We'll need to keep it for evidence, but I thought you might want to read it."

Billie read it first. "Damn!" she said, and handed it over to me. "You were right. Zuccari played us *big*-time."

It was a letter in what looked like Chuck Zuccari's hand, laying out his itinerary for the days surrounding the shooting, along with a second sheet that I was sure Leykis and Ybarra hadn't shown to Mario. "Remember, your final payment is contingent on only <u>one</u> person being killed," it read, then gave the name and address of a bank and an account number for funds that apparently were being held in the names of Chuck Zuccari and the two men. "I have several accounts at this bank," he wrote, "so Alma will be taking the death certificate to them soon after the job is done. Ask for Sandra Smith, the bank manager. She'll be sure the funds are released directly to you."

"I knew there was more to it than we thought," I said. "Zuccari had contracted with Leykis and Ybarra to have *himself* killed."

"And in a way that would preserve his reputation and keep his secrets," Billie added.

"Or so he thought."

Thor appeared on the unit, an unreadable look on his face. "Charlotte, we need to get you up to Cedars right away."

"Why, what happened?"

"Chief Youngblood called. It's your brother."

From the ticket found in his car, the police figured Paul Taft must have been camped out in the parking structure of Perris's building since Sunday night. "But your brother had been in depositions all day and didn't get to his office until three," Uncle Henry explained when I spoke to him from the car. "Taft accosted him, they argued, and Taft shot your brother in the arm."

Perris managed to get back in his car and exit the structure, Taft in pursuit. The chase continued as Taft pursued Perris through L.A. and West Hollywood, driving north along San Vicente. "We think Perris was trying to lead Taft to the West Hollywood sheriff's station, but we're not certain."

By the time they got to Santa Monica Boulevard, there were black-and-whites from the LAPD, Beverly Hills, and the L.A. County Sheriff's Department in pursuit. The chase ended when Perris ran a red light and was hit by a Toyota, spun out, and was hit in turn by Taft's SUV, which flipped over, pinning the FBI agent inside.

Perris had been taken to Cedars-Sinai Medical Center, where he was in surgery. Taft was in custody at the jail ward of L.A. County–USC Medical Center, undergoing surgery as well. "They'll charge him with attempted murder and extortion if and when he comes out of surgery," Uncle Henry informed me. "All because he was trying to locate and shake down Cinque Lewis's heirs for the money he thought Lewis had hidden from his years dealing drugs, according to what he told Perris."

"And he was trying to use Keith's files to get to the heirs, just like he tried to use the Smiley Face shootings to get to Eddie Aycox."

"When Perris refused to give up their names, Taft shot him," my godfather concluded. "That man's got a lot to answer for."

So did my godfather for not telling me the truth about Keith assisting the LAPD. But ultimately, I couldn't have cared less about Uncle Henry, Paul Taft and the days of reckoning they had coming. My energy was focused on Perris and on comforting Louise, who was pacing in the waiting room outside of surgery when I got to the hospital. "I don't know how I'm going to tell the kids," she sobbed when she saw me.

"Where are they now?"

"Your mother picked them up from school. She and your father have them over at their house."

"What have the doctors said?"

"He was pinned between the Toyota and the SUV. In addition to the gunshot wound, his right leg is shattered, and he's got internal injuries, too. They said they might have to remove his gallbladder and his spleen."

"Oh, God!" I crumpled into a chair, overwhelmed by tears and guilt. I felt around in my pocket for my yellow marble, felt nothing but car keys and lint. "I was so horrible to him Saturday night. I can't lose him like this!"

My sister-in-law came to my side and put an arm around me. "Perris finally told me about what he and your husband had done. The last thing he said before he left the house this morning was that he hoped, after the dust has settled, you might find a way to forgive him."

"I will, Louise." *God help me, if You let him live, I will.*

A man in scrubs and a white coat entered the waiting room and made his way toward us. I could see blood—my brother's blood—on his bootie-covered feet.

"Mrs. Justice?" He looked uncertainly between the two of us.

Louise gripped my hand. "That's me."

He wasn't smiling? Why wasn't he smiling? "Your husband made it through the surgery, but we've got to watch him very closely for the next twenty-four hours."

Through my darkening vision, I could see Louise nodding, tears spilling from her eyes.

The surgeon was saying something about how to get to the ICU when my phone rang. The prefix told me it was from within the department, but the number didn't look familiar. "If that's Matt or Joymarie—" Louise began.

Head spinning, I started to shut it off. "It's just my office."

"There are a few other things you should know," the surgeon was saying as he pulled Louise aside.

"Take your call, Char," she said over her shoulder. "I'll catch up with you in the ICU."

A voice on the other end said: "Detective Justice?"

My ears were buzzing, making it hard for me to hear. "I'm sorry, but I can't talk right now."

"Charlotte, is that you?" The voice was male, and sounded concerned. "This is Dr. Wychowski."

"I know I missed my appointment." My words came out in a tumble and I could feel myself start to tremble. "But I can't—I can't do this right now, Dr. P. There was a shooting—"

"At the hospital in Orange County, I know. It was on the radio."

I steadied myself against a wall. Why couldn't I stop shaking? "Not that. My brother. The doctor said we could see him. I have to see him, then talk to the detectives and the D.A.—"

"What happened to your brother?"

"See, I was so awful to him on Saturday. I have to see him. If the shooter survives, they'll charge him with attempted murder, but I have to see Perris—"

"Charlotte, listen to me. You need to come into the office right now."

"Didn't you hear what I *said?* I can't!"

"Detective, if you have any hopes of keeping your job, you'll get yourself down here, do you understand? I'll give you *one* hour, no more."

I made it to Chinatown in fifty-six minutes, fully intending to kick Pablo Wychowski's ass. But when I got to his office, and saw the worry in his brown eyes and that bowl of marbles on the end table, all I could do was collapse on his love seat and cry.

Dr. P. sat facing me in a chair, holding out the box of Kleenex and listening to the hell I'd been through since I'd seen him on Wednesday. "Charlotte, you can't go on like this."

I pretended he was talking about my crying, but I knew what he meant. "You're going to have to stop and deal with this."

"What are you saying, that I'm losing it? Like I lost that goddamn marble?"

"No, what I'm saying is you need time and a safe place to sort through your emotions and heal. And from what you've just told me, this is about the safest place you have right now."

I shuddered, knowing there was truth in what he was telling me. "So you want me to reschedule? I probably can't come in until after we meet with the D.A. on—"

"I don't think you understand. You can't heal and investigate homicides at the same time."

"You're kidding, right?" When I realized he wasn't, my tears started anew. "What will I do without my job? Who will I be?"

"That's what I'd like to help you find out. If you'll allow me to do that."

I sat on that love seat, feeling Dr. P.'s concern, knowing that neither the job nor my family, Perris's recovery nor even Aubrey Scott's lovemaking could make this pain go away. And that my life wouldn't be right until it did.

"Okay." I fished a new marble out of the bowl, slipped it into my pocket without even looking at it. "Where do we begin?"

Acknowledgments

To my untiring editor, Joe Blades, thank you for your wisdom, support, and belief in this book. To trusted agent and advisor Faith Childs, you have had immense faith in me, for which I am grateful.

Thanks also to: Special K, Terry, and Pat for keeping Charlotte and me honest; Irene for insights into Charlotte's psyche; and Debra F. Glaser, Ph.D., of the LAPD's Behavioral Science Services, for her generosity in sharing the BSS's history and methods in assisting troubled officers.

To Professors Daniel L. Simmons, Evelyn A. Lewis, and Thomas W. Joo of UC Davis's School of Law for their insight into legal matters affecting publicly traded companies. And to Bill Shuttleworth, who, unlike his smarmy namesake, provided excellent advice on finance and audit matters.

To Nancy Goldman, M.D., for help in determining the effects of gunshot wounds on my pregnant victim; to D. P. Lyle, M.D., for information on treating gunshot wounds; and to Ms. Pam Sinclair of the Brain Injury Program at Mission Hospital for assistance in understanding vegetative states.

To Ann duCille, gratitude for directing me to *Skin Trade* and its essential chapter on dolls and African American representation; to Sean McGowan for highlighting issues in the toy industry; and to Melissa Gilkey Mince, for valuable history and anecdotes on Chatty Cathy.

To Eddie Muller and Jim Quay, thanks for introducing me to great Oakland landmarks; to Rhea Cortado and Sam Domingo, for insights into Filipino culture; and to Jason Thomas, of Cal State Fresno's Interdisciplinary Spatial Information Systems Center, for statistical information on Filipino populations in the Central Valley.

To California Highway Patrol Deputy Tom Killian for insight into CHP procedures and the dangers of tule fog; to Sergeant Ron Yelder of the Oakland Police Department's Ranger Section, for Joaquin Miller Park lore; to Robert Nardoza and Tom Fallati for a crash course on the workings of the U.S. Attorney's office; and to Paul Hudson, for a reminder of the effects of the 1992 uprising on Broadway Federal Bank.

Special thanks to Carol Topping for her website wizardry; to Thomas Görden for assistance in developing that German headline; and Heather Smith and Marie Coolman for longtime friendship and PR support.

And to all of the team at the Ballantine Publishing Group—Kim Hovey, Mary Siemsen, Paul Taunton, Anna Chapman, and many others who have my back—your support and patience have meant more than I can say.